DIVINE AND CONQUER

J. C. JACKSON

Divine and Conquer

J.C. Jackson

Copyright © 2021 J.C. Jackson

Published by Shadow Phoenix Publishing LLC

ISBN-13: 978-1-7322835-8-9, 978-1-7322835-9-6

Cover designed by J. Caleb Design

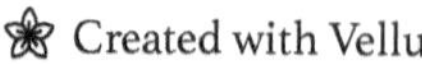 Created with Vellum

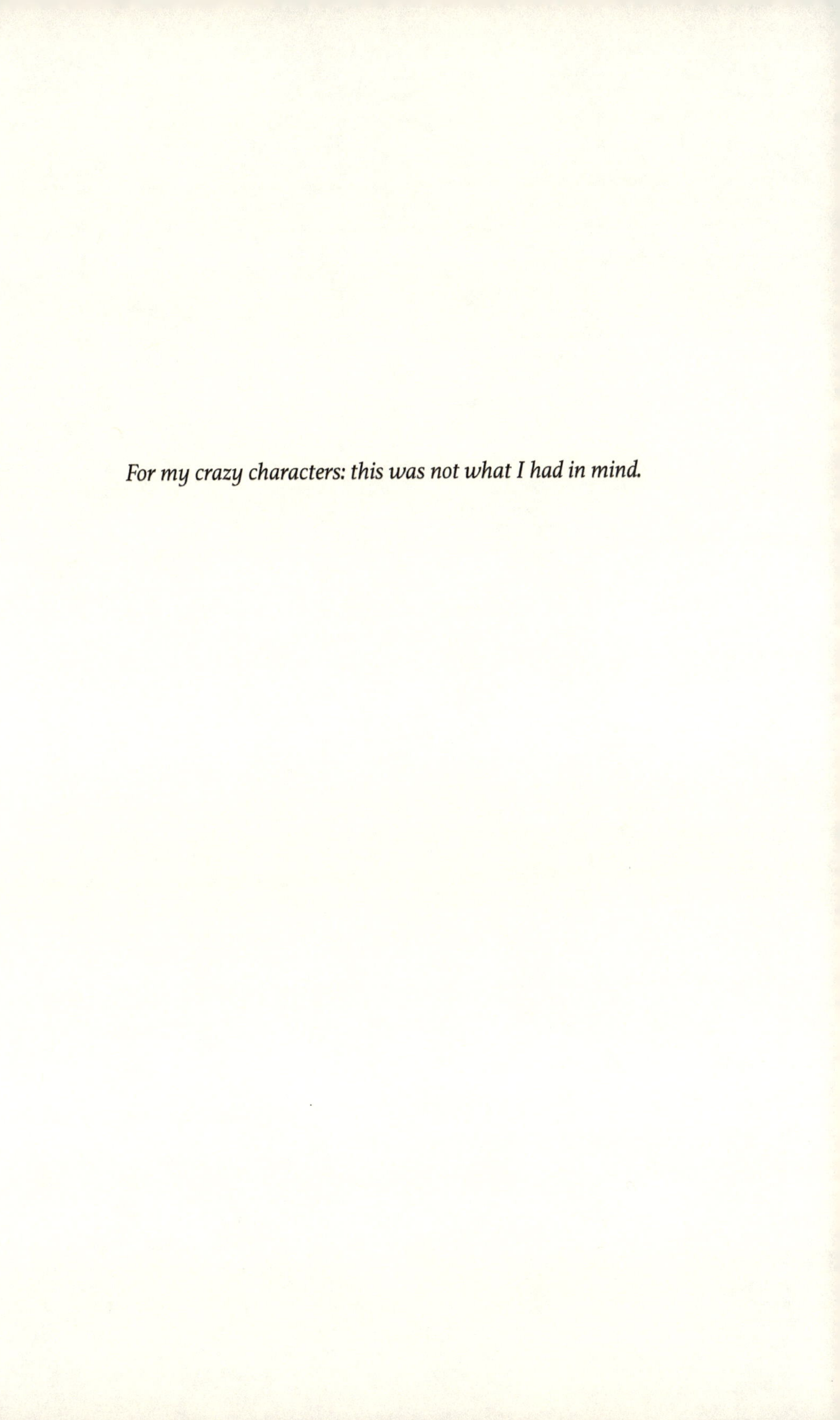

For my crazy characters: this was not what I had in mind.

FINALLY! All of the classes the Elven Arcana Consortium required me to take to obtain a rank as an arcane caster were over. Now I could devote my time to other things.

I swung my arms slightly, unable to hide the small bounce in my step as I headed back to my motorcycle, enjoying the early summer breeze. With as tired as I was after the final round of tests, I would likely need to take a few breaks on the way home. It was not enough to dampen my good mood. There were plenty of scenic spots to enjoy. Perhaps I would buy some snacks for the ride back and have myself a picnic. I giggled softly to myself at the thought.

"Ketayl, may I have a moment," a familiar male voice called from behind me.

I turned as Marsen hurried over.

The older Elven man smiled at me. "I'm glad I caught you before you left. I guess we won't be seeing you too often now."

I turned and smiled at him. "I'll stop by when I'm in the area." How often that would be, I had no idea. I imagined Magus Engelil would want to meet with me on occasion. Obtaining a rank was not going to end my working with her.

He pushed his shoulder length brown hair back. "Oh, that's right. Your parents live in Great Tree."

Adopted parents, I corrected in my head.

Marsen bowed. "It was a pleasure having you as a student, though I think I learned more from you than you did from me."

I shook my head. He and the other teachers often gave me similar praise. I personally thought they overestimated whatever small contribution I may have given.

He signaled for me to keep walking. "You're too modest. Anyway, I wish you the best of luck. What are your plans now?"

I bit my lower lip for a moment. "I don't think anything is really going to change. I'll just have more time to devote to my work."

He laughed, shaking his head. "Why am I not surprised? You should take some time for yourself. It was hard watching you work yourself into the ground. Even when you were testing out of classes there for a bit, I can only imagine how many sleepless nights you spent studying. Especially to get the scores you did. That's not even touching on the trouble you get yourself into in the course of your job."

I frowned at the implication and was about to respond when people started screaming from a nearby building. I did not even look to Marsen before I ran in that direction.

"Ketayl, wait!" Marsen shouted after me.

People poured out of a lecture hall. I managed to squeeze through the door against the panicked flood of people. Once I pushed through the bottleneck, the sight of a giant bubble greeted me.

There were a few people, several bags and notebooks, and a number of floor cushions already trapped in it. And it was growing. Anything within a couple of feet was being sucked into it.

Marsen came up beside me, shoving his messy hair out of his face again. "Oh Hells. Someone's final project went wrong."

I took a step forward, needing to get closer so I could analyze what went wrong.

He grabbed my shoulder. "Don't - you'll just get caught in it."

"We need to get those people out of there. The least I can do right now is contain it," I argued.

Marsen held onto my shoulder and looked at the bubble. After a moment he nodded. "Go. Do what you can. I'll find the caster."

I nodded and took a step away.

"And Ketayl," Marsen called and I turned back. "You get yourself stuck and I'm taking away points."

I rolled my eyes, shaking my head. I had noticed over the years that Marsen had a strange sense of humor.

It took effort to get closer to the bubble - the people still escaping kept knocking me back. One person tried to pull me with the moving crowd who I had to tear myself away from.

Once I reached the watery orb, I put my hands out in front of me and started forming my shield spell around the uncontrolled magic.

Unfortunately, I did not account for how fast the bubble was growing and had to drop it and back up. I used a small flight spell to jump farther than I normally could on my own.

Getting into position, I managed to get my shield spell completely up and around it this time. I only had a few seconds to attempt to analyze the spinning bands of arcane text and attempt to figure out what this spell was supposed to be before my concentration would be on keeping it under control.

Water, containment... it was difficult to make out the information with as fast as the bands were moving.

I grunted as the bubble pressed against my shield. I was still worn out from earlier so I would not be able to hold it long under the strain. Whatever the spell was did not matter. I needed to get those people out of there.

Holding my shield spell with one hand, I reached through it into the bubble, needing to do more to fix this. I felt myself getting pulled and adjusted my stance so I could brace against it.

With power still being supplied to the spell, I would have to dismantle it one piece at a time. As sweat slid down my face from the exertion, I prayed Marsen separated the caster soon.

I glanced at the people struggling. The first thing I did was send air bubbles so they could breathe. It was slow going to push through the dense liquid. Once I was satisfied they would be okay for the moment, I returned to the problem at hand.

My focus went to water first. I bared my teeth as I tore it apart. While I worked on that, the race I had to outpace the energy supplied ended. Marsen must have finally gotten the person separated.

The work to dismantle the spell went quickly once I did not have to fight someone. A few minutes later and I staggered, exhausted. People were rushing around helping those who had gotten trapped. I knew I needed to help, but it was taking everything I had to stand.

A number of people were trying to talk to me, but I could not make out their words. I swayed on my feet.

Marsen pushed through and grabbed my shoulders, pushing me down. That was all it took for me to fall unceremoniously onto my butt on the floor. I half-sat on one of the scattered floor cushions. I felt rather than heard the unpleasant squelching sound accompanying it.

He turned over his shoulder and was yelling something, but again, I heard nothing.

In a blink Magus Engelil was kneeling next to him. She reached out and touched the side of my face. "She'll be okay," she said, her voice sounding faint and distant, "She's just exhausted. If you would be so kind as to find out what happened, I'll take her back to my office."

"Of course, Magus." Marsen stood up and bowed to her.

She smiled and took my hand. Being teleported by someone else was always surreal. I was in one place and then suddenly somewhere else with no effort. I always expected to sense something, but outside of seeing the teleport line Magus Engelil left, there was nothing.

She helped me up and to a chair in her office. "If I had known that this was going to happen, I certainly wouldn't have pressed you so hard earlier. Just rest. I'll contact Lockonis and let her know what happened and that you'll be delayed returning."

"It's okay. I can call her." I began the hard task of moving. Everything ached.

Magus Engelil held up her hand. "You rest. I need to speak with her anyway. There may be an abnormal delay in assigning your rank."

I looked down toward the floor. It seemed I was problematic.

"Thank you, Ketayl. I'm not sure what would have happened if you hadn't reacted so quickly. We have been truly blessed to have you here." She left before I could formulate a response.

I sighed and slumped back in the chair. Even with dealing with the bubble of death, it still had not ruined my mood that this particular chapter of my life had come to a close. I let my mind wander about what I could do with the extra time. Having time to tinker with creating more useful tools for my day-to-day work came to mind and I decided to chew on that possibility.

———

IT WAS a while before Magus Engelil returned. She carried a tray of tea and fruit. Her long, light-blue hair shifted to a gentle purple at the ends, matching her simple summer dress. "I apologize for the delay. Marsen came by to tell me what had happened. Someone attempted to enhance a cleaning spell without being familiar enough with the base spell."

I shook my head. *Of all the things.* The fact that I did not recognize it immediately concerned me more.

"In one regard I'm glad your departure was delayed. I've been wanting to talk to you about your rank." The magus' words broke the train of thought I had.

I tilted my head, I thought she had told me earlier that there would be a delay. Under normal circumstances, the announcement would take a couple of weeks anyway and I had just finished my last class not an hour earlier.

"In an effort to speed up the process, your evaluation has been ongoing. Right now, the decision rests with the Archmages, but I've been informed that they are likely going to be pushing it up to myself and the other Magi."

I bit my lower lip, trying to make sense of her words. "I don't understand."

Magus Engelil smiled as she handed me a cup of tea. "Ketayl, do you have any idea how much skill you have?"

"I assumed I would be starting as any other within the school." It made the most sense.

She paused, halfway to her seat and stared at me a moment. Then she sat the rest of the way down. "You bypassed mage long before you came to us."

I bit my lower lip, still not getting what she was hinting at. I took a moment to pop a berry into my mouth to contemplate her words. "I haven't done the work for a higher rank than that."

"On the contrary, you may not have done the larger projects and research that would normally be required when wanting to obtain a higher rank within the school, but considering your work with the Terran Intelligence Organization..."

I shook my head.

"Ketayl, I'm not sure the full evaluation of your abilities can be contained within the Elven Arcana Consortium. We're following the guidelines, but I may need to take this to the Magi of the other schools. I want you to be aware of that."

I took a deep breath. That meant she would be contacting the Arcane College where I had been kept as a Researcher for over 40 years. "I don't think that's necessary."

"Hm." She sat back with her tea, eyeing me. "I would be doing you a disservice if I do not. Besides, I have not had the pleasure of the company of the heads of the other schools for quite some time, but that's a possible future. For now, I will await the decision of the Archmages."

I sipped at my tea, hoping it meant she was done with that conversation. She was implying that my rank was far higher than most people likely expected. *I could never be a Magus.*

The door opened behind me and I turned. Magus Engelil's assistant stood there, holding the door for my adopted father.

"Ah, Dayko, thank you for coming," she said. "I fear we unintentionally exhausted your daughter. I was too concerned for her safety to let her depart on her own."

"It's not a problem. I've already loaded her bike onto the trailer so whenever you're ready to go," he said, putting his hand on my head.

I frowned. Ever since I temporarily lost my arcane abilities several months ago, he had treated me like a child. I disliked it, but he had made a point that even at the age of 61, I was still a child by Elven standards. I had given up fighting him on it and let him dote.

"You should be proud. Not many, even among other Arcanists, are as talented as she is. Especially at such a young age," the Magus said.

Father smiled down at me. "I am. Marsen was telling me the same thing on my way in."

I rolled my eyes. Of course I was going to be the topic of conversation right now.

Magus Engelil laughed lightly. "And yet such a stubborn one. Soon hopefully you'll greet me as a peer."

I shook my head.

She made a shooing motion. "Go on home. There is much I need to do to close off the semester."

I put my teacup back on the tray, got up, and bowed.

"And be proud of yourself, Ketayl. You have done much in such a small amount of time."

I bit my lower lip and nodded, unsure how to respond.

I walked in silence next to my father as we left. I eyed the black and purple bike loaded onto the trailer behind his large white truck and frowned, crossing my arms. I should have been headed back to the main office by now.

"Easy, honey, it's just a delay. There's nothing wrong with taking time for yourself," my father said softly.

I shook my head. "I should be getting back to work. I'll be fine to ride back. I can stop on the way if I need to."

"No. Lockonis doesn't want you risking it."

I got in the passenger's seat and folded my arms again. Even as annoyed as I was at my current situation, I kept drifting back to idly considering what I could do with the extra time.

Father got into the driver's seat and started the truck. "Besides, now I can spoil you by taking you out for a late lunch."

I flopped back against the seat and sighed. I started to think Father's doting was less because of what happened and more because I was the only one close by. My sister, Kitteren, had moved to the other side of the territory over a year ago, leaving only me in the general area.

He tossed me a sidelong glance with an amused smirk on his face. "Since you're going to have some free time now, you should consider finding a romantic partner."

I rolled my eyes and groaned. Not this conversation again. I spent the rest of my time trying to convince him it was an unnecessary waste of my time. I was happy with the friends I had. I had no desire to go looking for more.

2

I LOOKED LIKE A FOOL. I knew I looked like a fool, but I could not tone down the big smile on my face even a day later.

Whatever case crossed my desk mattered not - even the most boring and tedious assignment would not phase me. Despite having an extra day delay to think about it before returning, I had not decided where to apply the available time.

"Ketayl!" a male voice called. The Gnome with dark green hair down the hall waved at me. He stood next to a cart with mail and other supplies.

"Good morning, Yosjin," I replied, keeping my voice as close to neutral as possible. This was where I fumbled. I never knew where to continue to carry on a conversation like this. I knew him enough to know his name, but not much else since I rarely requested supplies.

"Oh, hey, since you're here, mind if I give you your stuff now?"

I nodded. "Did Silver order more pens?" If he had, I would have to talk to him about throwing them at the ceiling again. I would eventually find them, but some had broken beyond salvaging.

He put down the stack of mail he had been holding and went digging through the tray. "For once, no. I've actually got mail for him."

I raised an eyebrow. We never got mail at the office. I rarely even got mail at my quarters. Worse was if Kitteren sent me anything - she would make me drive all the way to our parent's house in Great Tree to get it even though she knew the address here.

Yosjin handed me the envelope. "Thanks. I better finish my rounds. Someone had to go and rush order a crazy amount of printing."

I gave him a slight bow and continued on my way. I turned the envelope over. There was something stiff inside. I recognized the logo - it was similar to the one Silver had received months ago in his quarters. It was from the Central Seat of the Order of the Paladins of the Holy Sun. I crossed my eyes at the mental mouthful that was.

Silver had not said anything about being in contact with his Order. The last time I had seen him get a letter like this, he had gotten upset and thrown it out saying it was unimportant.

Whatever it was, it was not my mail and certainly not enough to dampen my mood. I put my hand on the scanner to unlock the office.

"You're positively beaming today," Silver said just as the door unlocked.

I jumped, not having expected him. I turned to see my partner coming down the hall. The broad grin on his face told me he was entertained by something. Likely that something was me. I rolled my eyes and entered into the office, holding the door open for him. "I am not."

"Yes, you are. You were practically skipping down the hall. Let me guess... you started courting someone," Silver said, his tone teasing. Every so often he would say something like that.

I grinned, deciding I was in the mood to play along. "Maybe I did." It was not my normal reply. I would always deny it. I had no time previously to pursue a romantic relationship if I even had the inclination to.

Silver's face fell and he stared at me with wide eyes. He opened his mouth and closed it again. Then he turned away and looked at the floor.

I tilted my head at his behavior. I had expected more teasing or at least curiosity, not this. "I'm kidding," I said quickly.

My partner tugged on his braid hard. "Don't do that to me. I thought you were serious."

I rolled my eyes and shook my head. He should know me well enough by now.

"Okay, so what has you in such high spirits? I know your birthday was recently, but this is something else."

Now that I thought about it, the whole thing seemed rather silly. "I, uh... I guess it's rather trivial when you think about it. It's just... I'm done with those classes. That's all."

Silver picked me up and spun me around. "That's great! You've been working for so long to get ranked. What is it?"

I shrugged once I got my bearings again. Why was I still walking around with his mail? I held his envelope out to him. "I don't know yet. I've been warned it's going to take longer than usual to finalize a decision. All that matters is I can devote that time to something else."

He glanced at the envelope, frowned, and then tossed it on his desk. "We should do something to celebrate."

"No. I'd rather use the time to get back to work. There's got to be more information about necromancers somewhere, but I may have to travel to access it." I shooed him out of my way so I could wake the computer table and the wall screen.

Silver picked up his envelope and opened it. A card fell out and onto the floor. He did not seem to notice as he walked around his desk, looking at the letter. He sat down, propping his feet up in front of his keyboard. "Come on, it's been quiet. And you should use your new free time for yourself. Maybe give courting a try."

I swore he had a one-track mind sometimes. I picked up the fallen card. "You know most people call it dating, and no, I don't need... to..." I trailed off as I read the card. I reread it again to make sure I understood the information presented on the small invitation. My chest tightened and my previous good mood vanished in an instant. I could not bring myself to look at my partner. "I, um... I'm..." I forced a smile to my face. "I'm happy for you."

The card was torn out of my hands while I tried to wrap my head around what I had just read.

"I... You know what, I think I'm going to go make myself some tea. I'll be back." I kept tripping over my words and hurried for the door. Why had he not told me he was getting married? Why did it matter if he did? I knew he had been romantically interested in someone for a long time, but I had not had any idea it had gone anywhere.

Silver grabbed my arm before I could escape. "Kela, wait. Please. This isn't what you think."

I refused to turn around despite his use of that name. "It's quite clear." *Please let me out of here. I can't be in this room right now.*

He sighed and put himself between me and the door. "No, it isn't and now I have another reason to be angry with them. This is from my former Order. I had no part in this."

I pinched the bridge of my nose, completely lost now. "I think you better explain then. I'm not following what is happening."

"The Order has been trying to recall me to the Central Seat since I decided to leave the church," Silver said slowly. "Every time we went out on a mission, I would get another set of letters when we got back. I don't know how they know, but it's been a pattern. Even after we got back from Mystic Port there were letters waiting for me. This arranged marriage is a new tactic to get me to return."

Now it started to make sense. "Why didn't you tell me before now?"

"It was my problem to deal with." Silver took a deep breath. "And now I can't ignore them. Not when they're dragging others into this."

I sighed. "You don't need my permission. Go ahead and take as much time as you need to deal with it." Why did my chest still feel tight? Must have been the shock of the announcement. I hoped under normal circumstances that I would see something like this coming.

"Kela, if I go alone, I might not be able to come back." A finality could be heard in his voice. It was something I rarely heard from him.

I bit the inside of my cheek. What was I supposed to do? This was not my problem to deal with. Or was it because we were friends?

"Say something, please," Silver pleaded softly.

"I don't know what to say," I blurted out. "I don't know what you're asking of me." If I knew what needed to be done, I could do it, but there was no plan.

Silver stood up straight and let go of my arm. "I... I'm not sure what I need other than to get out of this and make sure this woman doesn't get hurt because of it. Can you help me figure it out?"

I closed my eyes for a moment to help focus. "Okay." It sounded like both of us were equally lost about the situation. "How about you start with telling me what has been going on? What has been in those letters? Likely what we need is in there."

He gave me a soft smile. "I think I can manage that."

"After I make myself a cup of tea," I said and left. It was really to get some air since there was little I could contemplate without more information. Perhaps I should see if I could make a whole pot. I had a feeling I was going to need it.

Silver patiently explained what he had received in the letters. At first the requests had been gentle. A wish for him to return to the fold. The tactics changed over time and turned to bribery of giving him his own church and group to lead then to demanding his presence and now this.

"What would be the reason to arrange a marriage?" I asked. "It sounds too complicated for just calling you back."

My partner frowned and sat back in his chair. "Personally, I thought they would've been happy to see me go," he grumbled. "It doesn't make sense. If I held a lineage then I could see the reasoning, but I'm Elven. I'm not even supposed to have become a paladin let alone have a recognized lineage."

"Lineage?" I crossed my eyes. This whole set up was far too complex for my liking.

"It's kept in both blood and valor. A particular family would be known for valorous deeds and typically the oldest male would be expected to keep the line continuing even if they themselves did not add to the family story. My master, Blaise Sutton, was part of such a line, but that died with his son, James, since he never had children. The lineage holder also commands a group. At this time there are only two of us left loyal to the Sutton line, but neither of us holds lineage."

"There's someone else?" Another had managed to escape the massacre of his church in Ocean's Edge?

Silver lowered his gaze. "Marzena. She's been stationed at the Central Seat for several years. You'd like her."

Raising an eyebrow at him, I sat back and crossed my arms. That explained why I had not known about another. "How come you've never mentioned her before?"

Silver took a deep breath. "When I left, as much as I didn't want to leave her on her own, I needed to break all ties." He paused for a moment, "And I forgot how to get in contact with her directly. I didn't want to use the main line to get to her. That would've ended up in an argument with the Elders."

I frowned at him before chewing on my bottom lip for a moment. This lineage thing was an old tradition obviously, but I wondered if there had been some alterations to it over time. "What about a woman? Could she hold the lineage if there was no male child to carry it?"

Silver flipped the tail of his braid back and forth and stared at the ceiling. "Yes. There have been instances. When they marry, the husband takes the name of the family with lineage. Why do you ask?"

"Does this..." I trailed off, reaching for the card. "Does Amanda Sayer hold lineage?"

My partner shook his head. "No, I don't recognize the family name at all. And before you ask, it would take more than one or two generations to build a lineage. Besides, there would be no reason to marry someone with lineage to me. To them, I would dilute the line."

I pinched the bridge of my nose. "This is getting us nowhere. Maybe we need to take a break."

He nodded and I followed him out the door silently. Silver and I had finally gotten back into the easygoing friendship that we had before we had been kidnapped by pirates, but now I was about to lose that. Possibly lose him permanently by the sounds of it. *He's my best friend. I should be happy for him.*

Though Silver was not happy about it and I had no idea how to help.

"You're awfully quiet, even for you," he said softly.

"Just thinking," I replied automatically.

"About?"

Of course he would push now. Normally he left me alone after that. "I'm not sure how I can help. I'm too unfamiliar with the rules and traditions of your Order."

"Well," he started and then paused. "the whole arranged marriage thing really doesn't make sense."

"I thought we already determined that." I cringed slightly - it came out somewhat whiny.

Silver shook his head. "It's something more. Typically arranged marriages that aren't tied to lineage are meant to keep the Order populated. I'm too young and any Human woman at best is going to be too old to bear children when I do come of age. There is no reason to be pushing this."

"This conversation became awkward," I muttered. One Silver was enough of a handful. I did not even want to think of what his children might be like. "Can you simplify this and ignore them like you have been?"

He folded his arms and looked down as he walked. "As much as I want to, I can't. I don't know who this Amanda Sayer is, but I would not have harm befall her because of my stubbornness."

I raised an eyebrow at the change in his speech pattern. I had not heard him talk like that since we first met. But with the mention that he did not know her, that meant it was not whoever he had been romantically interested in. Though he had not spoken of that topic for a long time now, so I had no idea if it was even still valid.

All I was doing was confusing myself.

"Well, if you haven't met her, you don't even know if you'll like her or not," I pointed out.

"I'm not..." Silver started, his words sharp. He sighed and shook his head. "I won't be tied down by the Order. This... farce cannot be suffered to take place."

"Why are you talking like that?" I blurted out and then covered my mouth.

Silver stopped walking. "I... I didn't realize I slipped back. Sorry about that. Must be all of this having to deal with the Order. I thought my resignation would have been the end of working with them, but apparently even after two and a half years, my decision is unacceptable to them."

I walked away from him. I was the reason he decided to join the TIO. If that was the only thing, they might have left him alone, but Silver had told me that those at the Central Seat did not look kindly upon arcane casters. If they knew he worked closely with one...

"Ketayl, knock it off," Silver snapped.

I stopped and turned to look at my partner. Had I said something?

"Don't look at me like I can't read you. I know you're thinking it's your fault somehow." He gently brushed my long bangs back. "We'll figure it out. I have no plans of leaving this. Of leaving you."

"Ugh!" I turned away from him. "You don't have to sound so sappy about it."

Silver laughed behind me. We walked in silence for a bit and I let him lead to wherever he wanted to go. Once we returned to the office, he asked. "Do you have an idea of what your rank might be?"

I paused on my way back to my desk, thinking over the conversation I had with Magus Engelil before I left. "I haven't been given any direct information, so, no. To me it's really not important." I was not about to mention the roundabout wording.

"Aren't there certain things you would need to be able to perform for each rank?"

"Some basic things, yes, but that's only part of the application process. Each time one wants to try for a higher rank, there's more involved such as researching topics and presenting theory. I haven't done any of the extra work so I'm just going to assume I'm starting at the bottom." I knew that was a lie, but I would rather others thought that than what Magus Engelil had been implying.

"Didn't they want you ranked to figure out your ability level?"

I bit my lower lip, not wanting to continue this conversation. "Can we change the topic?"

"Sorry," Silver said quickly. "I'm just trying to take my mind off this mess."

I turned my gaze to the ground. "We need to deal with it. I assume the timeframe to respond isn't very long."

"No, it isn't." Silver blew out a long breath, looking at me out of the corner of his eye. "There is one way to legitimately break it, but I'm not in the position to exercise the option as things currently stand."

Why had he not said something sooner? I sat there staring at him for a moment. When he did not continue, I asked, "What is it?"

"You're not going to like it."

I rolled my eyes. "Just say it." There could be a way to make it an option if I knew what it was. I was certain we could locate the resources for it.

Silver hesitated, opening and closing his mouth a couple of times before he finally said, "I need to be courting someone else."

I sat back in my chair with my arms crossed. He currently was not dating anyone, which posed a problem. I was unsure why he thought I would not like his idea unless... I sat forward in my chair as the implication hit me. "Wait, are you wanting me to fill that role?"

Silver tugged with the end of his braid with both hands. I swore his cheeks had reddened. "Yes."

"I..." I looked down at my hands.

Silence fell between us. After a couple of minutes, the door unlocking broke it and the mental circle I had been running in.

Lockonis strode in with a big smile on her face like she usually did. "Hey, Ket, I thought I'd... um, what happened? You both look like you're attending a funeral."

Silver and I both looked at each other and then looked away again. What could I say? It was his problem and I had no idea how far he wanted to let the information spread.

"One of you needs to talk," Lockonis said flatly, crossing her arms.

"It's the Central Seat," Silver said quietly, "I can't ignore their requests any longer and we've been trying to figure out how to deal with it."

Lockonis came over to my desk and swiped the card off it, holding it up to face my partner. "I got one of these too. Wasn't planning on bringing it up, but obviously it's an issue. I suppose the first question is what do you want to do?"

I ducked my head lower with the knowledge that others besides just the two of us had been informed.

"I'm not leaving this if that's what you're asking," Silver snapped. He sighed and pulled hard on his braid. "I... we were trying to come up with a solution when you came in. The only thing that would legally work to dissolve the arrangement was if I was in another committed relationship. Even then I'm sure I would have to fight on the matter."

My boss turned to me with a mischievous smirk. "Oh, and I assume you just asked Ket."

"Not directly, no," Silver admitted. "I don't want to take her to the Central Seat though if I can help it. It's too dangerous for an arcane caster."

"Only if they know she is one," Lockonis said in a sing-song voice. "I assume that means the situation can't be handled from here."

Silver shook his head. "I can call and try, but there's almost no chance of them accepting a verbal, or even video response."

"We can set up a call and try that first. I'll drag Vince in to help," Lockonis said. Then she sighed. "I have a feeling you're right though. You two should prepare to travel in the meantime. Figure out how you want to do this. Take whatever time you need. Especially where there seems to be a lull in information right now."

I bit my lower lip as my boss spoke, the puzzle starting to form in my mind of how to deal with the situation. "I just have to play a role, right? I could always use the time to go through their library and see if they have anything useful to us. It wouldn't be a wasted trip." I knew I was rationalizing this to ignore the jumble of emotions, but the chance to also search through their library was too good to pass up.

"It doesn't work that way!" Silver was out of his chair.

I looked up at him with wide eyes. What had gotten into him?

Even Lockonis appeared to have been unprepared for his outburst.

My partner hung his head and sat back down, pinching the bridge of his nose. "Look, even if it did, they likely already know your name. They would know you were an arcane caster without you having to say or do anything."

"Then we create a name for her," Lockonis said. "It's common for undercover work."

Silver was tugging hard on his braid again.

I bit my lower lip for a moment trying to figure out why this was such a problem for him. "It's the lie, isn't it?"

His shoulders slumped. "Yeah. I'm fairly certain they don't know your other name, but..."

"Wait, what other name?" Lockonis asked, turning back to me.

I glared at Silver. I had kept his secret and he blurted mine out right in front of me.

"Ket, what other name?" Lockonis' tone became demanding.

I was busy trying to stare Silver down. He sat back and crossed his arms. The least he could do was look apologetic.

"Ketayl," she snapped.

I sighed. "It's the name I would have had if I had been old enough and gone through the naming ceremony in my village. But it didn't happen so I never earned it. Besides, my current name is a composite of it so it doesn't really matter."

Lockonis flattened her lips into a line. "I swear you two have or had the strangest traditions. Alright, spit it out. What is it?"

I folded my arms and looked away.

She put her hands on her hips and stared down at me. "I'll find out one way or another, kid."

I scrunched up my face. Why was this conversation now on me? We needed to focus on Silver's problem.

Lockonis glanced back at my partner. "I'll order Silver to tell me."

I sighed. That would put him into a bad position because he had promised not to tell anyone even though he had slipped up once and used it where others heard it. "Kela."

"Okay, how is Ketayl a composite? You have me curious now." Lockonis smirked.

I sighed, doomed to this. "It's parts of the first and middle names."

Both of them were looking at me expectantly.

Admitting the second name was dangerous. I looked between them, biting my lower lip. I trusted Silver with the first and he had respected that. He had known for a year and a half now and nothing bad had come of it.

But I had promised my biological mother to only tell people I trusted. I looked to Lockonis who was now playing with a pen she had taken off of my desk. She had never given me a reason to not trust her.

I got up and woke up the wall screen, grabbing the pencil for it. I wrote out "Kela Taylia" and underlined the "Ke" in the first name and the "Tayl" in the second. I turned as the pen Lockonis had been holding hit the floor.

My boss stood there staring at what I had written.

"Why hadn't you told me the second name before?" Silver asked.

I bit my lower lip. "I had promised my mother that I would be careful who I revealed it to. Within the village it wasn't an issue, but she seemed to think her name outside of it would be a problem."

"It's your mother's name? It's pretty," my partner commented.

I would have been embarrassed about Silver's words if I had not been concerned about Lockonis' reaction. She appeared to have paled. "Are you okay?"

She quickly retrieved the pen. "Yeah, absolutely. Hey, it's a nice day. Why don't you two go for a walk and iron out how to make this happen? I'll go over the information we have and see if I can't come up with more ideas. I would suggest just sticking with Kela for a name though. Keep it simple."

"I can—" I started.

"It's okay. I just want some time to think and it's better if the information stays in this room." She shooed us out the door.

Once we were outside, I looked up at Silver. "Did we just get kicked out of our own office?"

He shrugged. "I gave up trying to figure out Lockonis. She is right though - it is a gorgeous day. It'll also be easier to discuss this without her around."

3

WE PASSED VINCE, the director of the TIO, at the elevator. He stormed by quickly, muttering something under his breath. While I could not say I had ever seen him appear happy, this was worse than usual. I did not want to be the person he was heading to see.

It gave me something else to think about while we walked.

The forested area around the main office was a good place to take a walk and contemplate things. Without thinking, I headed down the path I liked that would go past a small waterfall. The sound of the water was often calming and helped me refocus.

Silver walked silently next to me. As much as I found his attempts to fill quiet times with small talk annoying, this only served to set me on edge.

"Kela," Silver said softly, "talk to me."

He was waiting for me to say something? "Um, I don't know. You're going to have to tell me what you're thinking. I can't really develop a plan with so many unknowns. Is there someone else you could ask who you would be more comfortable with?" That question should not have been difficult to voice, but I almost remained silent about it. *Maybe I'm too close to this. I really would like to go to that library.* That thought felt off, but it was the only logical reason.

Silver stepped in front of me. "No. I wouldn't want to take anyone else. I'm just not sure I can keep you safe."

I crossed my arms and stared at him, my mouth formed into a thin line. "I can handle myself."

He cupped my face with his hands. "I know, and I agree under normal circumstances, but this time you would fully be my responsibility."

I backed away from him. "All you have to do is not tell them I'm an arcane caster, right? You may not lie, but you're damn good at avoiding things you don't want to talk about."

Silver stood up straighter. Then he laughed. "Okay, so we know each other's bad habits."

I continued down the path, hopping up on the short stone wall someone had built. It meant I was close to the waterfall.

Silence fell between us for a minute or so. As he walked next to me, I realized that the wall put me about equal to him in height.

"You're like a small child when you do something like that," Silver commented.

"Like what?" I kept walking, focusing on my balance. I heard the waterfall to my left.

"Walking on the wall."

I shrugged.

Silver sighed loudly. "Kela, I don't think you get the full implication here. If you agree to this, you will be my intended. There's no playing a role here."

His statement threw me off enough that I slipped. He grabbed my arm so I could steady myself. *No, that thought had not crossed my mind. What does that even mean?* The new term only added another layer of complexity that I refused to acknowledge at the moment. It was enough right then that I understood that this would be real on some level. "I... um..." I could feel heat rising quickly to my face. This was worse than his proposal to explore our Elven heritage together.

"Easy. Sorry, I shouldn't have been so blunt."

I shook my head and got my feet solidly back underneath me. "It's fine. I obviously wasn't getting it otherwise. Are you sure? I thought there was someone you were interested in. You should ask them first."

"I am asking you." Silver touched the side of my face, gently pushing so I would turn to look at him. "Kela, will you allow me to court you?"

I searched his clouded blue eyes looking for something. Insincerity? Honesty? I had no idea. He trusted me enough to ask. After a moment I nodded slowly. If this was what I could do to help, then I would see it through. The arrangement would not be permanent. With any luck, we would not need to hold these titles for long. Perhaps not even beyond the planning stage if the calls worked.

Silver picked me up and spun me around before hugging me tightly. I could not remember having seen a bigger smile on his face.

"I can't breathe!" I managed to get out.

"Oh, sorry." He set me back down on the short wall. He took my hand and kissed the back of my fingers, his eyes never leaving mine.

I squirmed under his gaze.

Silver grinned broadly. "I suppose I owe you a proper date."

What did he mean?

"But there are some other details we need to discuss before we go back."

The unknown made me nervous and I stared down at my hands. "Is it necessary?"

"Not absolutely necessary, no, but it will help solidify the case of dissolving the arrangement."

I took a deep breath and reminded myself that this was all just to keep him from ending up under their rule again. "What is it?"

"Well..." Now Silver looked away, his cheeks reddening. "We should probably be comfortable with some show of affection toward each other in public."

"We're dealing with Humans, right?" I struggled to remember the differences between the races, but I had never paid close enough attention to begin with.

"Yes. It won't be much different from how we normally are except for one thing that I would request of you."

My mind went blank when I attempted to figure out what it was. "Which is?"

"May I kiss you?"

I stopped and blinked. I should have seen that coming. "I... uh... I'm not sure that's a good idea." I had kissed him before, but it had always been under extenuating circumstances. Most of that when he needed a more intimate connection to use his divine abilities on me. This was not like those times. There would be nothing else to distract me.

"Here." Silver stepped closer and took my hands, placing them so my palms were flat against the upper part of his chest. "This is a controlled environment so here you can push me away if it's too much. Will you let me?"

It's a kiss. We're Elven. It doesn't mean anything. I was now hating my lack of understanding in this area. "Okay." I had to be overthinking the whole thing.

He gave me a soft smile and ran his thumb lightly over my lower lip. "At least with you standing on the wall, I don't have to bend down."

I scrunched up my face at him.

Silver laughed. He moved suddenly and there was only the lightest of touch against my lips before it was gone.

Without thinking, I leaned forward to follow, but stopped, unsure of what I should be doing.

"You look so confused." Silver brushed my bangs back. "I guess that wasn't fair of me. Every time I wanted to kiss you before and it wasn't an extenuating circumstance, someone has always stopped me."

I raised an eyebrow at him. "Isn't this technically an extenuating circumstance?" It was a stretch, but I could justify it as such. *When had he wanted to previously? Why?* I shoved the thoughts aside, not needing to confuse myself further.

A finger was pressed against my lips. "Hush. I'll not let you ruin this." He was grinning. Then he leaned forward and pressed his lips to mine.

I fumbled to follow his lead, having no idea what I should be doing. I was never going to convince anyone with my lack of experience.

Silver backed away after a few long moments and looked down toward where my hand was near his right shoulder. "Should I take that as you enjoyed it?"

I looked to see what he was talking about and saw that I had held onto both his shirt and his braid in my hand. I let go as if it was fire. "Sorry!"

He wrapped his arm around my waist to keep me from falling backwards. I found myself pressed up against him.

"Um..."

Silver simply smiled at me. "You should probably get off the wall. I've been throwing you off balance all day." He leaned in and stole another short kiss before putting me on the ground.

My head swam. What had I gotten myself into? "What other details did you want to discuss?" If I had a list of what I needed to deal with, I could manage.

He took a deep breath. "This one you're probably not going to like, but if it acts the way it did, it might make things easier for you. Or harder. I guess it depends on your perspective."

I was about to ask when he pulled his necklace out from under his shirt. I eyed the golden sun pendant warily. The last time I wore it, it would influence me to physically connect more with Silver. "How is that going to make it easier?" I would be second guessing every decision I made when it came to dealing with him.

"It's something that's given to an intended. You figured out how to separate yourself from its influence, right?" There was that term again.

"To an extent, yes. It's not easy." Maybe it would make figuring out how to be openly affectionate a little easier. I hated the idea of relying on it though.

"That's why I wanted to share a kiss before offering this to you. Now turn around."

I took a deep breath and did as he asked. "You probably need to explain more of what I should expect when we get there."

Silver hummed in agreement. "We have time to talk about it on the way there."

I warily watched as he lowered the pendant in front of me.

While Silver latched it around my neck he said, "We should focus on us right now."

A warm sensation filtered through me as the pendant rested against my shirt. It felt familiar and yet I knew it was not. "Maybe I should work on making sure I can separate myself from the influence of your necklace."

Silver came around in front of me, putting his hand gently over the pendant, smiling softly. "Nothing says we can't work on both at the same time."

<hr>

AFTER CHECKING in with Lockonis who was far calmer when we returned, she ordered us to take the remainder of the day away from the office to work out what we were going to do. Though she and my partner remained behind to get in contact with the Central Seat.

If only we could have gone through one solution at a time to deal with this. I flopped onto the couch in my quarters, grateful for the breather from Silver. He wanted to go on a date tonight and insisted on leaving the planning to him.

What even was a date? I understood the concept, but I had never been on one nor had I any idea if there was something expected of me. That was something that other people did so I never concerned myself with the details of the ritual.

A warm, comforting sensation came from his necklace. I pulled it out from under my shirt and stared at it. "You need to knock that off. I've gotten myself into enough of a mess on my own. Don't add to it."

It was an inanimate object, so I received no response to my scolding.

Great, I was to the point of arguing with an enchanted piece of metal. Maybe I would get lucky and the Central Seat would accept that he was refusing this arranged marriage during their call.

My watch tapped my wrist, signaling a message. Reading it quickly, I rolled my eyes. What was Kitteren worked up over now that she wanted a video call?

I better get it over with.

Reaching for my phone, I saw that there had been a picture attached to the message that my watch did not show me. I opened it to find someone had caught Silver and I together. Heat rose to my face quickly.

How had I not sensed anyone nearby?

I started the call immediately so I could try to set the record straight. This was only temporary until he was free of the arrangement, right?

Kitteren narrowed her eyes at me as soon as the call connected. "Ket, did you forget to tell me something?"

"No." I knew my face had to be bright red with as fast as my heart was pounding. "It's not what you think." The words were out of my mouth in a rush. This had been a bad idea. I should have been more conscious of where we were.

"Uh huh." Kitteren smirked at me. "And it just so happens you're also wearing his necklace."

I grabbed it and shoved it back down my shirt. "It's complicated.

He needs me to help him get out of an arranged marriage." I shifted uncomfortably as the pendant settled - it fell low on my chest because of the length of the chain.

Kitteren blinked at me for a moment. "Okay, wow, I did not see that coming."

"It's just temporary," I assured her.

She blew a sharp breath of air through her bangs. "Ket... Okay, let's return to the 'you need to connect with someone on an intimate level' conversation."

I groaned. "Please don't."

"It could last past this," she pointed out.

"Kitteren, enough," I said, pinching the bridge of my nose, "I need to focus on the immediate future. I have some research I need to do before tonight."

"Tonight?" My sister grinned mischievously. "I have a feeling it's something you could just ask me, but you're too stubborn."

"I think I can find information about dates on my own, thank you."

She laughed loudly. "By the Gods you're overthinking this. You don't need to look up anything. It won't be any different than when the two of you went out together before."

I raised an eyebrow at her.

"Well, okay, he'll probably be much more affectionate now, but that's about it."

I rolled my eyes. Despite her teasing, I knew Kitteren would not steer me wrong. "How did you get that picture anyway?"

"Retanei. She sent me a bunch, but I liked that one."

I hung my head. "I didn't even know she was back."

Kitteren laughed. "I don't know about when she got back, but apparently she was testing out a training module when she saw the two of you. You better believe I'm sending this to mom and dad."

My face heated up again at the mention of our adopted parents. "Don't. Please don't." I hid my face in my free hand.

"Oh, come on. They'll think it's cute."

"Father has already been on my case about possibly finding a romantic partner. This will just confuse them when it's over."

"It'll be fine."

Before I could come up with any kind of reply, there was a knock at my door. "I better go."

"Have fun," Kitteren said in a sing-song voice.

I rolled my eyes and ended the call.

When I answered my door, Silver stood on the other side. "May I come in?" he asked.

I raised an eyebrow at him and moved aside. "Since when do you ask?" Normally he would just come in once I opened the door if he did not simply let himself in.

Silver closed the door behind him, grinning broadly. "Sometimes I can be courteous." He wrapped an arm around my waist and pulled me close, kissing me quickly. "And I figured you probably don't want that public around here."

The necklace warmed at his actions. I needed to figure out why it did that.

I frowned at him. "It's a little late for that." I fiddled with my phone, pulling up the picture to show him.

Silver took my phone from me and took a few steps away. "Who took this?"

"Retanei. She sent it to Kitteren."

He grinned and started typing on my phone.

"Hey, what are you doing?" I reached to grab the device from him and he held it out of my reach.

"Sending it to myself. I like it."

I jumped for my phone and he moved it further out of my reach. "No, it needs to be deleted!"

"Too late." He grinned, handing me back my phone.

I frowned and made a mental note to steal his phone from him later so I could delete the evidence.

"There's something more serious we need to talk about," Silver said, taking a seat on my couch. He held out his hand for me to come sit next to him.

I pinched the bridge of my nose. Of course there was more. I took the seat, uneasy at being so close. *This never used to bother me. Why now?* "Am I to assume the call was insufficient for them?"

Immediately he wrapped his arm around my waist and nodded. "I knew it was a long shot, but I had hoped to save us the trip. There's something else I need to discuss with you since we have to go to the Central Seat."

I squirmed and a wave of contentment washed over me. I

frowned, knowing it was his necklace again. It seemed easier this time to separate myself at least.

"Kela, I don't want to put more on you, but I'm going to need you to help keep me grounded through this. I was thinking we could come up with a signal so you don't have to be worrying about it all the time."

I bit my lower lip. It made sense. I would be able to keep my focus on gathering information and he would let me know when I needed to do something. Though I had no idea what that might be. "I don't know how to keep you grounded."

He gave me a soft smile and then kissed me. "I think that will be enough. You've always been an anchor for me in the storm." He lightly drew a crude anchor on my arm - a line down and then a curved line below it.

"I... um..." I stopped and closed my eyes, biting the inside of my cheek so I could focus past the contentment coming from the necklace. It was a simple and quick solution. "I guess that will work. Is that how you want to let me know when you need help?"

Silver raised an eyebrow. "I hadn't even considered it, but now that you mention it, it'll be better than a verbal que."

"When are we leaving for the Central Seat?" I needed to focus on preparations.

He took a long, deep breath. "In a couple of days. I won't be around much as I make travel arrangements. Lockonis will book our flights as soon as I've gotten information on when the ferries run. We'll have to travel commercial this time, sorry."

I shrugged. As long as I knew ahead of time, I could plan for it.

Silver gently ran his hand over my hair. "I'm hoping Marzena won't be too mad at me. She'll be someone you can go to if I'm not available."

I doubted I would want to go to anyone. I was going to have my hands full when dealing with people to make sure I kept my power hidden.

My partner fidgeted with his hands a moment. "Can I ask one more favor?"

I rolled my eyes. "Now what?"

"If you're still planning to go through the library, can you copy it? Some works will be written in divine and last I knew you can't read that. Plus, it'll be good to have on hand."

I bit my lower lip. "Going straight to my tablet will be obvious that I'm casting and I don't have anything that would be more subtle. I don't think my watchband will be enough for a library. For short things it works."

Silver grinned. "I'll worry about that." He got up and headed for the door. "I need to get back to work on getting preparations made. I'll come by later so we can go on our date."

After he left, I stared at my closed door. I was utterly useless at the moment. The least I could do was get back to my normal job. With that thought, I gathered my things and headed back for my office where it would be quiet.

4

THE SOUND of the office door unlocking broke me out of the staring contest I was having with the wall screen. I certainly had not been making any headway, my mind was too preoccupied with making sense of the situation I found myself in.

Lockonis strode in. "I had a feeling you would sneak back here."

I raised an eyebrow at her. "There was no reason to not try to get some work done."

"You have a date tonight. Your first one if I'm understanding correctly. I'm surprised you're not neck deep researching it," she said, crossing her arms and looking me over.

Seeing as I was not getting anything done, I cleared the wall screen. "I doubt it's going to be anything special. Likely just reviewing the information I need to know before we get there."

Lockonis sighed loudly, rolling her eyes. She pointed at my desk. "Get your things. You're coming with me."

"I don't understand," I replied while I did as I was told, grabbing my bag. There was little reason for me to remain here anyway with as distracted as I was.

"Exactly. You may be seeing this as simply playing a role, but Silver isn't. The difference is going to be noticeable if I don't coach you on this. And please tell me you were going to wear something nicer."

I looked down at the loose sleeveless shirt and cropped pants I wore. "This... is not appropriate?" It was fine for work, why would it not be for going out?

Lockonis grabbed my wrist and dragged me toward the door.

I stumbled for a few steps, not having expected the action. I managed to wrench myself out of her grasp, rubbing my wrist to get rid of the sensation.

Though that did not seem to faze her as she pointed out the open door for me to go. She would drag me along again if I did not move on my own.

Once we were in the hallway, she continued. "This is a *date*, Ket. Doesn't matter the race - people are always trying to look nicer to impress the person they're going out with."

"But Silver's already seen me dressed up," I argued. I usually suffered a dress for the Winter Solstice.

"Yes, he's seen you at your best, your worst, and everything in between. All of that was him as your co-worker. This is personal."

I bit my lower lip thinking through what she had just said. We arrived at the elevator by the time I had come up with a response of any sort, still not understanding what she meant. "I don't think there's any difference."

Lockonis groaned and pinched the bridge of her nose. "I'd debate this with you, but I think I understand why you're not getting it. You don't have a clear separation between personal and professional, do you?"

Folding my arms, I stared at the floor. "In most instances, yes, but..."

"But?"

"It's not that way with Silver," I admitted softly. Even from the beginning there had not been much of a separation between the two. When we lived together for a few months about a year and a half ago, it blurred the line even further.

"Hm..." Lockonis led me to my quarters in silence. As I opened the door, she asked, "Has Silver said anything about his plans for your date?"

I shook my head.

"Well, that's not nice of him to give you no clues. Good thing I know." She smirked and pushed me toward my bedroom.

"Hey!" Why was she being so physically pushy? I scrunched my nose up at her, unhappy, but knowing I could use the help in selecting a better outfit. Obviously, I was too clueless to do it myself.

Lockonis immediately went to my closet, searching through the few things I had hanging up. "A dress or a skirt would be an easy go-to, but you're lacking in both. I know you own some."

"I left those items at my parent's house," I replied as I scrunched up my nose at the thought of either. I greatly disliked dresses and skirts.

"I'd pull something from my closet, but you're smaller than me so none of it would fit right," she said as if she was idly musing. She moved from my closet to my dresser.

Without thinking it through, I voiced my thoughts, "I don't see why this is such a big issue. It's just Silver."

Lockonis stopped and turned around to face me. "And that's the problem," she started angrily and then paused. "Or quite possibly the solution." She hummed for a moment while she returned to going through my dresser.

I would find her actions embarrassing if I had not been distracted by her words. "Solution?"

"Well, you're supposed to have been in a relationship long enough to have become his intended. That level of comfort and familiarity will serve you well, but you need to put it in a romantic perspective and that's where you're going to fall short."

The conversation I had with Kitteren earlier came to mind. She had said something similar, but she was unconcerned about my convincing others. I rubbed my face with my hands, groaning softly at the complex situation I had ended up in.

"Don't think too hard on it. I think our best solution is to see how you do tonight and go from there, but you still need help getting ready." Lockonis' attention turned from going through the shirts I had to the top of my dresser. "Where'd you get this?" She held up the silver crescent moon hair clip. Clear crystals hung at various lengths from it on delicate chains.

My face heated up at the reminder. "It was given to me," I said softly.

"I've never seen you wear it. Granted, you wear your hair the same way all the time. Who gave it to you?"

I hesitated and my boss looked at me expectantly. "Silver," I managed to squeak out.

"Well, you're wearing it tonight then," she grinned broadly, setting it aside. "That gives us a good starting point. Let's put something together."

What had I gotten myself into?

***

ANOTHER MINUTE PASSED. I turned my attention from the clock to my door, wringing my hands. Why was this so nerve wracking? I had gone out to dinner with Silver many times before. At least that was what I assumed was the plan. Lockonis gave me little else to go on.

I sighed and resumed my pacing. This was no good. This whole situation had me distracted. It was taking much of my restraint to not rub the light amount of makeup off. As it was, I had gotten an earful about my lack of makeup and clothing options.

A warm, comforting sensation broke through my emotional turmoil and I pulled Silver's necklace out from under my shirt. "I told you to knock that off," I scolded it quietly.

Not that the inanimate object would listen. It continued to push the sensation at me gently. Sighing, I stared at the golden sun pendant, hoping for some answer as to what I should do.

A soft knock on my door made me jump. I hurried to tuck the necklace under my shirt and get to the door. My hand hovered inches away from the knob. I bit my lower lip, mentally arguing with myself to stop hesitating. It was only Silver.

I scrunched up my nose at the knob, wishing it would open itself and end my internal debate. Lockonis should never have said that it had to be different.

Taking a deep breath, I reached for the door, opening it as normally as I could manage.

"Oh, wow," Silver said, his eyes wide, looking me over. "You look amazing."

I squirmed under his gaze. Lockonis had found the black halter I had buried in the bottom of my drawer. It was there for good reason - the open back was not something I was comfortable with in public. The only saving grace was my long hair covered it.

Nervously I ran my hands over my black dress pants. "Um..."

Silver held out his arm. The only real change to his attire was he wore a short-sleeve, blue Elven tunic. Given the sheen on the material, it was a more formal variation. His hair was out of its normal braid, hanging loose. Even the waves from it being bound were gone.

What were we doing that forced us to play this farce? This was wrong. This was not who we were.

Despite those thoughts, I hesitantly reached for it, wrapping my fingers around the metal bracer on his forearm, unsure if I was doing this right. All of this was to save him from a fate others thought to push on him. It was just a part, right?

Silver smiled down at me. "I hope you're hungry."

I nodded silently - I just wanted to get this over with. I had missed lunch already because of this, but nerves had mostly destroyed my appetite anyway.

He reached over brushing his fingertips along my temple. "You seem nervous."

"You haven't told me what your plan is." It was only one of the reasons, but the easiest one to voice.

"Nothing we haven't done before," Silver said softly. "But to be fair, I'm nervous also. This is a little different from our previous outings."

"Does it have to be?" The words were out of my mouth before I could stop them.

Silver took my hand off his arm and kissed the back of my fingers before putting it back. "It doesn't hurt to change things up once in a while." Then he paused and looked behind me.

I turned to see what it was.

"I haven't seen you wear that in your hair in a while. It still looks good on you."

My free hand went to the crescent moon hair clip holding the top part of my hair back. "I..." I paused. Telling him Lockonis insisted would make the situation more awkward than it already was. "I never found a good reason to wear it." It always seemed too fancy for work.

The smile that graced Silver's face was gentle. "Let's get going."

I took a deep breath and stepped through my door, uncertain about what laid ahead, but willing to give it a chance. It was now up to me to figure out how to play my part or lose my closest friend.

I HID my amusement at Silver's story behind my hand as we walked through the nearby town after dinner. "Sparks seems less forward whenever I talk to him."

"Well, part of it was some liquid courage there. Not to mention he views you on a high pedestal so you're not likely to witness something like that." Silver put his hand over mine that was on his arm, smiling down at me. "I'm glad you're finally relaxing."

I turned away from him as my face heated up. So far the evening had been strikingly similar to our previous outings, though I was still wearing something I normally would not and needed to make unfamiliar gestures such as taking his arm. It was not so bad though. This seemed less complicated than Lockonis made it out to be.

Though the metal under my fingers instead of skin probably made this a little easier. His necklace had been quiet or at least I had not noticed if it was attempting to push its influence.

"No reason to get tense on me now. I…" Silver trailed off.

When I looked up, his attention was ahead. I followed his line of sight and saw the park was lit up with a festival. I had never paid much attention to the nearby festivals the entire time I lived here so I had no idea what it was for.

Silver slid his arm down, taking my hand in his. "Come on. It looks like fun." He tugged at me.

I rolled my eyes and trailed behind him by a couple steps or so, our fingers the only thing keeping us connected. *Ever the child.*

My attention was on our intertwined fingers, contemplating the gesture, so I had not realized where he had taken us. When we stopped, I looked at the crowd warily. Soft, slow music came from the people on the temporary stage. Being as short as I was for an Elf, I could not see over the taller members of my race.

Before I could voice my unease, Silver tugged me along again, through the crowd to the area where couples were dancing. He found a darkened spot off to the side before stepping closer and wrapping his arm around my waist. "It's been quite a while since I have had the pleasure of a dance with you." He grinned down at me, gently brushing a lock of hair out of my face with his free hand.

I scanned the crowd around us, every muscle prepared to flee. "I don't think this is a good idea."

Silver kissed my forehead the moment I turned back to him. "You can stand down. No one here is going to hurt you," he said softly. "Trust me, okay?"

I nodded, the movement stiff. This outing was not work and yet it was. I had no idea what *this* was anymore.

He stepped closer, eliminating the space between us, resting his head on top of mine. "When was the last time we danced?"

It took me a few moments to figure out where to place my hands. "Um... while we were in Ghost Forest?"

Silver led us in a slow dance once I figured myself out. "Oh, yeah, it was at the Alpha Prime's estate for the werewolve's Winter Solstice celebrations. It took a lot of effort, but I finally managed to sneak you away for one dance."

I rolled my eyes at the reminder of the chaos that evening. Being the temporary head of the Ghost Forest branch, I had ended up in more political conversations than I cared to have attended.

"Do you ever wonder what things would be like if they had decided to leave us there?" Silver asked, his tone sounded like he was idly musing.

"I thought you wanted to avoid talking about work," I countered, not having really thought about the question he posed.

"Hm. I did say that, didn't I? I suppose it's a little hard seeing as it's so much a part of our lives." Silver stroked my hair. "I suppose idle chatter will only ruin this anyway."

I moved stiffly while we danced in our little darkened corner. Chatter would have at least given me a distraction. His necklace pushed calm and contentment toward me, warming against my chest. Now it decided to make itself known. What on Terra was the trigger? If I could figure it out, I could avoid it.

In this case, what harm would there be in following it right now? I rested my head against Silver's chest and closed my eyes, listening both to the music and the signals I was getting from the necklace.

My partner's arms tightened around me. Silver seemed content to dance until the musicians stopped playing.

I opened my eyes when Silver stopped. The musicians were thanking the crowd and people were starting to disperse.

He stepped back, taking my hand and kissing the back of it before tugging me along toward the waterfront. My curiosity at what was going on in his head overrode the discomfort of the unfamiliar behavior. However, it was not enough for me to break the silence between us.

As Silver stepped behind me, wrapping his arms around my waist, the one thing I was grateful for at the moment was my power seemed content. That had been a concern at the back of my mind, but playing my part correctly had taken precedence.

After a while of watching the lake, Silver tightened his hold for a moment before stepping away. "I, um... I have something for you."

I turned, seeing him digging in his pocket for a moment before pulling out a folded piece of cloth. Before I could tell him I did not need a gift, he held it out to me.

"I know I said I didn't want to talk about work, but hopefully this will suffice for copying to. I finished it not long ago, but I hadn't gotten a box or found the right time to give it to you." Silver's words came out in rush. He opened his mouth to say more and then closed it.

As I took the cloth from him, I felt something thin and hard inside and raised an eyebrow at him before slowly unwrapping it. A delicate bracelet sat coiled up in the fabric. I picked it up gently with two fingers. Small swirls of silver-colored metal linked together, each wrapped around a small color-changing gem. At first glance and in the dim lighting, I thought they looked like the stones similar to the ones from the mine in Ghost Forest.

I ran my thumb over the bracelet, giving weight to his admission that he had made it. I had no idea what I was supposed to say. This was not simply a tool being handed to me. The personal attachment made this hard for me to process. Why was he giving me this? I could not have possibly been the intended recipient. It was just for work, right?

Silver took the bracelet from me and opened the latch before clasping it around my right wrist. It hung loosely, but not so much that it would fall off. "I'm glad it fits. I wasn't quite sure if I got the sizing right."

"You didn't have to do this," I said quietly, staring at the foreign object around my wrist.

He tilted my chin up to look at him. "I wanted to." He ran his thumb lightly over my lower lip before leaning down to kiss me.

I reminded myself to keep playing my part and wondered if I might wake up to find this had been all some strange dream.

AFTER I PARTED ways with Silver for the evening, I changed up and cleaned the makeup off of my face. It might not have been much, but it felt uncomfortable. I reached for the clasp on the bracelet and stopped now that I had time to look at it in the light.

Why? It was the only clear question that came to mind.

The delicate work was not something I had expected from Silver. I knew he had reforged his circlet into ear cuffs, but that was the extent I knew of him doing metalwork. It made me wonder how little I still knew.

Leaving my bathroom, I looked at my bed. It was late, but I doubted I would be able to rest at this point. I padded barefoot through my bedroom and headed out onto the balcony to enjoy the warm summer night.

"I had a feeling you'd have a hard time resting after that," a familiar female voice came from the shadows.

Having not expected anyone, I jumped and scrambled behind the lounge chair on the balcony, arcane energy pooling in my hands. It took me a moment to put the voice to the person. "Dammit, Retanei! I could've hurt you." I kept my voice down and slowly came back out of my hiding spot while releasing the gathered energy and turning toward where her voice had come from. "How on Terra are you even up here?" I was on the seventh floor.

My Dark Elf friend stepped out of the shadows. Her long silver-white hair framing her ebony face making it easier to see her in the low light. "I'm good at climbing. I should probably be thankful you scrambled for cover instead of casting something."

I sighed and pinched the bridge of my nose, taking a seat on the chair. "I assume you were following me again." She was one of the rare people I never sensed watching me. I could never figure out why that was.

Retanei leaned back against the railing. "Lockonis asked me to. I didn't realize that this was some weird undercover thing. This isn't fair to you."

"Huh?" I looked up at my friend.

"This whole set up. You have to pretend to enjoy yourself. You have to pretend to like Silver in a romantic way. Somehow I doubt you've processed how you feel about this."

I hung my head, letting my hair fall around me. "My feelings don't matter. Silver doesn't want to go through with the arranged marriage and this is the one thing I can do to help."

"I'm not saying that the whole situation that forced you into this isn't wrong, but Ket, you can't ignore yourself on this one. Not this time. Not with Silver. You're going to need to figure out what *you* want when this situation is righted," Retanei said, her voice gentle.

"Are you telling me I failed miserably in my role this evening?"

"No, if I hadn't known better, I would've sworn you were a happy couple. You're shy and nervous, but it makes sense for a first date."

I sighed. That was not enough. "Lockonis is probably going to want to coach me again tomorrow," I muttered more to myself.

"Expect a meeting in the morning. I should get going and get my report to her filed."

Great, now my dating ability was being rated like my arcane abilities. This was why I had not wanted to get mixed up in anything like this.

5

SILVER PULLED at the high collar of his shirt. I had lost count on how often he had done it. It had been so long since I last saw him in the white clerical attire of his Order - not since we worked together on my first field assignment. The blue trim running around the edges of the short-sleeve top was the only thing that broke up the light color.

He had waited until we arrived to change into the outfit. I could only imagine how cranky he would be right now if he had spent the better part of the day traveling in it.

We sat outside at a restaurant near the docks waiting for our food. I dug my fingers into the hair near my neck, trying to loosen how tight the bun was. How had I managed to wear this every day?

"It's been a while for both of us, hasn't it?" Silver asked.

I blinked and looked up at him. "Now that you mention it..." It had been a couple of years since I last put my hair up in a bun. It had been my constant hairstyle for decades, but now it felt foreign. "Is it really necessary for me to wear my hair up?"

"It'll be expected. I can do other styles with your hair while we're there. Perhaps something not so tight." He gave me a sympathetic smile. "And before you ask, no, I don't know why we're supposed to keep our hair long and tie it back all the time. There are a few exceptions to the rule, but I don't remember all of them. I think the Elders and scholars are exempt from having to tie it back."

"*They couldn't exempt guests also,*" I muttered under my breath. I frowned, moving my hands away, needing to stop toying with my bun before I messed it up and had to redo it. "You don't think it'll be over quick?"

Silver shook his head and took a sip of water. "I know it won't. Not with their response when I told them you would be coming with me."

I sighed and rested my chin in my hand. The bracelet Silver had given me made its presence known. I shifted the chained gems so it would sit comfortably.

"I've really gotten you out of your comfort zone. I'm sorry."

I shrugged. Hopefully this would not take too long. "How come you're wearing that?"

Silver tugged on his collar again. "Trust me, I'd rather not be." He sighed and quit fidgeting for the moment. "I'm hoping it'll appease the Elders enough to listen."

I frowned at his statement. The lengths we were going through for his former Order. Though, if faced with needing to return to the Arcane College to deal with something, would I behave differently?

A couple of Human women sat down at the table next to us.

"Oh, did I tell you about the spider last night?" the one with black hair asked.

Silver's attention turned to the table as he took my free hand.

The woman with light pink hair shook her head.

"I was working on something when my daughter started crying. There was a spider on the floor near her. So, I killed it," she explained briefly, her tone never shifting from neutral.

And here I had been hoping for a more interesting story. Anything to distract me from the current situation.

The woman telling the story continued, using her hands to help. "And then it exploded into like twenty babies. I spent half my evening stomping spiders."

"That suddenly escalated," Silver said softly.

I laughed lightly as their conversation turned to more mundane things. Even he had taken to eavesdropping to take his mind off the Central Seat for the moment. I shifted in my chair now that I had nothing else to focus on.

My partner reached across the table to gently brush my bangs back with his free hand, running his thumb over my hand that he held. "Kela, talk to me."

I shifted in my chair and thought about moving my hand away, but squeezed his instead. We were in this together after all. "I... I'm not sure what I should be doing. I know what we discussed on the way here, but there seems little I can actually do to help."

Silver ran his thumb over my knuckles lightly. "And that's fine. Let me do the hard work this time. The Gods know I haven't been much help."

I rolled my eyes. He underestimated his contributions. "You shouldn't have to handle this alone." And I needed something more to do. Copying the library was not going to keep my mind occupied enough.

He kissed the back of my fingers. "I'm not. I'm also not going to put more on you than I've already asked."

Catching sight of a server headed our way with our food, I pulled my hand back. Silver initially reached for it, but realized my attention was behind him and turned to see what was going on.

It was not the same server who took our order. He figured out which plate went to who and paused. "You're a paladin, sir?"

Silver paused and looked up at him. "Yes."

The young Human man wrung his hands. "I... sorry, I'm interrupting your meals."

My partner shook his head. "It's fine. What did you want to ask?"

The server bit his lower lip for a moment. "I've seen a fair number of paladins around all my life, but you're the first Elven one I've had the pleasure of meeting."

"I'm visiting," Silver said. His smile was visibly forced, or at least to me it appeared that way.

"Ah." The server bowed. "It was a pleasure. Enjoy your meal."

Once the man had left Silver's shoulders slumped.

"You okay?" I asked softly. *What should I do here?* I knew I needed to help him somehow, but was at a loss of what. Trying to guess was not the best strategy.

"I don't want to be associated with the Central Seat right now," he muttered, picking up his fork and stabbing a carrot with more force than necessary.

I hesitantly reached out and squeezed his hand. Why did I have to second guess every action with him?

Silver gave me a small, forced smile. "We better eat. We don't want to be late getting to the ferry."

He wanted my help and yet Silver was running away from me. Pushing him was going to do neither of us any good at the moment so I worked on getting through my meal. I filed away my concerns for later.

———

WHILE I WOULD NORMALLY FIND the gentle sea breeze calming, all I could do was worry. I stood next to Silver on the dock, forcing myself to not pace or shift my weight from one foot to the other. Could I keep Silver from having to go through this arranged marriage? Would Silver change his mind after he met Amanda Sayer? Would I be able to keep my arcane abilities hidden? What should I expect when we arrived at the Central Seat?

Fidgeting with the bracelet Silver gave me to copy the library to, I hoped the minor usage of my power would help me keep it hidden otherwise. At least the spell showed no outward signs, which unless there was someone arcane sensitive around, I should remain undetected.

Silver put his hand over mine. "It's okay. You'll be fine." He tugged at the high collar again. "It'll be nice to get out on the water and away from this heat."

I raised an eyebrow at him. "I thought you said that was enchanted so the weather wouldn't bother you." I vaguely remembered him telling me about it when we first met.

He sighed loudly, tugging harder at his collar for a moment, twisting his head before giving up. "Enchantments wear off after a while. I never thought I'd be donning this again, so I didn't bother recharging it. I also don't plan on being stuck in it long enough to go through the hassle of re-enchanting it."

Yet he had obviously kept the garment. Just as he had kept his original full plate armor. I wondered why. I glanced back at the trunk he had brought with both his original armor and his current one. Though he wore parts of the new one since it had been built into some of his original gear. Or, glancing at his ear cuffs which had once been a circlet that he had altered.

A large ferry came into view. I shifted from one foot to the other. Last time I had been on a similar type of boat, I had nearly gotten thrown through a wall by a Troll. I had not needed that reminder hanging over me with everything else going on.

"If that was me, I would never have heard the end of being late," Silver muttered. It was enough to break me out of my memories.

I tugged lightly on his braid to get his attention. He had grown more and more agitated the closer we got to the Central Seat. "You'll get through this."

Silver leaned down, kissing me lightly. "I'm still worried about bringing you, but there's no one else I would want by my side." He smiled gently, picking up the sun pendant that hung around my neck. "I do love seeing this on you. I should have gotten another chain though - this one is too heavy and long on you." He had insisted I wear it out so it could be seen.

I rolled my eyes and shook my head. He had been over the top with compliments since I agreed to court him so he could deal with this. It was only temporary, so I wondered why he bothered. Perhaps to make up for where I fell short.

Silence fell between us as we watched the ferry dock. I glanced around, realizing we were the only people waiting. "Why is it so big?"

Silver turned to look down at me. "There used to be a lot more people who visited the Central Seat, but we likely caught it at an off-time. It also doubles to carry supplies. I doubt we'll depart right off."

Once the ferry settled, a Human woman came down the ramp. "Brother! I heard you were coming back!" she called, waving in our direction.

I looked to Silver. His face had softened. Relief?

"Oh, and who is this lovely one you brought?" She stood in front of me. She wore an outfit identical to Silver's, including the metal bracers on her forearms and fingerless leather gloves. The one difference was she wore a circlet still. Her honey-blonde hair was pulled up in a simple ponytail. I caught a few strands of white running through it.

Silver had a genuine smile now. The contrast was so different from the ones he had given people on the way here. "This is Kela, my intended."

"You best be treating her right or I'm taking her from you." She smiled broadly. "I'm Marzena Nowak. I've known this knucklehead my entire life. It's about damn time he found someone who could put up with him."

I fidgeted with my hands. I had no idea what to say. Silver's change in attitude had thrown me off. As if I had not already been confused by it all.

Marzena signaled for us to follow her. "Let's get onboard. They sent this one out special for you guys."

I bowed to her and followed them onto the ferry. Both walked with ease while my legs wobbled up the ramp. I managed to at least appear to be stable by moving slower. I could always claim my suitcase was heavy. Silver would likely have taken it if he had not had his hands full with his gear.

Once we settled, Marzena brought bottles of water over to us and eyed me for a moment before turning to Silver. "Please tell me she can talk. It'd be horrible to have to listen to you constantly."

"I still do," I said quietly, accepting the water.

Silver had begun to drink and sputtered.

Marzena laughed loudly. "I like her already."

"You hardly know her," Silver argued.

His friend smiled broadly at him. "Well, I can tell right now that Kela is a much better match for you than Amanda."

"You know the woman they selected?" Silver asked.

Marzena stretched out, propping her feet up on the small table. "Of course I know Amanda. I'm weapons master - I know everyone. That girl won't listen to a damn thing I try to teach her. Her skills in combat are sorely lacking. I would never allow her to go into battle as she is." She looked me over. "Something tells me you've seen your share of fighting. Probably his fault." She thumbed at Silver.

"Hey!" My partner kicked her feet so they fell off the table.

I laughed lightly, trying to hide my amusement behind my hand while they stared each other down, both smiling.

"I can get into trouble well enough on my own," I replied once I felt I could speak without giggling. So, this was the friend Silver had spoken of. With my partner visibly relaxed at her presence, I figured I could let down some of my guard around her at least for now. She seemed nice enough.

Mostly just the two of them talked over the couple of hours it took to get to the Central Seat. All of Silver's worry might be for nothing and we would be headed back to normal life in short order.

"What can you tell me about Amanda?" Silver asked as the Central Seat came into view on the horizon.

Marzena narrowed her eyes as she stared at the table. "Outside of her lack of martial prowess, she's eager to please the higher ups. She's never been much good at any one thing from what I can tell, but whatever they order her to do, she'll throw herself completely into it. Including this arrangement."

I frowned. She was likely going to be unhappy to see me then.

Silver sighed, folding his arms. "I don't even understand why they're pushing this on me. I hold nothing of value."

Marzena sat there staring at him with wide eyes. "Nothing of value. Silver, you hold the Sutton lineage."

My partner sat up fully. "No, I don't. I'm not related by blood." He flicked the point of one of his ears, likely to remind her of his Elven heritage.

She sighed, crossing her arms and sitting back. "You were Blaise's first son and he had performed the right for the lineage to go to you years before James was born. Didn't he ever tell you?"

It was Silver's turn to sit there, staring. "No. It doesn't make sense. I'm Elven. I'm not eligible."

Marzena rolled her eyes. "Yeah, and he also trained you to be a paladin so don't give me that 'not eligible' crap."

Silver folded his arms and sat back, frowning. "So, you're telling me that they're acknowledging something that I didn't even know about?"

"It's my fault, actually," Marzena said, looking down at her hands in her lap. "I had been caring for the vault when I came across it. I've been fighting for them to recognize you. Then they came out with this."

Silver's shoulders slumped. "Marzi... I appreciate what you were trying to do, but..."

"No," she said sharply, "they've treated you like crap all of these years. They drove you away. I know what happened in Ocean's Edge. I just... you're obnoxious, but you're family."

Silver tugged on his braid hard. "You could've just called."

"Nuh uh." Marzena waved a finger at him. "I'm not letting your deeds be ignored. Besides, I had no idea how to contact you. *You* could've called, you ass."

"I couldn't remember the number and I couldn't look it up after I left. You're a pain, you know that?" he shot at her, but there was no anger in his face or voice.

They really did act like siblings. More than I did with Kitteren. Why was I here if he already had someone he could turn to?

She laughed. "Well, we're almost there. Time to go tell them where to stuff this stupid tradition."

As the Central Seat grew larger out the windows, I could not find as much entertainment in their banter as I normally would have. From their conversation, it did not sound like there would be many others with whom Silver could connect with like this.

I followed the two out on deck silently. In just what I had heard on the ride I had learned more about Silver than I had in the entire time I had known him. The thought of what was I doing here resurfaced. Marzena was going to be far better support for him.

"Hey, Marzi..." Silver said softly, stepping forward to stand between us. "Can I ask you a favor?"

She turned to him.

"Keep an eye on Kela for me when I'm not able to. She can handle herself, but..." Silver reached out and brushed my bangs back.

I closed my eyes, content at the gentle touch of his calloused fingers.

Marzena smiled broadly. "Oh, I was going to without you even asking. She's too damn cute."

What had I gotten myself in the middle of?

<hr>

I walked silently next to Silver and behind Marzena through the grand halls of the Central Seat. Initially I started behind Silver also, but he had taken my hand and pulled me forward to be in line with him.

Two more people in the same garb as the paladins around me stood outside of a large set of doors. They opened them for us. I hesitated, but Silver holding my hand allowed me only a moment.

My partner leaned down and whispered, "This is the Court of the Elders."

There were older Human men sitting behind a long, curved desk - similar to what I had seen of government councils - facing the center of the room. A younger Human woman stood off to the side. I was wholly out of place here not wearing a white clerical suit with blue trim, though I noticed the older men also had gold piping on theirs between the white and the blue. Denoting rank? I wished Silver had given me more information, but I had bet something like this had not even crossed his mind as important.

I bit the inside of my cheek. Here I would have to remain silent.

"Silver Blaise," the one in the center began. "It is good to see you return."

Why did the man's words sound insincere? I had to be imagining things or perhaps it was simply the situation. I took note of the older Human men behind the desk. Were there not any women? Perhaps they were simply not here. Granted, the Circle of Magi at the Arcane College were all men the last I knew.

There was also an emphasis on lineage being held by men.

I would have shaken my head to clear the random thoughts if I had not been standing in the Court of Elders. Figuring out the strange traditions of the Order could wait until I was not in the presence of others.

"Elders, I'm here to clear up a mess you began, not pleasantries," my partner shot back. "Let me make my intention clear right now: I am here to nullify the arrangement."

The woman off to the far-right side of the desk stared at him with a shocked expression on her face and then looked at me, narrowing her brown eyes. Until she had moved, I had not done more than note another person. Her light brown hair was pulled back into a bun at the base of her neck, similar to how I wore mine.

Another of the Elders spoke. "We are willing to discuss that. However, you will take the time to get to know the person we have chosen for you before a decision is made."

"There is no need for that," Silver argued. "Kela is my intended." He put a hand on my back and I forced myself to remain still. Should I smile? Bow? While I debated, the seconds ticked by too quickly and I simply stood there stiffly.

The Elders looked at each other, a couple whispered between themselves. The one in the center spoke again, "We will need further discussion on this matter. For now, ladies, please see him... them to their room. You're dismissed."

I followed Silver's actions and gave the Elders a short bow before following him out the door. Marzena was ahead of us and Amanda quickly passed me to catch up to her.

That meeting seemed short, but they had not immediately agreed to ending the arrangement either. Silver had said it would not be a fast process. Why had they been so quick to dismiss us?

Once we were away from the room, Marzena stopped us. "I suppose introductions are in order. Silver, Kela, may I present to you Amanda Sayer."

She bowed to Silver. "It will be my honor to be your bride if you will have me." Then she turned to glare at me.

Silver stepped in between us. "I'll not have you disrespect my intended."

Amanda stood up straight, her eyes wide. "My apologies. Please grant me the privilege of your time so you may get to know me."

Marzena shook her head, pinching the bridge of her nose. "Let's go. They need to rest, Amanda. They traveled a long way."

We followed the women outside and away from the main building of the Central Seat. At one point we passed a training area.

"Silver, think I can get in a sparring session or two with you while you're here?" Marzena asked over her shoulder.

My partner smirked. "I'll wipe the floor with you."

His friend laughed. "I'd like to see you try. I might have to see if your intended will indulge me also. I could certainly stand to learn something new."

"I'm not very good," I said softly. Especially without my power. The reality of how much my hands were tied while I was here had finally sunk in.

Marzena turned and smiled broadly at me from over her shoulder for a moment.

Silver leaned down and said, "She's not going to take no for an answer."

I rolled my eyes. It must be a paladin thing.

"Paladin Blaise, would you see fit to spar with me also?" Amanda asked.

"I won't allow it," Marzena said. "Your skills are abysmal and I won't see you hurt trying to prove yourself. As it is, you shouldn't have been allowed to be named a paladin because of that."

Silence followed.

Eventually we walked into a building that seemed to have been purposed for housing.

"You're lucky - they gave you one of the nicer guest suites,"

Marzena said. "Okay, I might've been in charge of arranging things here."

Silver reached forward and clapped her on the shoulder. "You've done a lot for me and I don't know how to thank you."

Marzena winked at him as she reached for a door. "It's the least I can do. Besides, the new seekers have been driving me mad, so it was a nice change of duties for a bit. Here you go."

It was massive. A large bed was against one wall toward the back near where doors were opened to show a balcony overlooking the water. Couches and chairs were closest to us and I could not tell what the room off to the side in the bedroom area was. I clutched my hands to my chest. I should not be here.

"Marzi, this is too much," Silver said quietly.

"Bah! In Ocean's Edge you got the bottom of the barrel for accommodations. It was free so I took it. You're a tall freak of nature - I figured you'd like to not feel cramped." Marzena was smiling broadly at him. "At least Kela is about my height."

"Paladin Nowak, we should show her to her room." Amanda gestured at me, avoiding looking in my direction.

Marzena raised an eyebrow at her. "What are you talking about? This is her room also."

"It is highly inappropriate—!" Amanda started.

"Enough!" Marzena cut her off. "Kela deserves to be with someone she knows. With her intended."

"She won't be for long," Amanda muttered.

"If you'll excuse us," Marzena said, pushing Amanda toward the door. "You two get some rest. I'll come by in a bit - I need to take care of a few things."

As soon as the door closed, I let out the breath I had not realized I held. "This seems overly complicated."

"Tell me about it," Silver muttered. "Something isn't right." He started pacing.

My attention had drifted a bit to taking in the room, but not so far that I could not continue the conversation. "In regards to what?"

"The whole lineage thing. It doesn't make sense why they would honor it. Less why my master would have wanted me to have it in the first place." His pacing turned into stalking.

I stepped in front of him and put my hands on his chest to get him to stop. "Hey, you're not going to be able to make sense of it if you get worked up. We just got here. We don't know the whole story yet. We'll figure it out."

Silver lightly grabbed my shoulder. I felt him draw the anchor. His whole posture was rigid and his eyes wild.

I nodded. That we had barely arrived and I needed to ground him spoke volumes about what I had missed. How could I have been blind to how this was affecting him?

His lips were on mine in an instant. This was far more demanding than any other time he had kissed me. The term desperate seemed more appropriate. I struggled to keep up with his lead, having been unprepared.

When he finally backed away, I was winded. I could not separate my thoughts from the emotional jumble coming from the necklace. Without realizing what I was doing, I was on the balls of my feet, wanting to continue.

Silver kissed me lightly before pushing me back down so I was flat on my feet. "Thank you. I think I'm okay now."

I looked away, my face heating up. "Sorry, it's hard to separate myself from it sometimes." I fingered the chain around my neck.

He gently brushed my bangs back. "I'll keep that in mind. Let's get some rest. A quick nap might help both of us."

I nodded, heading for the couch. I hated admitting he was right, but between travel and the time change, I was tired.

My partner grabbed my arm. "Come on, we'll rest together."

"Silver, I..." How could I explain the need to separate from him for a bit?

"We've been cooped up for too long." He slid his hand down my arm until he took my hand and tugged me along to the balcony. The view over the ocean made me pause and forget I wanted to argue with my partner. It was beautiful out here. I paused to take a deep breath of the ocean air. The salty sea air had a calming effect.

Then I took a moment to look around the outdoor area: one side of the balcony held a small table with a couple of chairs while the other was a couch and a couple of lounge chairs.

Silver tugged me toward the latter. Somehow, he situated us so we both fit on the couch, but I was mostly on top of him. I went to ask if I was too heavy, but yawned instead.

"Just rest, Kela. I'm not going anywhere."

When I woke, I was still stretched out mostly on top of Silver. I raised my head to look at my partner. His eyes remained closed and his breathing was soft and slow. He was still asleep.

Then I turned my attention to what was soft and silky in my hand. I dropped the bound hair as soon as I realized I had been holding onto Silver's braid again.

He laughed and I jumped, scampering to get off him, unceremoniously falling onto my butt on the balcony floor in the process.

"Are you okay?" Silver asked softly, still laughing lightly. He propped himself up on one arm to look down at me.

I scrunched up my face at him and folded my arms, turning away.

My partner leaned over and kissed my forehead. "Looks like just your pride was hurt. And if you like my braid that much, I guess I better keep it."

So much for him being asleep. A knock on the door to the suite stopped the admonishment I had been preparing to unleash on him.

Silver got up and helped me to my feet before heading inside. I followed him toward the door, curious, but cautious about who it might be.

Marzena stood with one of the Elders I had seen earlier. She looked unhappy, but the older Human man simply smiled at us.

"I hope you were able to get some rest," the Elder said. His voice was gentle as if he was talking to a child.

Something was not right here. That did not match the harsher tones from when we were in the Court of Elders. Granted, this man had not spoken by my recollection.

"Is there something you needed?" Silver's words were clipped.

"A couple of things, actually. I would like to speak with the lovely lady you brought with you and while we talk, the remaining Elders would like to begin scheduling out meetings with you."

I bit my lower lip and looked to Silver.

"I'll be with her," Marzena said quietly. Her eyes were locked on my partner as if she was trying to tell him something without outright saying it.

Perhaps I was still too tired if I was reading that far into things.

Silver turned to look down at me. "You could use more rest."

I shook my head. "I'll be fine. Go ahead."

"Are you sure?" My partner glanced at the two standing outside the suite door.

I forced a small smile, still uneasy about this sudden call. "I wouldn't mind stretching my legs."

Silver kissed my forehead. "Alright. I'll catch up with you when I can." He turned to Marzena and held her gaze before letting me out the door. "Keep her safe."

Marzena tossed him a smirk. "Absolutely. Besides, she could use a tour of the grounds."

I took a deep breath while Silver locked up the suite and headed off.

"It's okay. I'm here," Marzena said quietly.

I nodded, eyeing the Elder cautiously.

"Kela was the name I believe I heard. I'm Valere Bisset, an Elder within the Order. Forgive me for not giving you the long version. Even I find that painfully dry and overdone, so I thought I'd spare you," Valere said, laughing lightly.

The only thing I could do was nod and force a smile. What could they want with me?

"Come, let's walk while we chat. I would like to meet the person that the head of the Sutton line has chosen." Valere started walking without waiting for a response.

"Does that mean you'll nullify the arrangement?" I asked. Then I mentally kicked myself for it - I could make things worse if I was not careful.

The Elder glanced over at me. "That is not such an easy thing to do. Much time and thought went into creating the arrangement and much time and thought must be given before nullifying it. I understand you're eager to get back to your normal life and we'll see to it that proper consideration is given to you as well."

I frowned and turned my gaze toward the floor. Silver was right - this was not going to be quick. What would happen if they decided against nullifying the arrangement? I put a hand to my chest as it tightened. Work would not be the same without him.

A hand landed on my shoulder and I looked up at Marzena.

She squeezed my shoulder. "I'm certain that the Elders have already seen how close the two of you are."

"Yes, it's quite apparent," Valere said, his tone off. "If he had remained in contact with us and let us know that he was involved with someone, we would have held off on creating the arrangement. Now, while we normally prefer to choose someone from within the group associated with the line, there are no viable candidates."

I looked to Marzena. This process seemed overly complicated.

The female paladin walking next to me frowned at the Elder. "I'll explain later. I believe Elder Bisset has forgotten that you aren't as versed in our traditions."

"Ah, please forgive me. I don't often deal with people outside of the Order." Valere tugged at his collar, clearing his throat. "While Amanda may not be the best paladin, we have found that she would be a perfect balance for Silver which we need to weigh before coming to a decision."

Balance? What does that mean? I was essentially Silver's opposite. I bit my lower lip. I had barely met Amanda, so I had no idea what they used to base this opinion.

I followed the pair to a room down on the first floor. When I walked in, there were rows of white garments hanging with blue occasionally mixed in. Some were of the same styles as what Marzena and Valere wore. Others were longer. Some appeared to be simplistic in their design and padded. I raised an eyebrow at the choice of destination.

"Kela, since you are a special guest of ours, we decided that it would be best if you wore a seeker uniform while you're here." Valere walked over and put his hand on a rack with what looked like white dresses. "It will help distinguish you from the visitors we receive and grant you access to areas that might otherwise be closed off."

"At least long enough for people to realize that you're not a regular visitor," Marzena jumped in. "I'm sure after a few days people will get the idea that you're part of our family."

Valere glared at her for a brief moment - just long enough for me to catch. "It would be preferable if you continued to wear it when out and about. I'll leave Marzena to help you find one that fits. And please, see that she is familiarized with the grounds." He turned on his heel and left.

For wanting to get to know me, he left without asking anything. Whatever his idea was, that meant they were likely going to have a close eye kept on me.

I bit my lower lip and eyed the rack of seeker uniforms warily. I hated dresses.

Marzena growled at the door as soon as it was closed. "My brother is going to be unhappy about this when he finds out, but hey, you get to try on a new outfit."

"Is there more to it than simply wearing the uniform?"

She shrugged and started searching the rack. "Damned if I know. They'll likely leave you alone as long as you don't go poking your nose into things you shouldn't. I'll try to keep an eye out for you, but I still have my own duties to attend to. Granted, that doesn't account for much these days."

I scrunched up my face as I fingered the uniform closest to me, looking over the design. "I hate dresses," I muttered.

Marzena laughed. "It's not a dress. I'm sure the men who have to wear this would not be happy to hear someone call it that. Think of it as a really long shirt." She pulled one off the rack and held it up, parting a couple of the panels - the slit starting at what I would guess was about the hip. "There's pants to go underneath. It's meant to be a mix between the scholar robes and the paladin clerical uniform." She picked at her own top to emphasize the second one.

The garment she was holding went back on the rack and she looked through others.

"Let's see. You look to be about my height, but you're scrawny."

I rolled my eyes at her statement. She was not the first and I doubted would be the last to call me that. I made a face at the rack and reminded myself not to cause Silver more problems than he already had.

"You can say no to this. It isn't an order. Or rather, they can't order you around. They can't really order Silver around either. I guess he's mellowing out now that he has you. He would never have been as diplomatic as he has been."

I bit my lower lip, considering her words. "You make it sound like he was out of control before."

"Hm..." Marzena took a moment. "That's not what I would have called it, but he certainly had a chip on his shoulder."

"Chip?" I tilted my head at her, not understanding the phrase.

"Oh, sorry, uh..." She stopped looking through the garments on the rack. "He was confrontational. Easy to provoke. He seemed angry a lot about something. It took a while for people to get used to him though he seemed to have a lot more patience and calm when working with parishioners. Anyway, it never was directed at someone.

Well, except maybe James, but he was a jerk to everyone. Silver was the only one who would stand between him and the rest of us."

I crossed my arms and turned my attention to the floor. "The way you say it, I'm starting to wonder if I don't know him as well as I think I do."

"You probably know him better than anyone else. Certainly more than the Elders. They might have known him when they themselves were becoming paladins, but they haven't had to deal with him for decades. No offense, but it is a bit irritating seeing him looking like he had the last time I saw him and I've gotten gray hairs since."

I smirked as a thought crossed my mind. "Well, you could always make fun of him for always having gray hair."

Marzena gave me a broad smile. "Oh no, I'm not repeating that. I did that once when I was around 15 years old. I was mouthing off at him over something stupid. Not exactly the brightest idea I ever had." She pulled one of the long white tops off the rack. "I think this will work. Let me find some other things for you and then you can try them on. Though I'm somewhat curious what you'd look like in some of the other uniforms."

"This will be more than enough to deal with." I took the hanging garment thrust at me and held it up while she hustled to find more parts to the uniform. What had I gotten myself into?

6

—————

WHEN I RETURNED to the suite after much help from Marzena to find a seeker uniform that fit right, Silver had already gotten back. The two of them argued back and forth about me wearing it, though Marzena was of the same mind that it was a ridiculous request. I put an end to their bickering by pointing out to my partner that if it made things easier, I could deal with it.

The next morning, I got ready while Silver was away at morning prayers. By the time he returned, I was tugging at the collar, regretting my decision to agree to wear the uniform. These things were uncomfortable. I had not remembered it being so bad when I tried it on the day before. The loose blue pants underneath made me feel better that this was not a dress, but the fabric from them and the four long panels of the top got caught together easily.

Silver sighed as I moved about the suite, trying to figure out how people managed with all of this. At least I did not have to contend with sleeves as well. "Kela, stop."

I turned and looked at him, crossing my arms and prepared for him to argue with me about wearing it again.

"You're all tangled," he said, coming to kneel down in front of me. He grabbed the front panel at the top of the slits and shook it out. "If you start getting tangled again, it's usually this panel that's the problem, but if you don't catch it early, it'll mess up the others as well.

They really needed more form fitting pants with this." He moved around me, repeating the process with the side panels and the back one.

"Thanks," I said, knowing I must have been bright red at how pathetic it was to be getting caught up in a garment.

"I'd try to convince you to not wear it, but you're too damn stubborn. It does look good on you though." Silver stood in front of me and got his fingers under my collar, pulling on his necklace that I wore. "Wear that out. It'll be a good reminder to the others." He settled the chain on the outside of the tall collar and gently rested the sun pendant on the front of my top.

I nodded silently. I was out of my element here. When this began, I had not expected to be needing to rely on Silver quite so much. I would not have believed him if he had told me that I would have problems dressing properly.

He ushered me over to the vanity and prodded me to sit on the stool.

I opened my mouth to argue with him as he picked up my brush, but stopped. He had enough problems to deal with. Letting him brush my hair would help calm him before any meetings he needed to attend.

"Are you still planning to head to the library after breakfast?" Silver asked after he finished brushing my hair. He was in the process of pulling it up.

"Yes. If nothing else, maybe I can get a better understanding of how everything works."

"You're not likely to find that information in a book. Even I'm unsure of the changes since I was last here. It's been a few decades. Last I had seen any of the current Elders, they were the ones wearing seeker uniforms. Honestly, I didn't recognize them until they said their names."

His words put into perspective the differences between his Elven lifespan and the Human ones around him. "I'm sure I can find something to entertain myself."

Silver grinned and then leaned over to kiss my cheek. "You do lose yourself in books."

I put my hand to my cheek, ignoring the warmth from his necklace. "Why'd you do that? It's just us."

"Indulge me, would you?" His attention was on my hair.

I frowned and crossed my arms. I was the one who agreed to this nonsense. For a few minutes I watched my partner working on my hair. If it was me doing it, I would have been done by now. *"I'm starting to regret this,"* I muttered to myself in my dialect of common.

Silver paused. "I'm sorry. I'll make it up to you after we leave." He tied off the end of a small braid. "There. That should hopefully not be as tight as you had it yesterday."

I turned my head, trying to make sense of what had taken him so long. He had put my hair up into a softer updo with a pair of braids wrapped around it. They hung off the bun to my right, not quite touching the collar of my shirt.

"Better?"

Biting my lower lip, I nodded. He was only trying to help and I was being fussy. "Thank you."

He kissed my cheek. "Come on. I'll walk you to the library after breakfast. It's the least I can do." He paused and looked at me once I stood up. "Actually, there's one benefit to you wearing that."

"What?" I tugged at my collar. At least now that he adjusted the panels, I could move a little easier.

My partner held my shrunken staff in its holster out to me. "You'll be able to hide that easily."

I rolled my eyes and sat down to attach the holster to my thigh. If nothing else, at least it would hold down some of the loose fabric of the pants. "Do you think I'm going to need it?"

He frowned, crossing his arms while he watched me. "I hope not, but if nothing else, just consider it you staying on even ground with the paladins. We're all constantly armed."

That was not something I had considered. I was always armed as well with my arcane abilities, but I had to watch my usage here. Copying the library was one thing - it would go unnoticed. Weilding it to defend myself would be a dead giveaway that I was an arcane caster.

Once finished, I followed him out the door. While he locked it behind us, I asked. "Do you think you'll have time to point me at where I should start in the library?"

Silver smiled at me gently. "I can make the time."

THE SCHOLARS in the library did not seem pleased with my presence, but not a one spoke to me and they all kept their distance, occasionally shooting a frown or glare in my direction. I sighed, got up, and put the book I had been pretending to read away. Scriptures held no interest for me, but picking a book at random off the shelves I scanned and stopping to read for a bit made my activity hopefully look less suspicious.

A few shelves later and I found another good stopping point. I collected my book and sat down at an empty table. Granted, they were all empty in the main part of the library. I would look for a quieter corner, but Silver asked for me to wait for him here and the last thing he needed was to go hunting all over the library looking for me.

Marzena took a seat next to me. "Well, you look like you fit right in."

One of the scholars tossed me a nasty look before disappearing into the stacks, their long white robe fluttering behind them. At least I had not been asked to wear that. I might have objected. I reminded myself that the seeker uniform was not a dress.

Sighing, I forced a smile. "I think my presence might be interrupting the people here."

"Nonsense. They're just worried that you're going to be better at whatever it is that scholars do. I'm honestly not certain. I just see them studying all the time." She shrugged. "I do spend a fair amount of time here and I still haven't figured it out."

I managed a small smile for Marzena. "Though I fear if you're looking for something, I'd be the worst person to ask."

She gave me a broad smile. "Well, it's only your first day. Given enough time, I have a feeling you'd have this place memorized."

How could she possibly make that kind of assumption? I tilted my head at her.

"Come on, let's head to lunch." Marzena stood and signaled for me to follow. "The crowd should have thinned out by now."

What time was it? I looked down at my watch. If she had not come by and said something, I would have missed it. But... "Where's Silver?"

Marzena sighed, crossing her arms. "When I went looking for him, they said he was in a meeting with the Elders. I hope they don't try to make him miss a meal. That never ends well."

While I found some amusement at her statement, knowing Silver's eating habits, I wondered if the Elders would attempt something like that. Though it would be more accurate to say I was concerned about how rash my partner might be if they did. Being here and the little I had learned about him from Marzena, I was afraid I would lose him to the past.

Silently, I followed her out of the library. I had not thought they would demand this much of my partner's time. What would his mental state be like when I saw him again?

"Worried about Silver?" Marzena asked once we had left the library.

I raised an eyebrow at her.

"Please, it's written all over your face. Has been since I mentioned that he was still with the Elders."

I sighed, apparently I was too easy to read. "Just wondering what he's going to be like when he gets out."

She toyed with the end of her long ponytail. "Well, I'd like to tell you, but I have a feeling your guess is better than mine. He's changed a lot in the handful of years we've been apart. Though he's still heavily guarded."

"Heavily guarded?" I tilted my head at her. He was not one to give up information about himself easily, but all of my interactions with him had seemed genuine.

"Well, mayhap less around you. I wonder if he's ever let anyone all the way in. To see who he really is inside. I know I haven't and before you came along, me and Maria were the two who were closest to him."

The name sounded familiar, though Silver had not mentioned Maria much after the first time we worked together. I chewed on the thought for a bit, wondering how much he hid from me also. It was his right to do so just as it was my right to maintain my walls.

We arrived quickly at the dining hall.

"Lunch is over," one of the paladins said as we approached the counter. He glared at me.

"You just served someone right in front of us," Marzena argued.

The blond Human man sneered at us. "Last one. You'll have to wait for dinner now."

Marzena turned to me and shrugged. "Guess if lunch is ending early then that means I can call whoever was on duty for some extra training time."

"You wouldn't…" he started and then trailed off.

She turned back to the man. "Why not? You obviously have the extra time if you're closing down early."

"Fine." The man grabbed a couple of trays and set about putting two more meals together. "Don't come so late next time."

Taking the trays and setting them down on the counter in front of us, Marzena tossed back, "I'd be more concerned about treating a guest poorly. It could cause you problems." She winked at him, picked up her tray, and signaled with her head for me to follow.

I gave the man a short bow and grabbed my tray, hurrying to catch up. The dining hall was mostly empty and she took the nearest unoccupied table.

Sitting down across from her, I kept my voice down when I said, "You didn't have to do that. I'm okay with skipping meals."

Marzena scrunched up her face at me, her mouth full. As soon as she swallowed what she had eaten, she replied, "Well, I'm not. Not for me and certainly not for you. You're scrawny. Toned, but still scrawny." She reached over and poked my upper arm. "I need to remember to give Silver a hard time about making sure you eat better."

I rolled my eyes and pinched the bridge of my nose. So it was not just my partner.

"Eat, Kela. It won't taste better cold."

These paladins were certainly a confusing lot.

***

THE ONLY THING lunch provided was stares. I had not tasted my food as it felt like the entire dining hall, as sparse as it was, was judging me. Marzena kept trying to distract me, but it was not so simple with feeling like every alarm in my head was going off and none of them making sense.

It did not change when we went to leave.

Silver caught up with me and Marzena as we left the dining hall about the time the alarms in my head started dying off. He fell in line with us and wrapped an arm around my shoulders before kissing the side of my head. "Sorry I missed lunch with you."

"You're lucky I went and got her. I have a feeling she would have skipped it," Marzena tossed at him, her tone teasing.

My partner squeezed my shoulder. "Kela..." he warned.

I rolled my eyes and crossed my arms. "I lost track of the time." This was a habit he should know by now.

"Says the girl wearing a watch." Marzena folded her arms, smirking.

"She doesn't pay attention to it when she's deep in something," Silver said. "Where are the two of you headed?"

"Library," I replied, toying with the bracelet he had given me that I had been storing the information in. It was either return there or go to our room, but I had a task to complete. The library was not nearly as big as I imagined it, but it would still take a long time to copy everything.

"You need to get out of that stuffy place. Get some fresh air," Marzena argued.

Silver brushed my bangs back. "She's right, though you don't do well being idle. I've got an idea." He took my hand and tugged for me to follow.

"*You gave me a task*," I said quietly, using my dialect of common. It was highly unlikely that Marzena would understand. "*It's going to take time.*"

"You need a break." My partner kept his eyes on his path, not even bothering to turn around to reply. "You never rest well when we're in a new place. This might help with the transition."

"Wait, what did she say?" Marzena asked, jogging to catch up with us.

Silver laughed. "Just her usual trying to get out of something, though you don't even know where we're going." He turned his attention down to me on the last part.

I scrunched up my face at him. At least I had enough time this morning to figure out how to stop getting tangled in layers of fabric that constituted the seeker uniform. Unfortunately, that meant I had nothing to slow me, and subsequently him, down.

We passed by the training grounds which gave me some relief that it was not our destination. He led us to the next building that was back against the forest line. It had been set away from the other surrounding buildings.

"Why come here?" Marzena asked. "They stopped using it a couple of years ago."

"I noticed," Silver said, rubbing his temple. "People have been using the main hall all morning to practice. I don't know how the Elders tolerate it. At least when they decided we should have lunch we retreated to the Chamber."

"You actually ate with the Elders? I'm impressed," Marzena commented. "They don't like having guests. Not unless they want something from them."

Silver snorted and frowned. "They only offered for me to dine with them because I was about to walk out."

Marzena crossed her arms, grinning. "And yet here you are."

My partner shrugged. "Well, lunch was over and I had no patience for their idle chatter. All these meetings so far have been nothing but a waste of my time."

I pinched the bridge of my nose. He had a knack for aggravating people. I only hoped he knew what he was doing. I would also have to ask him more about his meetings when we were alone. Perhaps there was another perspective I could offer.

Once we reached the doors of the offset building, Marzena put her hand against them. There was a click and she pushed them open. I tilted my head. A magical lock?

Silver leaned down to whisper in my ear, "She's always had a knack for getting into places she shouldn't."

"I heard that," Marzena called back to us. "They only keep it locked to keep visitors out. Though no one ever comes here anymore anyway."

As I stepped through the doors, daylight shown hazily through the dirty windows and dust in the room. Several large white sheets covered furniture and what looked like a piano in the room.

The female paladin moved about, opening up windows. She coughed as she stirred up more dust. "The least they could've done was keep this place clean. Well, I know what I can do now when I have to dole out punishments for skipping training. The hard part is going to be making sure they do it."

"What is this place?" I asked, my voice quiet. The building was mostly this one room. A couple of smaller bathroom or closet sized rooms were toward the back.

"A music practice hall. Or at least it was," Silver said, moving further into the building, helping to open windows. "Now they seem to prefer practicing in the main hall. They really should be back here instead of assaulting people audibly. That has to be a crime of some sort."

"I've gotten creative about skipping major services when the musicians are performing. I know there was a big fight over moving away from here. Too many wouldn't show up because it was set so far out. I suspect that's also part of the reason I have to hunt down people for training. They're more than content to let themselves get rusty," Marzena said. "Nolan also complained that they sounded too different from here to the main hall. Frankly, I think they sound worse now. Care to tell me why you wanted to come here? You used to prefer training when you were frustrated."

Silver turned and smirked at me. "I still do, but Kela left without packing anything to practice."

I scrunched up my face at my partner. "I was trying to save on space. This really isn't necessary." Shifting from foot-to-foot, I looked about the practice hall. Empty instrument holders hung on the walls. The only one in sight was the piano. If it had been a couple of years in this humid environment, I could only imagine how out of tune it was.

"Well, they took most of the instruments with them to the main hall. This was all they left," she waved at the piano. "It sounds like what you play is more portable than this."

"She can play that also or sing," my partner commented, the mischievous grin never leaving his face.

I glared at Silver. He had caught me a few times playing various instruments when we were staying at my adopted parent's house for one reason or another. I was definitely regretting that they had given him an open invitation to stay there when he wanted.

Marzena laughed. "And here I thought maybe you expanded your horizons, brother."

"I did. Just not to music yet." Silver came back over and took my hand, tugging me along. "Come on, Kela. This place won't bite."

"I might," Marzena interjected with a broad, sly grin on her face.

"Marzi..." Silver warned.

She gave him a broad smile and held up her hands in defense before heading to the covered piano and pulling the sheet off. Dust flew everywhere.

I hurried to escape outside, coughing. Silver was not far behind and eventually Marzena found her way out also.

"Okay," she said in between coughs, "that was a bad idea."

"Well, you were always full of them," Silver said with a smirk.

"You have plenty of your own," I grumbled at my partner. I looked down at myself after seeing how dust-covered the other two were. Out of habit, I raised my hand.

Silver quickly took my hand and squeezed it. Right, I could not use my power here. Not within view of someone who did not know.

Marzena touched her hand to her chest, closing her eyes. The dust lifted off and away from her, drifting into the forest. Once she had finished after a minute or two, she reached out for Silver and repeated the spell.

That my partner did not use it meant he likely did not know it. Or he was lazy. It honestly could have been either way.

I took a step back when Marzena turned to me. Silver I might have gotten used to, but I was not keen on others using their magic on me.

"It's okay. It won't hurt," she said gently. "It beats having to go all the way back to your room to shower and change."

My partner nodded. "It's okay. She won't hurt you."

Biting my lower lip, I remained still and unsure, but it seemed similar enough to my own version of the spell. I just could not sense what she was doing because it was divine. Though something had pulled at my senses while she was casting. Likely my mind was trying to fill in the blank.

No sooner had Marzena finished, a young male seeker came running over to us. "Paladin Blaise. The Elders are looking for you." His words were clipped and he seemed upset about something.

Silver growled low. "I guess this means my break is over," he muttered. He gave me a quick kiss. "I'll be back as soon as I can." Then he turned his attention to Marzena and nodded before leaving with the seeker.

I tilted my head, uncertain what that was about.

"Come on. We might as well spend some time cleaning. Or I guess I will since I can make it go faster." My guide shooed me toward the practice hall. "You can entertain me while I work."

I kept my eyes on Silver until he was out of sight. What could have happened?

7

THE REMAINDER of the day passed quietly. After dinner, Marzena walked with me back to where I was staying. Silver had been absent again.

"Sorry we spent the afternoon cleaning that mess. And we barely made a dent," Marzena said. "This is your first visit here and I've got you cleaning."

I laughed lightly, hiding my amusement behind my hand. "It's okay. I don't mind." What had bothered me was I could not use my power to do so. I would have had the whole place cleaned within the hour. Her spell seemed limited to small areas and it took longer than mine. Not to mention she had run out of energy to keep using it after the first hour. Or had given up - I remained uncertain.

"Well, at least it's good to know that the enchantment to keep that piano in tune hasn't faded." She smiled broadly at me. "Too bad my brother escaped helping. So, who taught you music?"

Biting my lower lip, I hesitated before answering, "My adopted mother." My voice was quiet. Speaking of Lindale was a touchy subject if only because of her fame, but it was better to speak of her instead of another.

"She taught you well. My parents were too set on us kids following the path." She was animated as she spoke, trying to mimic someone stern sounding. "Me, it really wasn't a question if I would, though don't tell the others I mostly nap through morning prayers. I'm not exactly the most devout."

I hid my amusement behind my hand again. "How many siblings do you have?"

"Had," she corrected, her face solemn. "There were five of us - three boys and two girls. I was the youngest."

I bit my lower lip, unsure if I wanted to continue this conversation. I knew what happened to the others of their group. It did not sound like someone else in her family managed to be away at the time.

"You know what happened at the church in Ocean's Edge, don't you?" she asked softly.

I turned my gaze out over the water and lowered my voice. "Yes. I was part of the team investigating. I'm sorry I didn't figure out what was going on sooner."

Marzena shook her head. "I was wondering how Silver met you. I'm glad you were there with him at that time." She took a deep breath and let it out slowly. "I would suggest not repeating that information to anyone else though. And you have nothing to be sorry for. I trust the words he wrote to me before he left the Order over the whispers from around here."

Silence fell awkwardly between us and we both ended up staring out over the water for a few minutes. I was trying to figure out how to change the conversation.

"Do you have any siblings?" she asked. "I know you said you have an adopted mother."

"And adopted father, but yes, I have a younger sister." There was no need to go into the detail of Kitteren and I only sharing a biological father. The last conversation I had with her over the picture she sent came to mind. "She can be a right pain."

Marzena smiled broadly, bumping my shoulder with hers. "But that's what younger sisters are for."

I rolled my eyes and shook my head.

"I miss my sisters. Maria may not have been blood, but we were as close as I had been to my own blood relation. Sometimes I wish I knew what had happened to Maja." She laughed. "Oh, you should have heard our parents yelling at us as kids - they'd go through every name before getting the one they wanted. Serves them right for giving us all names that started with M. At one point I had a single combination name to yell at my brothers at the same time. It didn't last long."

"What happened to Maja?" I asked, confused by the statement. Was it before the events I was part of in Ocean's Edge?

Marzena folded her arms and looked at the ground. "Funny, isn't it? I barely know you and I feel like I can talk about this." She dropped her arms and stepped toward the edge of the walkway. We were the only people out here. "It was my three brothers, then Maja, and then me in terms of birth. I think my parents had been wanting to create their own line, but it takes a few generations for it to be accepted. Anyway, most of us embraced eventually becoming paladins. Maja... I knew it wasn't for her."

I stepped up next to the female paladin and turned so I could keep an eye on the area. This was a private conversation.

"Don't get me wrong - she was good at it, but I think she would have been happier outside of the Order. Anyway, like our brothers before her, she was sent here to the Central Seat to train. Within a short time, the letters stopped coming. It was like she had simply vanished. My parents decided to keep me in Ocean's Edge for my training. That's all I know."

I bit my lower lip and considered the information. There was too little to go on. Unless there were records somewhere in the library that I might be able to trace. That would take a while to find. Perhaps Silver knew something about it, but where was he?

"You look like you're thinking about something," Marzena observed.

"A couple of things. I'm not sure what I could do to help you," I admitted. There was too little information of what she had told me.

She shook her head. "I didn't mean for you to join in the search. To be honest, after several years of going through the records and trying to trace her path, I don't think I'm going to find her. I'm getting to the point of being okay with that. Besides, if she was lucky, she ran away from all of this, changed her name, and started a new life. Though I'd love to know if I have any nieces or nephews to spoil." The gentle smile on her face told me that her narrative brought her comfort.

The problem was neither of us had any idea if it was true.

I sighed and looked over the grounds as the sun set behind the mountains. Paladins, scholars, and seekers all roamed about, but none came anywhere near close to where we were.

"Thanks for listening. It's been a long time since I mentioned Maja to anyone and it's nice talking to someone that hasn't known me since birth." She tossed me a lopsided grin and then paused, turning to face me fully. "Is something bothering you?"

"Silver," I said quietly.

"Hm..." She turned to scan the area. "He's a tough one to miss. If he missed dinner and the Elders didn't decide to be nice this time, he's probably raiding the kitchen. I miss his cooking. He hated kitchen duty, but he always made the best meals."

"I miss it too." Until she mentioned it, I had not thought about all the times he would cook while we were living together in Ghost Forest. Especially after we both figured out that I had no talent for it.

Marzena smiled broadly and signaled for me to follow her, already taking off. "Then let's go find him and see if we can't get treated for having to wait so long."

Shaking my head, I hurried to catch up. It was hard to follow her changing moods.

THE NEXT MORNING, I again found myself sitting in front of the mirror while Silver did my hair. I needed to get up earlier to beat him apparently. I had just picked up the first hairpin to begin securing the bun when he returned from morning prayers. He already seemed tense, so I did not fight him when he expressed a desire to do my hair.

Glancing at his lengthy braid, I should return the favor. The least I could do was brush it out for him in the evening. Maybe it would help him relax.

While I watched him put it up in the same style he had yesterday, I asked, "Do you think you're going to be in meetings all day again?"

Silver took a long, deep breath while he tied off one of the small braids. "It's highly likely. I'll do my best to at least have mealtimes with you."

I bit my lower lip for a moment before deciding it was okay to press him on it. "How are the meetings going?"

"Nowhere," he said flatly. Then he kissed the side of my head and smiled at me in the mirror. "Don't worry about it. This is just their way of dragging it out."

"I'm not sure it's a good idea to be away from the office this long. We could be missing something right now."

Silver tied off the second braid. "You know they'll call if something comes up that they need us for. Come on." He patted my shoulder before moving away.

Slowly I got up, crossing my arms. I did not move from where I stood. "None of this seems right. Why won't you tell me what's going on?"

My partner came back over with my holstered shrunken staff in hand. He placed it down on the stool I had been sitting on before running his hands down my arms and taking my hands. He kissed the back of my fingers before he said, "I know. I don't like this either. There's nothing worth telling in detail right now. Can you trust me that I have everything under control?"

I nodded without thinking about it, knowing I was too conflicted. I let the influence from his necklace guide me for the moment. I could worry and fret about it all when he was not around. He certainly did not need me adding to the problems he had.

Silver gave me a quick kiss before grabbing the holster and kneeling in front of me.

I took a step back, bumping into the vanity. "I can do that."

My partner made a face and waved at me to come back. "It'll be easier if someone else does it when you have that top on. I watched you struggle to get it around your leg yesterday."

I crossed my arms and frowned, refusing to look at him as he parted the panels to secure the straps around my right leg. Letting people coddle me was getting on my nerves. I thought Father could be bad...

Once he finished, he stood up, wrapping an arm around my waist before leaning down to kiss me. "I still don't like you wearing this outfit. I might have to complain about it."

"It's fine. I don't mind," I said in a hurry. Not wearing it could cause him problems.

"Kela, I don't think you understand. I've never seen them demand another guest wear any of the uniforms. You're not on the path so it doesn't make any sense."

"You haven't been here for decades," I pointed out.

"And even Marzi thinks it's strange." Silver picked up the sun pendant around my neck.

A warmth radiated from it toward me. That piece of metal still stumped me on what was enchanted into it.

"I don't know what to do," I finally said, breaking the short silence.

Silver leaned down again to kiss me. "Keep doing what you're doing."

HOURS HAD PASSED in the library again. Some of the scholars at least seemed to have warmed to my presence. Others scurried away whenever I got near. I had no intention of bothering any of them.

The words in the open book on the table in front of me became a blur. I was hungry from having eaten little at breakfast and it had become a distraction.

I sensed Silver's presence only a moment before he wrapped his arms around me from behind, squeezing gently. His necklace warmed and sent a wave of contentment.

"You look positively bored," he said quietly before kissing my cheek. Then he rested his chin on my shoulder.

There was no way I could turn to look at him. "I'm reading - I don't think there's a way to make it look interesting. Are you done with your meetings for now?"

"Something like that. I need to remind them that this visit is on my terms, not theirs. Since words weren't getting through, I'm trying actions." He pressed his cheek to mine.

I sighed and shook my head at his statement before closing the book and standing up. "I assume you're hungry." There was little point in arguing with him over this. Especially when I had no direct information of what had been going on in those meetings.

Silver moved away for a moment before he bent down and kissed me lightly. "For that mostly, but yes, it's time for lunch."

I rolled my eyes and shooed him out of my way so I could put the book back.

"Just leave it," Silver said. "The scholars will put it away."

"It's no trouble." I forced a smile and hurried to put it back. If it had been just a random book, I would have left it, but I had managed to find records of seekers. I needed to at least try to figure out what happened to Marzena's sister. It helped to break up the monotony of just copying with the occasional pause to pretend to read something.

Neither of us spoke until we were well away from the library.

Silver pulled me aside and folded his arms, staring down at me. "Okay, what are you getting yourself into?"

I bit my lower lip. "It's nothing important." At least not to him.

He narrowed his eyes at me. "You had a book of records. That's research material, not reading."

I sighed and hung my head. "Marzena told me about her sister. I thought I could at least take a look and see if I could piece something together while I was here. Sometimes another set of eyes helps."

My partner frowned. "I know you love puzzles, but... Listen, I don't know what happened to Maja either. Anyone could tell she wasn't meant to be a paladin and I doubt she would have been happy as a scholar either. Though you couldn't tell her parents that. I was grateful when they decided to have Marzi take the path at the church. Granted, her weapons skills were impressive even then."

His words pointed out how little I knew about his life before joining the TIO. It seemed unfair given how much he had managed to pry into my background.

"Kela, under normal circumstances I'd be more than happy to let you have a try at it. As things are, you should leave this alone. Just keep to your task. We can come back to this later." Silver leaned down and kissed me again. "Please?"

My shoulders slumped. I had found something less mind numbing and now I was being asked to ignore it. Though he was right that I would have all of the information available in the library for later if I kept at my primary goal. "Fine." It was not as if rushing to do this now would matter any. Maja had been missing for decades.

"Thank you," Silver said gently, kissing my forehead.

I allowed myself to follow the influence from his necklace. With as affectionate as he was being, I knew I would start to pull away from him otherwise. That would not do well for keeping up appearances.

"Well, aren't you two adorable," Marzena called out as she walked up to us. "Thought maybe I needed to remind her to eat, but it appears you got to her first."

Silver gave her a big smile. "Marzi, this is our third day here and you've already pegged some of her bad habits."

I rolled my eyes and walked away in the direction of the dining hall. The two caught up and chatted energetically about random topics. It continued all through lunch, which thankfully the person behind the counter was not the same one as yesterday and seemed to have a much better disposition toward us.

Maybe the people here just needed time to get used to us. The glares from the ones who disliked our presence changed my mind on that thought. Perhaps it was more accurate that some were more open to our being here than others.

As we left, one of the paladins who had been glaring at us shoved me as he hurried past.

"Hey!" Silver shouted at him.

The paladin did not even bother to turn around and continued to hurry away.

Silver went to chase after him and I put my hand on his arm, shaking my head.

"I'm fine. It's no big deal."

"Kela, even I could tell he did that on purpose," Marzena argued.

"It's not worth getting into an argument over," I replied.

A large hand rested on my head and I looked up at Silver. "You're too kind," he said.

Marzena eyed my partner with a mischievous smirk on her face. "I'm impressed she's mellowed you out. A few years ago, you would have chased him down and torn him apart."

I knew he got hotheaded, but had he really been that bad? It seemed spending time with Marzena would grant me insight into Silver.

8

IT WAS our fourth day here and once again I had hidden myself away in the library. Silver seemed to be in constant meetings and was always aggravated by the time he was done.

I flipped idly through a book, not really paying attention, thinking about when I brushed his hair for the first time last night. He had argued with me initially, but he had been outwardly much calmer when I was done.

What I had not expected was to find it relaxing also. Part of me wanted to play with it, but I kept to simply brushing and running my fingers through the silky strands. I doubted he would be keen on letting me attempt to braid it. It gave me a little bit of perspective on why he liked doing mine.

As Silver requested, I dropped my search for Maja. I returned to spending my time in the library scanning the shelves, copying as I went. Only choosing something to sit down and read so it did not look too suspicious.

"Hey there," Marzena said happily, flopping down on a chair next to me. "You look bored. Want to read something interesting?" I glanced at my watch. It was far too early for lunch.

"Yeah." I had already copied this book, so I had no problem leaving it. The scholars could get annoyed with me all they wanted - I tired of the glares. Though one happily chatted with me this morning.

She grabbed my hand and pulled me from the chair.

I tripped over the long seeker top I wore. I thought I had finally figured out how to move properly in this, but I had not expected to be practically dragged out of my chair.

Marzena smirked at me. "I've got an idea for something fun this afternoon. But I thought maybe you'd like to know more about your intended. I doubt he'll have shared this."

Now she had my attention. "What do you mean?"

Marzena held a finger to her lips which did nothing to hide the playful expression on her face. She led me through the library and down a set of stairs I would never have seen with the way they had been hidden around a corner.

The hallway was barely lit, but it did not slow my companion down. I lost track of the turns and grew more uneasy with each one. Where were we going? There was no one else down here. I was going to be lost if she left me behind.

She did not stop until she found the door she was looking for. "Sutton" was written on it.

"Each line has people take turns coming down to care for what is stored in the vault, but it's only done by someone who is proven loyal to that line. Since I'm the only one here at the Central Seat, it falls to me. Well, was the only one."

I looked at the door across from us and sure enough another name was etched on it, but it had been worn down to being unreadable.

She followed my line of sight. "Just because we're supposed to care for the vault doesn't mean that people actually do. James had it before me and I don't think he ever set foot in it. Not with what I found anyway. That and there was a long period where no one was here before I came. It took me forever to clean it before I could even start working with the records and artifacts."

I pursed my lips. I wondered what kind of information might be hidden in the other vaults. Obviously, what my friend wanted to show me was not available in the main part of the library.

Marzena put her hand on the door. "Open to me the story of my line that I may care for the passages of time kept within your walls."

The door glowed a faint blue before I heard a lock.

"Does it open for just anyone with the spell?" I asked.

She shook her head. "Only those who have not only pledged their loyalty to the line but also have been granted access by someone within the line. Right now, it's just me and Silver. The Sun knows how much of an ass James was about granting me access when I was being transferred. I had to get Silver to do it. That was before I knew he held lineage. I sometimes wonder if James couldn't perform the right."

Behind the door, bookcases lined the walls. There seemed to be a visible chronological age to the tomes housed here. Some of the bookcases remained empty.

I lightly touched the books, hesitating only a moment at each to copy them. I should probably not do this directly in front of someone, but this might be my only chance.

"A book lover, are you?" Marzena said teasingly.

I gave her a small smile. "I have a certain appreciation for them, yes."

She laughed. "If only Silver did. I'm not sure if you know that he's actually a talented paladin. Definitely the most powerful I know. If he applied himself to his studies, I could only imagine what he could be capable of."

I paused and turned to look at her. "He's been doing more of his own research recently, but I don't know what he's working on exactly." Getting into the fact he was taking a more scientific approach would probably not go over well.

Marzena paused and stared at me with wide eyes. "Has he? Don't get me wrong, he's quite knowledgeable, but he would rather be at the training ground than the library."

I turned back to what I was doing. "He still likes to train regularly. Much to my dismay."

"Oh? Now I really need to get you over to the training grounds." The broad grin on her face told me I had walked into that one.

I shook my head.

Marzena went to a bookshelf near the end of the volumes. "These are all the stories of valor from the generations. I've been wanting to bring Silver down here, but I can't seem to get a minute with him. I can only imagine how you feel."

"He's been stressed when he gets back at night," I admitted.

She turned and made a face at me. "I'm talking about you."

"I... uh..." Why did this conversation have to be about me? "I'm okay. He's got a lot to deal with. You should bring him down here when next he's free."

"And keep him away from you? No. He's a man in love and I'm not getting between that." She reached behind a row of books.

I rolled my eyes. At least she was convinced. The Elders seemed to be giving me space, but I wondered how much they were just trying to wear my partner down. I was going to have to put forth more effort to keep him grounded.

"Ah, there you are," Marzena said, pulling out a smaller leather-bound book. "I'm not sure why this was in here, but I couldn't bring myself to move it from the safety of this room. Or its hiding spot."

"What is it?" I glanced at the shelf I had just copied, making a mental note of where I left off.

"It's one of Blaise Sutton's journals. He talks about when he found Silver. The official records don't match what he wrote in here. I'm torn as to what to do about it." She handed me the journal.

The second I touched it, I copied the information. "Have you talked to the Elders?"

She shook her head. "No, and I dare not. There's been something strange going on over the past couple of years. It's probably been going on for longer than that, but being weapons master doesn't put me within the inner circle. That and other things. They don't approve of people like me since I'm not helping breed the next generation. My parents were so mad when they found out. Needless to say, Silver saved my skin. He's got Hells of a protective streak, but you've got to give him good reason to care about you."

"His protective streak is obnoxious," I muttered. Then I bit my lower lip, trying to parse what she had both said and left unspoken. "Why tell me?"

"You're an outsider. You can move much more freely. And you like books. Here," she said, taking the journal from me and flipped through it, "read this and then read the historical records from that time."

I raised an eyebrow at her before reading the beautifully scripted entries in front of me. Blaise Sutton talked about his group coming across another group of paladins who decided to slaughter an Elven village along the northern coast of the Inner Sea Region.

He spoke in detail about coming upon the murder of an Elven couple and managed to stop the men before they could kill the baby.

"*I decided then to take the boy as my own. Without a name, I've taken to calling my new son Silver,*" the entry concluded.

Blaise's group killed the paladins who had broken some code or other.

"Silver doesn't know about this," I stated. I knew he did not. Even with what little I had heard about his past, I was certain of it.

"No. I'm too young to have known Blaise all that well since he worked with the adults. I couldn't tell you very much about what he was like other than what I've read and what others in the group have told me." Marzena took the journal back.

I took a deep breath. "Silver will likely do something rash if he learns about this right now."

She crossed her arms and stared at me. "I see you do in fact know my brother well."

I gave a short laugh. "I'll try to find the records in the library and see what I can piece together."

Marzena gave me a knowing smile. "I'm putting my faith in you."

"Why?" The word came out before I could filter it. Well, I was already this far. "You hardly know me."

"You're right, but I know Silver. I see how much he trusts you. How much he loves you. I might give him a hard time, but I know when to listen."

I gave her a soft smile, wishing I could tell her the truth about the relationship I had with him. "Can you teach him that? He gets so hardheaded about things sometimes."

Marzena laughed loudly. "You have a better chance at that than I do. We should probably head back. It's getting close to lunch and I'm certain Silver will want to spend time with you if he can get free."

I nodded.

"There's more of Blaise's journals hidden in here," she said as she put the leather-bound book back, "but that's the one with the most controversial accounts that I've read so far. I've been making copies when I can. I'm partially regretting trying to get all of the records in here into a digital format, but there needs to be a backup."

And I had just made a copy of that one. "Can you show me the others sometime? I'd like to get to know the man who raised Silver."

Marzena smirked. "Oh, you're going to love some of the stories then.

My brother was such a brat growing up. Probably a good thing we weren't brought up together - we'd have terrorized everyone. I'll bring you back later." As she closed the door behind us, she put her hand on it once again, closing her eyes. It glowed blue and then the lock slid home.

When we reached the main area of the library I had been keeping to, we found Silver searching through the stacks.

"Awe, he did come looking for you," Marzena said softly.

I saw his braid down his back. "This isn't good." I left her, jogging quickly to my partner. I touched his arm lightly as I came up behind him. "Hey, what's going on?" His braid was normally over his right shoulder.

Silver turned quickly, pulling me into a tight hug. "Where were you?"

"I borrowed her. She looked utterly bored," Marzena said as she caught up.

When he finally gave me room to breathe, I reached back and brought his braid forward to where it belonged. "What's going on?" I tugged on it lightly.

"I'll explain later. Let's go get something to eat. I'm famished." Silver wrapped an arm around my waist. He leaned down and gave me a quick kiss. "I bring you all the way out here and then hardly get to spend time with you. Hasn't been fair, has it?"

His necklace warmed in agreement with his statement. "You have business to take care of." I decided a neutral answer was better.

"You're too understanding." He looked to Marzena. "Thanks for keeping her company."

She grinned broadly. "Maybe I'm working on stealing her from you."

Silver shook his head and led the way out of the library. I had to have missed something there.

MARZENA CONVINCED me to join her at the indoor training grounds for the afternoon. I guessed the search into the history was not an immediate need. Not like it was going to go anywhere. Just as any information about her sister was not either.

I watched from the sidelines as the seekers worked through drills.

There were only three of them, all Human men. They had immediately shed their long tops, identical to the one I wore, as soon as they arrived. I could see the four long panels becoming problematic to fight in.

Marzena walked between them, correcting as needed. She would use a hand or a foot to push them into the position they needed to be in, barking orders. This was vastly different from the person I had met so far, and yet, despite the rough nature of her teaching, she seemed caring.

Turning my attention away for a moment, I eyed the various martial weapons lining the walls, all neatly organized. Most of them wooden. Swords were racked according to length. A stack of shields sat next to them. Lances, staves, daggers, axes, war hammers - some weapons I could not identify were all around me.

It was nice to be out of the library, but I remained wholly out of place. And I had nothing to do. I wished I could have brought my tablet with me, but Lockonis had insisted that I leave it and work behind. I had only been granted my phone and my watch, but was to keep communications to emergencies only.

So far, I had found nothing of interest which might give me a better perspective on necromancers either. Perhaps instead of looking through scriptures, I should be looking through history.

"Kela, come here for a minute," Marzena said, signaling to me.

I sat up straighter for a moment, not expecting to have been addressed. I did as I was asked, the seekers eyeing me cautiously.

"Now, Kela hasn't trained with us, but she's trained elsewhere with another paladin."

"What? That pointy-eared freak that showed up recently?" one of them said. The others laughed. "Elves can't be paladins."

Marzena stepped away from me and swept out her leg, kicking the back of his knee. He instantly fell to the floor.

She stood over him with her arms crossed. "I would not recommend insulting a brother that way. I've trained with him as well and he's more of a paladin than you'll ever become."

I folded my hands together and stood there silently. I had mostly been hidden away so I had not heard the racism before that had come from the seeker who was getting himself off the floor.

Marzena slapped him hard once he stood, knocking him back

down to the ground. "And that's for insulting her intended. Now, onto the lesson at hand."

I bit my lower lip and took a step back. She was not one to be messed with when she was mad.

She came back over to me. "I can teach you all I know within these grounds, but out there on the battlefield is another matter altogether and it will not harm your integrity to learn from others as well."

What was she planning? She had no idea what I was capable of. "I'm not good in a fight," I said quietly. Not without relying on my power at the very least and I could not show my arcane abilities here.

"You'll be fine. I'm sure Silver has taught you some grappling." She grabbed my wrist.

Instinctively I twisted to break her hold. The panels on my top spun out around me as we went through a dance of grapples and breaks. All of it was things I had done in training with Silver.

"Oh, and here it is," Marzena said after a few minutes. "I haven't seen someone do that before. Now I've learned something and all because I was open-minded enough to let her teach me. Alright, head on out, seekers. I'll see you in a couple of days. Don't forget to train on your own time."

I watched the seekers leave. I remained unsure I was sufficient for what she was trying to teach them.

"Sorry about that. When I was learning, no one ever had to emphasize that lesson. Now they're so focused on keeping things 'pure' that they're doing themselves a disservice. They don't believe they'll ever have to do more than hold a sword in ceremony, but..." Marzena trailed off.

"Pure?" I asked, tilting my head.

She sighed. "It's the word they use so they can be closed-minded and bigoted. It seems to be more and more common, but there are also less and less people wanting to follow the path."

I frowned and crossed my arms.

Marzena smirked and signaled for me to follow her. "Let's have some fun." She pulled a wooden sword and shield off the wall, handing them to me.

"Um..." I took them, holding the weapons awkwardly. "I've never used something like this before."

She waved me off. "That's fine. I'm in the mood to teach someone who will listen."

I lost track of time as she walked me through drills and sequences. Soon she had her own set and we were moving through a sequence.

"That's it," the weapons master encouraged, "Don't show an opening."

Suddenly Marzena switched what she was doing and I was reacting to her attacks, fumbling with the awkward weapons. *How can Silver fight like this?* I tried to mimic some of his movements, getting a better idea of why he would move in particular ways. All of it while trying not to trip over the long top.

As she withdrew an attack, I flipped my grip on the wooden sword and slashed at her, spinning to bring the shield to bear as an offensive weapon.

Marzena stumbled backwards to get out of range and then started laughing. "Now I know you've trained with him. What do you use normally?"

"A staff." Not that I felt all that proficient with it.

The weapons master raised an eyebrow at me. "Really? Then what is attached to your thigh?"

I walked away from her, hanging the wooden weapons back up. "A staff."

Marzena made a face at me and pointed at the rack of long wooden poles. "Yeah, staves aren't that short."

I sighed and pulled it out of its holster. It made a soft metallic sound as it extended.

"Oooh, I want one." She was next to me in an instant. "Has Silver used it?"

I bit my lower lip while I thought through all the training and the fights we had been in. "He's toyed with it, but he's never fought with it. I've only ever seen him use a sword, shield, and dagger."

She let out a short laugh. "Those are his preferences. By all rights, he should have become a weapons master with his ability to use anything in this room. He's the one who taught me."

A movement near the door caught my attention and I turned to see Amanda entering. "I should probably go back to the library. Thank you for your time."

"No, Kela, stay. Perhaps you're here for some one-on-one training?" Marzena directed her question to Amanda.

Amanda narrowed her eyes at me. "No, I came to fight her for what is rightfully mine."

"Oh, you've got to be kidding me," Marzena said, pinching the bridge of her nose. "How archaic can you get?"

I looked down at the floor. Why was she doing this? "There's no reason to fight - it's Silver's decision and his alone."

Amanda called forth her weapons in the same manner Silver did: her shield appearing on her arm and she drew the sword that materialized on her hip. "Stop insulting me!"

Marzena stood between us. "She hasn't insulted you. Now stop this nonsense."

"It's okay," I said softly. "Paladin Sayer is frustrated, and I understand that."

"You understand nothing!" Amanda yelled as she stalked up to us.

Marzena turned to look at me from over her shoulder. "Are you certain?"

"No, but I don't think she's going to back down anytime soon," I said quietly.

As Amanda and I went to the areas Marzena designated, Silver arrived. He stood there frowning with his arms crossed. At least his braid sat where it should be.

"Begin!" Marzena called.

Amanda charged at me and I stepped to the side, sweeping her legs out from under her with my staff. I walked away to give myself distance.

"Oh, you never mentioned she was this good," Marzena said.

"You should see when she can let loose," Silver replied.

Our fight continued in a similar pattern: Amanda would make some wild attack and I would simply dodge and trip her. There was little reason to put much effort in here.

"Please let the girl be learning something here," I heard Marzena mutter. I had gotten over near them.

Silver stepped between us. "I think that's enough. Put your weapons away."

I shrank my staff and put it back in its holster, fumbling to move the panels out of the way. *Damn this outfit.* Amanda, however, made no move to comply. Seeing no reason to be part of the staring contest between her and Silver, I walked over to Marzena.

"Excellent job keeping your composure. Too often I see people feed off the energy of their opponent. While it can be good to some extent, people tend to take it too far," Marzena said.

I bowed to her. The other two were having a quiet, yet heated conversation. Amanda had yet to put her weapons away.

"Though I do have to ask you one thing," Marzena said, grabbing my attention. "Do you always do what Silver tells you?"

I stopped and stared at her. "No. I just saw no reason to continue."

"She actually gives me a hard time most of the time," Silver said as he approached.

"Good, someone needs to since I haven't been around to do it," Marzena tossed at him.

I looked over at Amanda who stood in the center of the room, weapons still at the ready.

She followed my gaze. "Though there's a time and place for every-thing. You're little sparring match is over."

Amanda remained as she had been, glaring at me.

Silver called his shield to his arm and threw it. It hit Amanda's hand, knocking her sword away. "It's over." He reached out and caught his shield as it came back.

"That's still one of the dirtiest tricks in the book," Marzena said, smirking. "And one of these days you're going to tell me how you can control the flight of your shield like that."

Not all of the paladins could throw their shields like that? I tilted my head to the side. The topic had never come up, but he had also never let on that he had abilities beyond his peers.

"Come on, before anyone else gets any bright ideas," Silver said, wrapping his arm around my waist.

9

———————

SILVER LED us through the grounds and I realized it was far earlier than I expected. Usually, he did not show up again until it was time for dinner if he did at all. "I take it you had a short meeting this afternoon."

"Something like that. I mostly got tired of it."

"Silver..." I pinched the bridge of my nose. His impatience could cause him more problems.

He pulled me to the side, off the path. "It's fine. I realized I needed to set limits with the Elders. I had resigned and I don't actually have to listen to them. However, I can't leave Marzena to have to deal with them on behalf of the line."

"What about Amanda?"

"What about her? She's not part of this." Silver smirked and leaned down. He wrapped his fingers behind my neck. "You have no idea how much I enjoyed watching you fight."

"I didn't really do anything." I could not back up with how he held me.

I felt him trace the anchor on my arm a split second before he kissed me. I wished he would give me more time than he did. When we got back to the main office, I definitely planned on spending some time by myself and separated from his necklace to attempt to make sense of the jumbled mess of emotions in my head.

Life had been so much simpler when I used to keep tight control of all that. For now it was easier to follow what I felt, whether it was my own or from the necklace. I vowed to myself that once we returned to the mainland, he was taking it back. Waiting until we returned to the main office was too long.

"Come on," Silver said quietly, "Let's take a walk."

I bit my lower lip and looked in the direction of the library. "I should get back to reading." I dared not tell him what Marzena requested of me.

"You need a break."

I took a deep breath. "Have you spent time with Amanda?"

"I don't want to." Silver nuzzled my ear with his nose. "I just want to spend time with you."

"You should. Maybe she's not as bad as she seems right now. She's pretty devoted to this arrangement and you could try to dissuade her of it. Help her to understand the downfalls. It would be best coming from you. She sees me as the enemy so I can't do it."

Silver put his finger over my mouth. "Enough. I'll think about it, but right now I want nothing more than to enjoy the remainder of the day with my intended."

I knew I was fighting being influenced by his necklace, but he was not the one wearing it and ever since I had agreed to this, he had been acting strange. It had to be the stress of the situation. If only it could have been resolved when we got here. Or even better would have been before we had even left.

Having to share a bed with Silver was not horrible, but I missed my own. I missed home. I had no idea how long we were going to be here.

"Kela?"

I shook my head. "Just thinking about work."

"I know this is a horrible excuse for a vacation, but you need to stop worrying about it. Maybe after all of this is over, we can take at least a weekend for the two of us." He took my hand and kissed the back of my fingers.

Kitteren's words about the arrangement continuing past this came to mind. There were other people off in the distance, so I remained unsure if her words were becoming true or if Silver wanted to keep up appearances in public. Why did this have to be so complicated?

The question of should I consider continuing our current status past this crossed my mind. I shoved it aside assuming it was simply an influence from his necklace.

"What do you want to do?" Silver asked, taking my hand and leading us back down the path.

I shrugged. "I don't really know anything here. You rarely ever talked about this place."

"There's not too much to say. You've seen the seekers who are working on becoming paladins."

"Are there always so few?"

Silver shook his head. "No. There used to be twenty people in a class at minimum at any given time. Now there's probably at most twenty at various levels. Several would make it all the way to becoming paladins. Some would change paths to become scholars if only to stay within the Order."

"The remainder?"

"Devotees. Many would go help churches. That's not everyone, but I don't know all the stories."

I nodded and walked alongside him, holding his hand.

"You know, you don't have to wear that if you don't want to." Silver tugged on the shoulder area of the top I was wearing.

I shrugged. "I'm doing what I can to make things easier for you."

"Don't, Kela. You shouldn't worry about that. You wearing something you don't want to won't make things any easier."

"Well, if my fight with Amanda gets back to them, it's going to make it harder." I really should have thought about that before I agreed to letting her vent her frustrations.

Silver kissed the back of my hand. "Let me worry about that. I'm not giving this up."

We walked in silence for a few minutes when a thought crossed my mind. "Theoretically you could marry her to appease them and find someone else to be involved with. It's not fair to her, but... you are Elven. Our lifespans are—"

"No," Silver snapped, cutting me off. He paused and took a deep breath. "Even if I was inclined to think that way, it couldn't happen. In the Order, once I marry, it's for life. I refused to be tied to that."

"Sorry."

He ran his hand over my hair. "You didn't know." He stopped and looked out at the ocean. "At one point I might not have cared, but I do want a family someday. It will never happen if I go through with the arranged marriage."

I turned my gaze to out over the water. Silver had never spoken of his goals in life. Then I realized I had never considered my own. I was so focused on the tasks set before me in the here and now that I never gave thought to the future.

What did I want? Did it even matter?

"Kela?"

I shook my head. "It's not important."

"I think otherwise."

I glanced up at him quickly and sighed. "You're not going to let this go, are you?"

"You already answered your question."

"*You can be such a pain,*" I muttered in my dialect of common.

Silver kissed the top of my head. "Just say it."

I took a moment to organize my thoughts. "I guess I never really thought past the present. The future was always for other people to plan for."

"Well, maybe I can help you find what you want. You helped me find my path, it seems only fair."

I nodded and let the conversation fall there.

"I never did thank you for earlier." Silver tugged on his braid.

"Thank me for what?" I rubbed my arms. It had gotten chilly.

"When you found me in the library. I've been trying not to let it show how much this has been bothering me, but you saw through it."

I put my hand over his to get him to stop pulling on his hair. "Your braid was down your back instead of over your shoulder."

Silver stared at me. "I had no idea I did that."

"There's other signs also, but that one is when it's really bad."

He gave me a soft smile. "Thanks for looking out for me." He stepped behind me and wrapped his arms around my waist, holding me against him and resting his head on mine. "Mmm... you're the perfect height for this."

I followed the desire to lean back into him, but argued, "We should probably get back."

"Not yet. Besides, you were getting cold."

He was right. I must have wanted to lean into him because he was warm.

While we stood there a ferry went by. I wondered if they carried people or supplies.

Silver stood up straighter. "That makes no sense."

"What doesn't?" I was too content where I was to pay much attention to the tone of his voice.

"That boat - there's no reason to come this direction. The docks are back toward the main hall."

"The island is big. I imagine it would be easier to send supplies by ship."

"There's nothing else on the island. The Order has held it for centuries."

That got me out of my comfortable spot. "Do you think we should follow it?"

"No, it's moving too fast. Next time you're in the library, can you see if something has been built on the other side of the island?"

I nodded, adding it to my list of research tasks. It sounded more and more that things were not adding up. Perhaps I could sneak in searching for Maja.

I RUBBED MY EYES. I had been going through historical records for hours. At least with Marzena's request I had a timeframe to narrow it down, but what Silver asked me to look for was far more tedious and time consuming. It gave me no time to return to the search for Maja.

Marzena had been right though - the official records for that timeframe did not match with the accounts in Blaise Sutton's journal. The paladins who attacked the village were written in the public records as having been attacked by the village. There was no mention of a surviving child.

What was it that Blaise had called that clan? Moon Elves? They were dedicated to the God of the Moon if I remembered correctly. I found it a bit ironic then that Silver had spent his life worshipping the God of the Sun. Though there were several times I had caught him staring at the night sky.

I wanted to talk to him about the discrepancy, but then that meant alerting him to what Marzena had found. He had enough to deal with at the moment.

"Hey." Marzena plopped into the seat next to me. "You look horrifically bored again."

I sighed. "Silver asked me to look something up for him, but I haven't found it yet."

"Hm. Maybe I can narrow it down?"

"He's just wondering if there's something built on the other side of the island."

She sat up straight and looked at me. "No. There's nothing over there. They've always kept it that way so if needed, we could hunt on the island."

"Oh." I closed the book I had. "I guess I wasted my time then."

Marzena smiled at me. "Oh please - you've only been in here to have something to do while Silver wastes your time."

I could not argue with that logic.

"Did you read that story I suggested?" she asked.

I nodded, catching that she was being careful of her wording. "Yes, it was quite intriguing."

She smirked at me. "I am wondering something though. How on Terra did my brother wind up with a scholar? Seems incompatible, but you two are obviously a perfect match."

"I... uh..." I shrugged. *He likely wants to be with someone closer to his personality.*

"Marzi, stop tormenting my intended," Silver said.

I jumped at the sound of his voice.

"I'm not tormenting her - I'm trying to figure out how to steal her away from you." She grinned broadly at my partner.

Silver leaned down, wrapping his arms around me from behind while I still sat in the chair. "Not going to happen." Then he kissed my cheek.

I scrunched up my face. I swear I would never understand him.

"Are the training grounds open right now?" Silver asked.

"Huh? Yeah. There aren't many seekers and I've given up chasing down paladins to keep their skills sharp," Marzena replied. "Some still show up, but usually on the weekends when we have more visitors."

Silver stood up and patted my shoulder. "Time for training then."

I folded my arms and put my head down on the table. "No." It came out whiny. "Take her."

"Well, while I would like to wipe the floor with my brother, I am much more interested in seeing what you can do."

"Like you could," Silver said.

"I haven't forgotten your tricks," Marzena tossed back at him.

Maybe they would goad each other into a sparring match and leave me out of it if I stayed quiet.

"Come on, Kela. I've let you lapse for too long." Silver pulled my chair back.

I sat up and rolled my eyes. "I did some training with Marzena yesterday."

"Oh, did you now?"

Marzena smiled. "What? My teaching skills have been getting rusty with these lazy paladins and seekers who think they know it all. Kela is a wonderful student. Though while you were able to copy one of his signature moves, I don't think a sword and shield will be replacing your staff anytime soon."

"Well, when you get hit by it enough times..." I muttered.

Marzena laughed and led the way to the training grounds.

As we walked, I whispered to Silver, *"This isn't a good idea."*

"You'll be fine. You're good at working within a specific ruleset," he responded in my dialect of common. It was still odd hearing him speak it since he responded so rarely in it.

"What are you two talking about?" Marzena asked.

"Kela is still trying to get out of it," Silver replied.

When we arrived at the indoor training room, Amanda was there working her way through one of the drills I had seen the seekers practicing the day before. I hung back at the door. *Should I leave?*

"Kela, come on." Silver took my hand, dragging me further into the room.

Amanda stopped and looked at the group of us. Various emotions flitted across her face as if she could not decide what she thought of our presence.

"You could have told me you were going to come," Marzena said walking over to her. Their conversation became too hard to hear as they moved to the other side of the large room.

"Hey," I said softly, "Why don't I come back later? You should spend some time with Marzena."

Silver had started undoing his collar and paused. "No. Kela, you don't need to leave. Marzi has taken a liking to you anyway and she would follow you to drag you back here."

I sighed. "Are you going to take it easy on me?"

"No."

"That's not fair." I did not want to say out loud that he was handicapping me heavily. It was going to be incredibly hard to keep myself from using my power.

"You're good at playing by a rule set," he reiterated.

I rolled my eyes at his repeated assurance. "You won't get much of a workout then."

"We'll see," he said with a broad grin, shedding the clerical shirt he had been wearing along with the white tank top underneath. He called his sword and shield.

His missing necklace was such an odd sight.

"There's no getting out of this is there?"

"No."

Why could he not spar with Marzena if he was needing to vent his frustrations? When I reached for my staff, I could not seem to separate the panels with one hand and twisted to find the slit in all of the fabric. The seeker garb I wore would be another handicap. I had gotten relatively good at moving in it, but sparring with Silver would require a much higher level of ability. The little I had done with Marzena yesterday had not required me to move too much.

"Kela, there's a reason seekers don't train in that," Marzena called from the other side of the room. She jogged over to us, leaving Amanda behind, off to the side of the room. She reached for the back of my collar as soon as she was close enough.

I stepped away.

"You don't need to give him more of an advantage by wearing that," she said.

"It's okay," Silver said gently. "I know you're wearing something underneath."

I bit my lower lip and looked between the two. "It might not be appropriate."

"You'll be fine," Marzena said, stepping behind me again. "You look adorable in the seeker outfit, but they were never designed to fight in." She tugged lightly, unhooking the collar. "But it does generally keep the hotheads in order."

I squirmed when she pulled on the collar to look down the back of the top.

"Oh, you're fine with what you have underneath. Anyway, I better get back. Can't miss this opportunity to get that girl to train."

I sighed and finished getting the top off, grateful to be free of the mass of fabric. I was still unused to being around others with just a sports bra for a top. At least the loose dark blue pants would allow for ease of movement.

Silver took the top from me and tossed it with his. "You should go back to wearing your normal clothes. You haven't seemed comfortable in that."

I wrapped my arms around myself, hiding as much of my exposed stomach as I could, particularly the thin scar that ran from under my left arm to the front of my left hip. "I've worn worse."

He shook his head and took my hand, tugging me out to the main part of the hall. When he dropped my hand, I stopped and watched him walk farther, putting some distance between us.

I folded my arms while I waited for him to decide where he wanted to be. Suddenly he turned and threw his shield. I dropped to the floor to avoid it. As soon as it cleared me, I charged at Silver, drawing my shrunken staff out of the holster on my thigh, extending it.

Not having any spells to use was going to make this impossible.

Silver stood ready with his sword, but his eyes kept darting to where I assumed his shield was. I feigned an attack to get him to block with his sword arm high.

I switched and slid underneath him, shrinking my staff in the process. The second I got to my feet behind him, I extended my staff again to hit him in the back. The sun pendant swinging wildly around my neck had distracted me somewhat.

My partner turned and blocked the strike in time with his shield. It must have returned when I went underneath him. I pushed against his shield, gritting my teeth.

He was grinning madly.

I prayed to whoever might listen that he would not push me to the point of slipping with my power.

Silver turned, swinging his sword while throwing off my balance by moving his shield. I dropped to the floor and kicked out, aiming to sweep his legs out from underneath him.

I managed to unbalance him and swung up with my staff toward his head. He lost his balance completely when he moved to dodge the strike and I used the moment to scramble away, getting some distance between us.

My partner sat there for a moment staring at me. Then he laughed, getting back to his feet. I slid into a ready stance. I might have gotten myself into trouble with that. I worried Silver would forget that I was unable to defend myself as I normally would. Not without giving away that I was an arcane caster.

I heard laughing from the side of the room. I chanced a glance over at Marzena and Amanda. The weapons master was the one finding amusement in our fight.

"Normally I would say being on the floor is a disadvantage," she called over, "but it looks like you know how to use it."

"When you end up there often..." I muttered.

Silver threw his shield again and I stepped to the side, taking a swing at it with my staff to change its trajectory. He closed the gap while I avoided it and I managed to block his sword, but I ended up in an awkward position.

Before I could figure out how to get out of the odd twist I was in, he shoved against the block and I stumbled. I had to duck his next swing and found myself being pressed for a while to keep dodging and blocking his attacks.

As he continued, my reactions became increasingly sluggish. I would not be able to keep this up much longer.

I missed blocking his shield and ended up taking a hit to the ribs. I hit the floor and rolled. I dropped my staff in the process.

I managed to get to my knees and held my ribs, groaning, keeping my eyes closed. The throbbing pain in my side told me that I likely had bruised, but not broken anything. Normally I would continue, but I could not guarantee I would be able to keep to the handicap imposed. As it was, my power was agitated. It was good my hair was confined as I was sure it would have been floating about me.

"Get up," Silver ordered.

I shook my head. It was hard to breathe. My assessment of my injuries might have been wrong.

"You're not done yet." His voice was firm.

Footsteps rapidly approached. "Silver, it's over," Marzena said.

"I know how far she can go," he argued.

"No. Walk away," Marzena ordered.

"Kela, you know you can keep going," Silver argued with me.

I shook my head. "*Not like this,*" I whispered, sinking lower to the ground.

"Dammit," Silver said, "I'm sorry." I could tell by the size of the hand that he was the one brushing my hair back. "Can you walk?"

I nodded. "*Just need a minute.*"

My partner helped me up and I kept my eyes lowered, focusing on the sun pendant dangling from my neck. "Marzi, I've got her."

"You better, you ass," she snapped.

My partner held me tighter. "I deserved that."

"Silver needs someone who can fight like him," Amanda said as we passed by. "She obviously can't keep up."

"And that isn't you," Marzena shot back. "Last I checked Kela didn't even break a sweat dropping you to the floor and she was still wearing the seeker top. Get back to your drills."

"It wasn't fair - she wasn't using the proper weapons of a paladin," Amanda retorted.

"Sayer! Have you looked around this room? It's full of proper paladin weapons. There's a whole section of staves right over there. A sword and shield does not define a paladin. Now shut your mouth or I'll find you something worse than drills to do. The practice hall could certainly use a cleaning."

Silver helped me sit on a bench away from the arguing pair. He held the sides of my face. "Look at me."

I shook my head. I had no idea if the buildup of agitated power was visible.

He sighed and knelt lower, looking up at me. "Okay, keep your eyes lowered or closed," he whispered. "I need you to lean back so I can see how badly I hurt you."

I nodded, hissing as I moved.

Silver sighed. "I don't know how you continue to put up with me. Especially when I get out of control like that."

"Brother, I've seen you lose control and that wasn't it. You just don't always recognize when you've pushed too far," Marzena said softly.

A smaller hand gently stroked my hair.

"Though I have a feeling someone here was holding back," she said, her tone teasing.

Silver let out a soft huff.

"Well, said someone also bruises very quickly it seems," she commented.

"Not the first time," I said, my voice strained.

There was a pause before Silver said, "Okay, I get carried away a lot."

A healing spell washed over my abdomen, but it was unfamiliar.

"I can handle that," Silver said.

Marzena made a noise of disgust. "Ugh, knowing you, you'll torture her with that damnable restoration spell you found."

"Twice was two times too many," I said.

The healing stopped. "You *have* tortured her with that?!"

"Both times I used it only as a last resort." Silver sounded defensive.

"You and I will talk later," Marzena said firmly. Her healing resumed.

After she was done, I heard her go back over to where Amanda was. Silver knelt in front of me. "Hey, can you look at me?"

I did as he asked, but I felt so completely drained. All I wanted to do was sleep.

"Good. I take it you're feeling a little calmer."

I nodded. Once the pain had dissipated, my power had settled.

"Apologizing isn't going to make up for what happened. You did really well considering." He kissed my forehead.

I hoped he did not want to carry on a conversation.

Silver moved away for a moment. I heard cloth rustling. "Here, lay down and rest. I know healing drains you more often than not. At least you don't seem to be running a low-grade fever this time."

I looked at him - he had folded my seeker top up into a makeshift pillow. The suggestion was too enticing to ignore. As soon as I was stretched out on the hard wooden bench, Silver threw his own clerical shirt over me as a partial blanket.

He knelt down, brushing my hair out of my face gently. "I plan to train for a while, so I won't go anywhere."

I made a noise of agreement and let myself doze. Silver and Marzena would watch out for me.

When I woke, it was to a conversation between the two paladins of the Sutton line.

"Silver, what is she?" Marzena asked quietly.

The question set me on edge. What was she getting at? Had she figured out that I was an arcane caster?

"What do you mean?" Even he sounded defensive.

Marzena hummed for a moment. "I've been watching her interact with people. I can't quite tell if she's hiding it or if she's just not interested in men or women. Don't get me wrong, the way she looks at you is different, but it's also not the same as those other Elves you dated. Last I remember, one like her is extremely rare among your kind. How did you manage it?"

"Annoying her until she agreed, I guess. I really hadn't thought about the fact that she might not be interested in anyone that way."

Great, now my lack of desire in finding an intimate partner was a topic of conversation. Granted, they were not the first in recent weeks. At least it was not about me being an arcane caster.

Marzena laughed. "Well, the least I can do is kick your ass around this room for a while for hurting her. Especially since you've used that damnable spell on her."

Silver blew out a quick breath. "At least believe me when I say it was a last resort."

"Hm... I think you have stories to share then. Right now, though, I'm going to clean the floor with you." Her confidence was obvious even in just her voice.

I opened my eyes as they squared off. Marzena had shed her clerical shirt and simply wore a sports bra and the white pants to her uniform. She held a sword and shield as well.

"I hope you remember that the rule is if you drop it, you have to take a different weapon," Marzena taunted.

Silver grinned broadly. "Hm. Haven't had a chance to play this game since you left Ocean's Edge."

She held her shield up to him as if in salute. "Here's to hoping you still know how to use everything in here."

With that, they began their fight. It was like watching a well-rehearsed dance. I sat up, wrapping Silver's clerical shirt around my shoulders. They appeared evenly matched though Marzena seemed a bit slower.

After a few minutes of Silver simply blocking her attacks, they separated and she threw her shield at him. When he swiped at her shield, forcing it to the floor, he grinned. "That's out."

She flexed her arm, causing her shield to return, then it disappeared. "Strategy, dear brother."

"Well, if your strategy is to lose..." he trailed off, grinning madly.

At least they were both enjoying themselves without dragging me into it. I watched silently as they went through the different weapons in the room. I never knew my partner was able to pick up anything in here and use it effectively. He had toyed with my staff before, but that was the extent of what I had previously witnessed.

Marzena ran out of weapons to choose from first and struggled to get Silver to drop his last one with her bare hands.

Silver managed to get the staff he held locked under her chin. She struggled for a minute or so trying to get free, but eventually dropped her arms. "Okay, you win. Damn, I thought I might have had you this time."

My partner laughed. "I'm out of practice, but it doesn't take too much to remember how to use them. Oh, you're awake." He turned his attention to me.

"Are you feeling better, Kela? Silver told me you have some odd reactions to healing. Sorry, I wish I had known that ahead of time."

I shook my head. "I'm fine."

"Well, I don't know about you two, but I'm famished. Let's go find dinner," she said, her voice chipper.

10

"Divine and conquer," Silver said after I told him that Marzena said nothing had been built on the other side of the island and that I had found no evidence of it either.

"Don't you mean 'divide and conquer' and what does that have to do with anything here?" My attention was split between our conversation and me trying to figure out if the contentment of sitting with Silver like this was me or something from his necklace. It was warm leaning back against him with his arms wrapped around me.

"No, it's something my master would say. It means to learn the truth of the situation and then do something about it." He lightly stroked the side of my neck with his fingers.

The motion made me drowsy, which in turn made it difficult to concentrate. "Is there another island nearby? Could they have been headed there?"

"It's highly unlikely. There are closer ports than the one the Central Seat uses. And they would not be using the same ferry."

"Maybe the two of you should talk then. There's little I can do to help at this point." And maybe Marzena would talk to him about the vault. Either way I was comfortable where I was and had no desire to move.

"You're probably right." He nuzzled my ear with his nose. "Though I haven't thanked you for how much help you have been."

I turned as much as I could to look at him. "I haven't done anything."

Silver kissed me lightly. Did he have to do that when it was just the two of us? "You've kept me grounded. You researched things for both me and Marzena. Though I noticed that neither of you wants to tell me about that one. It's not about Maja again, is it?"

I sighed. "No, but it's not for me to tell either. She wants to wait until you're done with nullifying the arrangement. You haven't said how that is going."

He picked me up and shifted me to the side, still keeping an arm around me. "There's not much to say. They've been wasting my time by wanting to meet one-on-one to discuss my departure from the Order."

I frowned and rested my head back against his shoulder. We had been spending our evenings like this. Most of the time I had my nose buried in a book though. Some of the scholars had not been happy about me borrowing books, but Marzena had come and checked them out under her name for me.

Silver sat up. "Come on. It's nice outside."

"Isn't it always nice outside here?" I remembered him saying the grounds here were the same as the church grounds in Ocean's Edge: in a perpetual spring. Though I supposed that would not stop any precipitation that came through. I found it odd that I would still get cold in the evenings though.

"Yes, but... oh just come on." He was off the bed and tugged my hand to follow.

I sighed, but did as he asked. The hour had gotten quite late, but being Elven, we did not require as much rest as the Humans that inhabited the island. The rest would be asleep if they were to get up in time for morning prayers. Not being required to attend was the one saving grace I had been granted.

Silver walked out onto the balcony. He leaned over the railing, looking out over the water. His loose hair moving gently in the breeze.

The second I stepped up next to him, he wrapped his arm around my waist. It was a bit chilly out here with the ocean breeze, so I did not fight him. Not that his necklace would want me to anyway. I glanced down, watching the tide disappear below me to strike at the sheer cliff. It made me uneasy to be standing out over such choppy waters.

"I'm not leaving you, I want you to know that," Silver said after a minute.

"Have they been asking you to stay?" I pushed my loose hair back out of my face.

"Not directly, but yes. I know nothing of holding lineage and there's no reason to remain, but I'm worried for Marzi. We're the only two left." He turned and pulled me up against him. "I guess three left since you're part of this as well."

"Silver..." I warned. There was no way he could seriously consider me part of this. Thinking back to Ocean's Edge, I had failed him when he needed me most. I had not been able to save his family at the church.

He ran his thumb over my bottom lip. "You've always been there for me. Even when I wasn't for you. And it helps that you and Marzi get along so well. You're part of the line whether you like it or not."

I rolled my eyes, realizing this was a losing argument. "Let's get some rest. I want to figure out what to do tomorrow that doesn't put me in the training grounds."

Silver laughed lightly and pulled me into a kiss. "I'll let you get away from training only if you promise me to not wear that seeker uniform."

"Does it look that bad?" I turned my attention to where it sat folded for the next wear.

He shook his head. "Once upon a time I would have loved to see you in it, but now... well, let's leave it as it's not you. I'll still pull your hair up in the morning though. It'll be safer that way."

"But the Elders..." I trailed off. How could I explain that I tolerated it on his behalf? He had not seemed to accept my words thus far. "I'm trying to do what I can to make things easier for you."

My partner shook his head. "Ignore them. They have no say over us. I'll keep wearing mine if only to remind them I am trained and have been since they were but children at best."

I bit my lower lip, still not fully convinced, but he had been too vague about his time with the Elders. "Okay."

Silver kissed my hair before running his fingers through it. "Thank you."

———

THE NEXT MORNING, after I parted ways with Silver, I headed toward the library. I was nearly to the building when Marzena came up alongside me. "Can I borrow you again?" She had a bag slung over her shoulder.

I nodded. I had no idea when Silver was due back and it was still early.

She took my hand and dragged me to the library and down to the vaults. She wasted no time getting us inside where the Sutton line's history was kept. She dropped her bag as soon as the door was closed, turning on me. "Okay, you and I need to talk."

I bit my lower lip and took half a step back, remembering her temper with the mouthy seeker.

Marzena folded her arms and stared at me. "You're hiding something. I know you were holding back when fighting Silver yesterday. Tell me."

I took another half a step back, but where would I go if the truth got out? "It's not for me to tell."

"That's crap and you know it. Family doesn't keep secrets from each other." Her volume increased as she spoke.

Family? I tilted my head at the word. My confusion had not over-ridden my fear and I had backed up enough that I bumped into the bookcase behind me.

She tugged on her ponytail. It was odd seeing someone other than Silver perform the motion. "You can't possibly be that ignorant. You're Silver's intended - you're family. Now out with it."

"I... I can't right now. Silver's request," I stammered, my voice dropping. I had to keep myself under control, but teleporting myself away was at the back of my mind.

The weapon's master paced. "I saw your eyes when I was healing you yesterday. Different colors were swirling around where it's normally gray. You've got magical abilities."

I brought my tightly folded hands to my chest. "Please don't. It's not safe." Where would I go if I had to teleport?

Marzena's shoulders dropped. "I had a feeling you might be an arcane caster. Especially when I couldn't sense it. In here no one can overhear us, so it won't leave this room. You don't need to fear me. Our line accepts all."

I lowered my hands and nodded to her, thankful I did not have to defend myself or run.

She took a long, deep breath before letting it out slowly. "You are right to hide it though - the others won't be so forgiving. What was he thinking bringing you here?"

Biting my lower lip, I shifted away from the bookcase I had backed into. "Silver wasn't sure he would be able to come back if he came alone. I can handle myself if it comes down to it, but I'm trying to behave. Unfortunately, he forgot the handicap I had when he wanted to spar."

Marzena looked back at me and gave me a lopsided grin. "Perhaps I should take some time and come visit the two of you after this. It'll be much more fun to spar with you without restrictions."

I rolled my eyes, moving to where I had left off copying the volumes the last time I was in here. "I always have restrictions. Even if the location doesn't hold me back, it's too easy to go too far." I had nearly killed Silver once. The look of surprise he had given me from behind his shield, scorch marks leading up to and around him on the floor from the fireball... I had not forgotten that. Nor had I forgiven myself for acting without thinking.

"Okay, okay. So back to why we're here." She picked up her bag and went to the sole desk in the room. "I'm hoping you can help me copy Blaise's journals faster. I know they really can't force Silver to marry, but I'm concerned if they try to corner him. If he fails to the nullifying the arrangement, then that potentially opens up this vault to whoever Amanda's loyalty lies with. Though good damn luck to them in getting him to follow through with the marriage. His word games are equal to his skill in arms."

"How hard is it to give access to someone to one of these vaults?" I asked, slowing my copying.

"In the case of the one who has lineage it's insanely easy. I'd have to go look up the right to perform it on you, but Silver just has to verbally accept you as part of the line. There's a difference between accepting as part of the line and as part of the group."

I hung my head. He had done just that last night. "What about taking away access?"

Marzena stopped and looked at me. Her arm was behind the set of books to gather the journal she had showed me yesterday. "Did Silver give you access?"

I bit my lower lip for a moment, copying another couple of volumes. "He might have."

"Okay, first of all, what are you doing? I've seen you do that upstairs and I figured you were just looking for something that caught your attention, but now I'm thinking it's something else."

I paused and pulled my hand away. "Um..." How should I explain this without sounding like I was simply looking for something horrible? "Silver requested that I copy information so he can have access to it back home." That was accurate without being specific.

She folded her arms and eyed me for a minute. "Can you really do that?"

I nodded. "It's just useless to anyone except me in its current state. I won't be able to do anything about it for him until we get back."

Marzena hummed for a moment. "I'm thinking your process is a lot faster than mine." She pulled a laptop out of the bag.

"Not with having to wait to get back to transfer it all to a computer. It takes longer and requires a specific program to read my input." There was no point in hiding the information. Not when she sought me out for help.

"Damn, I was starting to get excited, but having a third backup and one that can't be accessed by others can't hurt. Let me get Blaise's journals out for you. He hid them all over the place in here." She paused while she dug another out. "I wonder what the chances are that I could get a copy of it when you're done."

"I'd have to ask. Separating it from our database might be difficult. Unfortunately, I don't know enough about it to give you a solid answer." I copied a couple more before I commented, "There must be some amazing stories in here."

"Speaking of stories, I bet you have some good ones. Let's focus on the current task though."

While she dug them out, I continued copying the shelves of books. I would be done easily before we had to break for lunch.

"I noticed you've declined to wear the seeker uniform today," Marzena said after a few minutes, her tone conversational.

I bit my lower lip for a moment. "This is going to sound like I do whatever Silver asks, but he didn't like it and honestly, it was uncomfortable and restricting."

She laughed. "You looked cute in it, but my brother has a point - it wasn't you."

"I thought wearing it would make it easier for him with the Elders, but it doesn't seem that way."

Marzena flipped a page in the journal she had open, not stopping in her typing. "It doesn't surprise me. I had argued against it before we came and got you. I came here about five years before we lost the remainder of our group to the necromancer. Someone had to come care for the vault and all. In that time, I've seen a change here in how the Elders do things. They demand blind loyalty. There are enough people still here like myself and Silver who could care less and continue to hold to the oaths we swore. The newer ones though, and those looking to curry favor for promotion, have gone to them as if they were the God of the Sun himself."

Her words had me think that perhaps something from here also led to the fall of the church in Ocean's Edge. I could not put my finger on it though. "It sounds hard to deal with."

"It's a pain, but we're waiting for the Elders to change out. I tend to be more vocal about things. Silver really does belong sitting as an Elder, but he'll never take it even though by all rights he should be one of them. My brother does not have the patience for politics."

"He has little patience in general," I said flatly. "You know he's still a child, right?" Though with that statement, I had also admitted I was still considered a child by Elven standards since I was a couple of years younger than Silver.

Marzena sputtered and then laughed hard, backing away from the desk to wipe her eyes. I had not thought what I said was that funny.

After she calmed down, I voiced a concern. "I don't understand why they're pushing the arranged marriage though. What's the point? He couldn't have children with Amanda - she'll be well beyond child-bearing age if she's even still alive by the time he's matured enough to produce any."

"Well, Silver will never actually mature - I'm fairly certain of that," Marzena commented. "I understand what you're saying though. It's almost like they want to make sure the line ends."

"What happens if a line ends?"

Marzena shrugged. "I don't think it's ever happened. That's why lineage can be passed on to someone not related by blood. I've managed to hear whispers of his deeds in working with the Terran

Intelligence Organization. The Elders haven't been happy that he's made a name for himself outside of the Order."

That gave me pause for if the name I normally went by had also been attached to that. "We should probably get back to work. The clues might be buried here in the past."

Marzena nodded and turned back to her task.

I SAT CURLED up against the side of the desk reading Blaise Sutton's last journal when something fell out of the back of it and landed on my lap. I jumped, not having expected it.

"You okay?" Marzena leaned over so she could look at me.

"Yeah, sorry, this fell out." I held up the envelope. Something hard was inside and it was addressed to Silver in the same handwriting as Blaise's journals.

Marzena took it and held it up to the light. "Huh? I don't remember seeing that before, but that's not one I've managed to get to transcribing yet." She handed it back to me.

I flipped the envelope over, trying to guess at what was inside with my fingers through the aged paper. "Should we give it to Silver now or wait?" The last time I had an envelope for him, it landed us here. I could not guess if it would make matters worse.

"Hm." She tapped her finger on the desk. "I think it will be a good one to give him when you guys leave."

"Are you sure he's going to be able to?" I asked before I could stop myself. I had not meant to voice my concern that I might in fact lose him.

"Kela..." Marzena started and trailed off. "I know I'm not good at this reassuring thing, but Silver won't agree to marry Amanda no matter what the Elders decide. He can't be forced into this. Not unless they've got something to hold over him. I'm surprised he's taking a diplomatic route with trying to get them to nullify it. And more that he's letting them drag it out like this. I have no idea what he's trying to do."

"He's worried Amanda will get hurt," I said.

She let out a long sigh. "Always the protector. One of these days he's going to be the one to get hurt doing that. With as obnoxious as she's been so far, I'm surprised he's still trying. Normally she's pretty quiet and I'd almost say timid, but when she gets her mind set on something, she won't let anyone stand in her way."

I looked down, flicking the envelope lightly. I had let him get hurt before. I almost lost him more than once. I could not do that again.

Before anything further could be said, the door glowed blue. Silver strode in, closing the door behind him. He looked at us and crossed his arms. "I had a feeling both of you were down here."

Marzena and I looked at each other. "She's been helping me preserve the vault," she said flatly. "I'm surprised you even remembered how to get down here."

Silver knelt down in front of me. He kissed me and I felt the envelope I had been holding disappear from my fingers.

"Hey!" I cried, reaching for it.

He smirked and stood up, the envelope well out of my reach.

Marzena leveled a look at him. "Brother, that wasn't fair. Give it back to her."

"It has my name on it," he pointed out.

"Now might not be the best time…" I started and trailed off.

Silver stopped and looked at me. "Is there something you haven't been telling me?"

I bit my lower lip and turned my gaze to my lap, holding tightly onto the journal I had been reading.

"We don't know what's in it. It fell out of the journal Kela was reading," Marzena said. "And given the differences in the official historical accounts and what Blaise wrote, I asked her to keep it quiet until you were in a better position to deal with it."

The sound of the envelope being torn open echoed loudly in the room. Silver paced as he read the letter that accompanied some small trinket he immediately hid in his hand.

I got up off the floor, placing the journal I had been reading on the desk. I was uncertain if I should interrupt him or not.

When he stopped, he kept his back to us. "It seems like there is a bigger issue here than a pointless arranged marriage. Something we've dealt with before, Kela."

I moved to stand in front of him. I had a rough idea that there was corruption hidden within the Order, but I had no idea what that letter contained. Then I realized tears had trailed down his cheeks. I reached up and wiped them away. "*Tell me what you need. This is your case.*" While I could likely trust Marzena, I needed to speak plainly enough so that Silver clearly understood that I knew what I was getting into. Especially with as vague as he was being. Even I remained uncertain what his words alluded to exactly, but it was enough to know it was time to take action.

Silver looked at me with wide eyes. He opened his mouth to say something and then closed it, pulling me into a tight hug instead.

"I think I missed something here," Marzena said, standing up. "But that you didn't immediately storm out of the vault to go deal with it is an improvement over your previous impulsive behavior."

"I may have been forced to learn patience over the past few years," Silver said, but did not let go. It was warm and safe here, so I did not fight him. "I don't know what to do. I don't know how to keep both of you safe if I try to do anything."

"You know I can handle myself," Marzena said flatly. "I'm thinking she can too if it comes down to it."

Silver put his hand on my head and I looked up at him. "You are the bigger problem. You'll do whatever it takes and not retreat." He whispered, "And I almost lost you the last time."

I frowned at him, folding my arms, not needing the reminder that I had lost that gamble and would have died if not for him. "We need more evidence of whatever it is before doing anything. I don't doubt the accuracy of what I've read in the journals considering how things were changed in the public records, but that's decades old. We need something current."

"Hm. I suppose you're right," Silver said, his voice even. "Marzi, are the paths around the island still intact?"

She folded her arms and looked to one of the walls as if she could see outside. "Not likely. Like the practice hall, no one has cared for them in a long time. Longer, actually. What are you thinking?"

A large hand stroked my hair and I looked up at Silver. "Kela, feel like going for a hike tomorrow?"

I raised an eyebrow at him. I had a bad feeling about this.

11

AFTER LUNCH I was on my own. Marzena had trainings to conduct and Silver was in more meetings. I glanced up at the library and then at the ocean. While I knew it was almost always nice here, I had been holed up much of the time, trying to stay out of the way. A simple walk around the grounds should be fine.

I kept to the outer paths that wound along the shoreline. Silver had not shown me what was in the letter nor the item it contained, but I could wager a decent guess. When I worked with him in Ocean's Edge, I had been warned that his Order had backed the Racial War. Given what I had read of Blaise Sutton's journals, not all of them agreed with the decision.

What bothered me more at the moment was the person following me. I had caught sight of Amanda keeping her distance, but trailing me all the same. I tired of this game and figured she would say something when she was ready.

I remained unsure about the plan for me to start my hike as the Order gathered for morning prayers. It would give me a chance to slip off the grounds unnoticed, but I had no idea where I was going.

"Couldn't be bothered to dress appropriately today?" A condescending female voice came from behind.

I rolled my eyes and did not turn to face her. I had more important things to deal with. Perhaps if I ignored her, she would move on.

"Hey, I'm talking to you!" she shouted, storming over.

I paused and took a deep breath before turning to face her. "I know. Unless you have something worth my time, I'll be on my way."

Amanda sneered at me. "You lack respect for our customs. I can only imagine the respect you lack for your so called intended."

Customs that seem to have been put in place for me only. I pinched the bridge of my nose. "You should ask before assuming. Silver didn't want me to wear the seeker uniform today."

Amanda folded her arms and frowned at me. "Why do you have to be here and complicate things?"

I shrugged. "Take it up with the Elders. Silver had resigned."

"He has the Sutton lineage. He can't resign," she argued.

A question came to mind that made me wonder if it had even crossed hers. "Do you even like him?"

"What?" The confusion playing across her face told me she likely had not even considered her own feelings in this matter.

"Do you have feelings for Silver?" I restated. "It doesn't seem like you two knew each other before this."

Amanda crossed her arms and glared at me. "It doesn't matter. Our pairing has been ordained. I will honor it."

I raised an eyebrow at her. "For what purpose?"

"Even to you it should be obvious that the lineage must continue. He can't ignore his duty and I will help him fulfill it. We will raise the line again. An outsider can't do that."

"Is that the only reason?" It truly did not sound like she had given the arrangement much consideration of her own. How could she so blindly follow these orders? What of her goals in life?

She sneered at me. "Does there need to be any other? I will bear his children."

"The line won't continue that way if you marry Silver," I said quietly.

"Your lies will not change anything," she snapped.

"I'm not lying," I snapped back. "Do you know anything about Elven biology? By the time his body matures enough to be able to produce children, you'll be long past childbearing age."

"I... I... You're lying!"

"Talk to Silver then. He's the one who pointed it out to me." I turned on my heel and walked away.

"He is mine by decree! I'll see that it happens. Then I'll make sure you never see him again," she shouted after me.

"Paladin Sayer... Amanda..." I sighed. "I'm not your enemy here. Talk to Silver. He's been worried about your safety since he first got word of the arrangement. He may not know you, but he'll protect you. Even if you don't want him to." I walked away before she could say more.

Her threats bothered me. Even if he did decide to go through with the arrangement, I guessed I always assumed he would stay in contact. Now I was unsure if that could even happen.

"I don't know what to do."

I PACED IN THE SUITE. I had not seen Silver at dinner and it had gotten late. My interaction with Amanda earlier made me more uneasy. What if he had no choice? What if I never even heard from him again?

I shook my head and headed out to the balcony, hoping fresh air would stop the incessant thoughts. Silver would choose his own path. If that meant I returned alone, then I would have to accept that.

Why was I so obsessed with this? I ran my hands through my bangs and tugged on the ends hard. Were these thoughts because of his necklace that I still wore? Was it filling me with such dread at the thought of never seeing him again?

"There you are," Silver said as he stepped out onto the balcony.

Before I registered what I was doing, I had gone over to him, lightly drawing the anchor with my finger on the backside of his upper arm.

Silver raised an eyebrow at me, running a hand over my hair. "What's going on?"

I tugged on his braid and repeated the anchor, not trusting my voice.

"I know I'm late, but what has you so worked up?" His eyes scanned my face for something.

Finally, I gave up and stood on the balls of my feet so I could kiss him. He had requested I help anchor him enough that he should not have had to think about it. I ended up pressing myself fully against him in trying to steady my precarious balance.

Silver hesitated just long enough I was about to stop and pull away at the rejection. Then he growled and pressed harder, demanding more and if it meant keeping him in my life then I would give it to him. Whatever he asked. I could not lose my best friend here. Not after everything we had been through.

Whatever it took to get him to stay. Part of my mind asked why I was doing this. I shoved it to the back for the moment, wrapping my arms around his neck to hold on.

Suddenly he picked me up, carrying me back inside. I had barely landed on the bed before he was kneeling over me. He pulled my hands from around his neck and pinned them to the bed. "Okay, now you're going to tell me what is going on," he said calmly.

I cringed at his rejection. "Am I doing something wrong? Is this not right?" What was it he needed? What if I had done something to push him away?

He growled, nuzzling my ear with his nose for a moment before backing away to stare down at me. "It's not right in that I know damn well this isn't you. I may be a hot-blooded male, but I won't take advantage of you."

I turned away from him. Rejection and relief fought for control. I had let his necklace take over and I had not even noticed. "Sorry."

Silver let out a long breath, easing up on how much weight was on me, but not enough to move. "Kela, I want an explanation, not an apology."

"I..." I squirmed. I hated being pinned.

Silver released my wrists and sat back on my legs.

It seemed that was the best I was going to get at the moment and got up on my elbows. "I... I guess overreacted to a conversation I had earlier."

Silver frowned and then moved to sit on the edge of the bed. "My missing dinner with you and being late likely only made it worse. Who was it?"

I followed, but left enough room between us that another person could easily sit. "It doesn't matter. What matters is I acted like a fool. I didn't even notice what was happening."

Silver hummed for a moment and then slid to sit right up against me. "Well, for what it's worth, I wouldn't have turned down the offer if it had been genuine." He grinned broadly.

I rolled my eyes. "*Child.*"

He laughed loudly. "Now I know you're back in control. Come on, let's take a walk. I need something to eat anyway and I think they've forgotten I know how to raid the kitchens."

"What about tomorrow? I might not be able to get started on time," I argued.

He stroked my hair gently, tugging playfully on one of the braids. "It can wait another day. You and I need to talk about that conversation you had and Marzena didn't have time to try to locate a map for you."

I frowned, but followed him out the door. At least now I knew he could tell when his necklace had taken control. *He won't betray this trust.*

1 2

I had taken a spot in the corner away from everyone else at lunch. Not that anyone outside of Silver or Marzena would likely have wanted to sit with me anyway. Both of them had been busy since breakfast today.

It did not help that I also stood out since Silver had gone and hidden the seeker outfit, so I was left with what I had brought. The stares had gotten to me and I took what I could carry in my hands and returned my tray and dishes.

Today was not a good day to be outside either. The rain had been falling steadily since just before dawn. I hurried and found an overhang to stand under away from where people would be entering and exiting the dining hall.

I leaned against the wall and ate what I had kept of my lunch. Not that I had much of an appetite, but Silver would be on my case if I skipped a meal.

"Did Paladin Blaise ask that you not wear the seeker uniform again?" Amanda asked as she approached.

I sighed and popped the last bit of sandwich in my mouth. I had no desire for another confrontation with her.

She stood under the overhang and folded her arms.

Apparently, she intended to wait out an answer. "In a way. He hid it."

"Can... would you tell me about him?" she asked, her voice quiet.

I raised an eyebrow at her. This was so vastly different from our confrontation yesterday.

Amanda wrung her hands. "Look, I was thinking about what you said yesterday. I don't know if you're lying or not about him being too young. I don't even know where to find out. And I realized all I know about him are the deeds recorded in our historical accounts. I tried to get Paladin Nowak to tell me, but she only gets on my case about my training."

"What have you read about Silver?" I asked, keeping my voice as gentle as possible. If I could avoid another confrontation, I would happily answer her questions.

"That he came from humble beginnings and often got stuck with menial tasks. I certainly know what that's like," she said, rubbing her arms. "But his story inspired me to push to become a paladin like him."

So, she knew something about Silver before the Elders ordered the arranged marriage.

Amanda smiled softly and looked out at the rainy day from where we were taking cover. "I've read his various deeds of valor. The stories about when he was up against what should have been impossible odds. How he helped begin and shaped the church in Ocean's Edge to become a place where many would worship. I had tried to get in with the group that went to rebuild that church after a necromancer destroyed it, but I had not finished my training at that point."

"He left after that though," I said.

She wrung her hands. "I know, and I don't understand why. I heard something about him calling himself a 'free paladin,' but I have no idea what that means. The Elders won't tell me more."

"I think it was he would not be tied down by the Order. He has his own code to follow, but even after knowing him this long, I couldn't tell you what it is." Granted, it had only been two and a half years. Some of that time we had been apart. Some of it seemed like we had been inseparable.

Amanda laughed lightly. "Thank you for being honest. I should probably have approached you like this, but..." she trailed off.

I forced a small smile to my face. "It's easy to see me as the enemy. Is this what you want though? To be married to him? I know he wants a family of his own, but you wouldn't be able to have that. Not unless you were planning to adopt children."

She folded her arms and leaned against the wall with me. "I don't know. I just accepted the decree and prepared myself for the duty that lay ahead."

"Even if it goes against your goals in life?" I was the last person who should be speaking of life goals since I had none, but if it got her to think, I was willing to have the conversation.

"I... I know it doesn't seem right, but how else can I prove my worth to the God of the Sun if I don't follow the orders I'm given?" The expression on her face was of someone lost or at least conflicted.

I bit my lower lip and looked out at the rain. "Well, if you want to use Silver for an example, he finds fulfillment through following his heart." It was the only logical way to explain his often lack of logic. "The God of the Sun hasn't forsaken him for it." At least as far as I knew.

Silence fell between us for a few minutes.

"Just so you know, I didn't read only Paladin Blaise's records. I read through a lot. About the only thing I'm good at is remembering otherwise useless information." Her laugh sounded strained. The toll this was taking on her was not something I had thought about and likely Silver had not either.

I took a deep breath. "In the end it's Silver's decision, but you should talk to him. If he keeps avoiding you or being a jerk, let me know and I'll talk to him about it."

"Wait, you're helping me?"

Out of the corner of my eye, I caught her staring at me with wide eyes and I shrugged. "I know how thick-headed he can be. I want him to be happy, but sometimes he gets too focused on one thing." Even if Silver being happy meant losing him, I would continue to stay neutral. I hoped we could at least stay in contact.

Amanda crossed her arms, but it was more like she was hugging herself. "If you're free, would you come train with me? Maybe Paladin Nowak is right and I'm using the wrong weapons."

"You don't want to admit that to her?" I asked, raising an eyebrow.

She shook her head. "Not yet anyway. She's scary when she's mad."

"THAT'S IT, just take it slow," I said, moving to match Amanda's sword and shield with my staff. "Speed will come."

She had spent quite a bit of time moving about the training area, trying different weapons, but came back to what she already had. While I had been waiting, I moved through different sequences and it caught her attention. Enough that she was willing to take the position Silver normally did. At least I had done these enough times with my partner that I could direct her.

"Do you do this with Paladin Blaise often?" Amanda asked.

"Sometimes. It'll switch up between this, sparring, and just general physical training. It helps him think," I answered honestly.

She moved slowly, but fluidly to the next strike. "Do you think he'd be willing to work with me?"

I let out a soft huff, matching the strike. "He has enough patience to deal with me and I fight him about training regularly."

Amanda laughed.

We continued through the slow dance with our weapons. As she seemed to get comfortable, I would increase the speed slightly. I lost track of the time. We had taken a few breaks in which she asked me more questions about Silver. Thankfully nothing had strayed into the realm of our work within the TIO and I offered none there. It would be too easy to slip and admit I was an arcane caster.

I caught sight of Silver and Marzena entering the training room, but Amanda was completely focused on her movements through the sequence. We were close to a stopping point, so I continued.

Marzena took a step forward and Silver put his hand out to stop her.

As soon as the point came up, I stepped back, signaling that I was done. I nodded to the two standing behind her.

Amanda turned and I could not see her face, but the rest of her body froze. "It's... it's not what you think! I swear I wasn't fighting with her."

"I know," Silver said calmly. "I recognized that sequence." He looked at me. "I can't say I expected to find you here like this."

I shrugged. What was I supposed to say to that? He had not given me much to do. I had gone through much of the library and it would have been rude to turn down Amanda's request. I shrunk my staff and tucked it into its holster.

Marzena folded her arms and looked Amanda over. "Thrice in

three days without it being an order. I'm impressed, though I'm not certain the first one counts. Learn anything?"

Amanda looked to me briefly. "I think I need to figure out if there's a better weapon option for me to start."

The weapons master stood up straighter and looked over to me. "Well then. Too few can see past the most common weapons used to find where their highest potential lies. We can discuss this tomorrow. It's getting close to dinner time and you two look like you've been at this a while."

Now that I had stopped, my arms had begun to ache. I was not about to tell anyone though.

Silver wrapped his arm around my shoulders. "You and I need to talk."

I rolled my eyes. "It's never a good thing any time you say that."

"Go ahead," Marzena said, "I have a few things I want to discuss with Amanda."

I nodded and followed Silver outside. He led us to a quiet area away from the training grounds.

The rain felt good and I paused before we reached the tree line, turning my face up to the sky and closing my eyes. I could care less that I was getting soaked.

I jumped when I felt an arm wrap around my waist.

Silver smiled down at me. "Feels good, does it?"

"Yeah," I answered quietly.

He leaned down and kissed me. It was gentle and something else I could not figure out. It was so different from the times he needed me to help ground him or what happened last night.

The kiss became deeper, but never demanding. I had no idea what Silver needed from me. He said he had wanted to talk.

He pulled back, smiling. "*I could definitely get used to this. Though I'm not sure about the both of us being soaked part.*"

I raised an eyebrow at his use of my dialect of common.

Silver grabbed my hand and tugged me along toward the forest.

As we entered the tree line I asked, "What did you want to talk about?"

He stopped a ways in before turning on me. "Your habit of turning people around."

I tilted my head at him, unsure what he was referring to.

"Last night you were upset over a conversation you had with that girl and today you're helping her train. I don't get it." He gestured sharply in the direction of the training grounds.

I shivered, rubbing my arms. "She asked if I would help her. Silver, Amanda is being used in this just as much as you are. At least get to know her. She didn't even know about you being too young to have children. She does know the stories they have here about you though."

"None of it good I imagine," he muttered, crossing his arms.

"Enough to inspire her to push to become a paladin," I argued. Why was he being so stubborn about this?

"Oh, come on! You're going to believe some sad story like that?" He continued being animated as he spoke, using his hands to emphasize his obvious frustrations.

"It doesn't matter whether I believe it or not. I believed you when you voiced concern over her safety before we even left. Before you had a chance to meet her," I countered.

"Are you trying to get me to agree to the arrangement?" Silver's voice started to rise.

I paced. "No! I know that isn't what you want, but could you at least talk to her? Maybe she could help nullify it. I don't think she even knows what she wants - she's just following orders."

"What do you want?"

I stopped and looked at Silver.

"What do you want?" he repeated. "I'm not even sure which side you're on."

I pinched the bridge of my nose. "I'll tell you what I told Amanda. It's your decision to make. I just want you to be happy. If that means pointing out that you haven't considered all of your options, then so be it." I dropped my arms and hung my head. "Even if it means losing you, I want you to make the decision that's best for you." Those words were far harder to say than they should have been. It must have been his necklace again that I was fighting against.

"Kela," Silver said softly, tilting my chin up with his fingers. "You are my intended. You have no idea how happy that makes me. I don't need to look elsewhere. Though I will talk to her and see if she'll help nullify the arrangement."

I nodded, not able to break eye contact with him. At least he seemed to be listening now.

He smiled before kissing me quickly. "And actually, I was looking for you to talk to you about hiking to the other side of the island. It sounds like all of the trails have been unkept for decades. Your best bet would be to travel south along the coast. It'll be too easy to get lost in the mountains."

"What if there's something in the mountains?" I asked. Letting paths deteriorate would only help keep people from wandering into something.

He stroked my cheek gently and I blinked as water dripped off his loose strands of hair onto my face. "I wouldn't concern myself with that. Without roads, it would be too difficult to haul supplies up there."

"Okay, I get it." My stomach made a noise, demanding to be fed.

"You didn't skip lunch, did you?" he asked, his tone warning.

I sighed and admitted, "I ended up cutting it short."

"Alright, let's make sure you're fueled up." Silver took my hand and led me out of the forest.

13

I WAS WELL out of sight of the Central Seat when the sky lightened to pre-dawn. Silver agreed with me that I should head out before the others started waking for morning prayers. He led me through back doors and passages, most of which had not appeared to have been used in a long time. The dark, tight areas had set me on edge. We parted at the forest line.

While this was not the familiar forest outside of Mystic Port, I still moved easily beneath the leafy boughs. I kept the water in sight between the trunks and underbrush to make sure I did not stray from my intended path.

Finding a spot to stop, I took a seat and dug into my backpack for the food my partner had pilfered from the kitchens. In an effort to minimize the weight, I kept my meals light with a few snacks for backup. At least now I could use my power if I needed to, but I planned on keeping it to a minimum.

The problem was I had no idea if I could make it down to the other side of the island and back in one day. Being absent for a day I could probably get away with. Two days would be suspicious. That and I would be hiking on an empty stomach on the way back. Not the best of plans, but I could manage if it came down to it.

Once I got going again, I kept my pace as quick as I could sustain. The island was beautiful and I wished I could slow down to a more leisurely pace to enjoy it better, but I had an assignment and I would see it through.

I wished Silver would have told me what was in that letter he got from the back of Blaise Sutton's final journal. For now, I would assume it was something to do with his past.

Perhaps after this was over, we could try to search for where his village had been. Something might have remained that could give him answers. The notes Blaise had left should make it easier to locate, though he used a lot of pre-Racial War names for places.

The cover of the forest had given way to open sky and tall grass before I stopped again, making me scan the ocean frequently for any boats. It would not do to be spotted from the sea. Just as I finished eating lunch, I caught sight of something on the horizon coming from the northern part of the island.

I hid in the tall grass, staying as low as possible. After a few minutes the ferry came into view. It was the same one Silver and I had seen the other day, but this was not the time it gone past before. The ferry continued by and slowed before turning, disappearing around a bend not much farther south.

The boat could not have docked far. Silver was right to suspect something was going on, but what? It could be as innocent as another town, though Marzena seemed to know nothing of it either.

I hustled, packing up my things before heading in the direction of the ferry. When I got back to the suite, I was going to take a long, hot shower. As long as this proved to be nothing demanding more immediate action.

As I crested the last hill which dropped down into another valley, I caught something on the edge of my senses. *Arcane? On an island supposedly solely of people devoted to the divine?* I pulled my power as much into myself as possible before moving. I kept low to the ground and crept up through the tall grass, staying low.

What greeted me as I got to the top, enough to see down into the next valley, I had not expected. A small settlement was nestled along the shoreline. The buildings were primarily large, heavy canvas tents. Some sturdier looking buildings sat on the perimeter, but they had not been built on a foundation. There was also a basic dock that stretched out to the ferry. Nothing seemed overly permanent.

Crates were being hauled off of the ferry at the moment while people in robes milled about the area - many with their nose in a book.

I slowly stretched my senses, trying to figure out what was arcane. There had to be some powerful casters down there for me to sense them this far. I wished I had my phone so I could take pictures, but Silver had insisted I leave it and my watch behind in our suite.

Why would there be arcane casters on an island with such a strong divine presence? And more so one that disliked anything arcane from what I understood.

I could not risk getting closer. If they were at the edge of my senses, I was barely out of theirs and I would only be able to keep myself hidden for so long. At least that was what I hoped seeing no one had yet raised an alarm at my presence.

People started coming off the ferry. Both children and adults. A couple toward the back got shoved. It did not appear they were here willingly. Not when the people doing the shoving had long guns in their hands.

I backed away from the edge and hurried down the hill. I needed to get back. I ran whenever the terrain allowed and moved as fast as I could otherwise. My lungs and legs burned. It was mid-to-late afternoon by the time I got back. I hid within the tree line near the training grounds, needing to catch my breath and compose myself.

I sat against a tree with my back to the building, using the trunk to hide. Once the dizziness was gone, I would find Silver.

I GROANED and rolled onto my side - my stomach felt like it was trying to turn into a black hole. Wait, where was I?

A calloused hand stroked my hair. "Welcome back," Silver said gently.

I looked around finding myself in the bed in our suite. "I thought I had stopped in the forest."

"You had. Marzi found you. I brought you back here. I still remember all the back ways around the island, so no one saw you," he said, sounding as if he was trying to be reassuring.

I struggled to sit up.

Silver pushed my shoulders back, resetting my progress. "Hey, easy. I don't know what happened."

"I came back as fast as I could. I stopped because I was dizzy," I said, struggling against him. The sight of the people being offloaded stayed at the forefront of my mind.

He sighed and helped me sit up. "Likely you didn't have enough fuel to burn for the run. Marzi had a feeling that might be the case and went to get some food for you. What happened? Something tells me it wasn't the local fauna."

I closed my eyes and hugged my knees to my chest and shook now that I had time to think about it.

Silver took one of my hands and kissed the back of it. "I'm right here."

I took a deep breath, focusing on our hands. "*That ferry does go to the other side of the island,*" I said quietly in my dialect of common.

"*How far?*"

"*I don't know. I didn't get down there until shortly after I stopped for lunch.*" I looked up at my partner. "*Silver, there were people being offloaded like cargo by armed guards. And I caught strong arcane presences.*"

There was a knock on the door before anything further could be said. Silver squeezed my hand quickly before going to answer it.

Marzena came in holding a tray. "Hey, you're up at least. Feeling any better?"

I forced a small smile for her. There was no reason for her to be concerned.

"We have a problem," Silver said quietly after he closed the door. "It sounds like people are being brought down there against their will."

She set the tray on the small dining table off to the side of the room and sighed. "I had hoped I was simply imagining things."

"What do you mean?" I asked. I slid over to the edge of the bed. The moment I started to stand, the world spun and I sat back down, holding my head in my hands.

Not before I caught sight of Silver jumping the couch to get over to me. "Dammit, Kela. You never do know when to stop, do you?" He picked me up off the bed.

"Put me down," I ordered.

Silver said nothing even as I pushed to try and get free of his hold. Unfortunately, I was unable to do so in the short time it took for him to carry me over to the table where the food was. He pointed at the tray of food.

I rolled my eyes. The food smelled far better than it had this whole trip so far. My movements were slow, but I managed.

My partner stood next to me. "Care to clarify about what you thought you were imagining?"

Marzena took a seat across from me. "It's hard to explain. It's been small things. The demands for loyalty from certain lines. The changes not only in the ferry runs, but also who is allowed to pilot it. There's been a decline on allowing visitors. Letting the paths around the island fall into disarray despite repeated requests for them to be reopened."

"It's a control of movement," I said quietly.

"And the demand for my brother to marry someone loyal to the Elders makes me think that someone wants control of the Sutton line," Marzena said flatly.

"Or to end it," Silver said flatly. "The vault will likely seal and the truth along with it."

"Silver, they've never made a move to end a line before," the weapons master pointed out. "I don't think a line has ever ended. That's why lineage can be passed to someone not related by blood. It's why this arranged marriage tradition exists."

"They have tried to end a line," I said quietly and closed my eyes as I thought about the events that led me to meeting my partner. That statement gave me the piece to start putting things together.

"Not just the church in Ocean's Edge," Silver said. "I'm fairly certain the failed settlement near Troll territory was another attempt."

"Wait, what?" Marzena was on her feet. "I know about the church, but that was a few years after I had come to the Central Seat."

"You hadn't been born yet," Silver said flatly. "My master had told them it was too close to Troll territory. He fought the decision. James had remained behind when the rest of us were sent. It was a constant battle. They left us there for about five years."

She returned to her seat across from me. "I remember those entries now. It was as if Blaise hadn't had enough time to write. Much of it was simply statistics of people lost or what had been damaged or stolen." She sat upright. "Brother, don't you dare try to take on the

Elders and their followers. We'll have to get help from others. I know many who have no desire to pledge their loyalty."

My partner shook his head. "I have no intention of storming into the Court of Elders and alerting them. I'm going to focus on continuing to nullify the arrangement. This corruption runs deep and long. It won't be solved by the swing of a sword."

Marzena raised an eyebrow at him before she turned to me. "Am I to give you credit for tempering him?"

I bit my lower lip. "I don't think I—"

"She is," he said, cutting me off. "As well as I can't let a sister get hurt because of my impulsive tendencies. I will protect my family."

"Now you sound like the head of the line," Marzena teased.

I put my fork back down and stared at the plate of food. I knew I was not included in that despite his words before. I barely knew him in comparison to Marzena. I had my sister and my adopted parents, but it seemed so drastically different than what he had just spoken of. Than of what I had seen.

"Kela?" Marzena asked.

I sat up straight. "It's nothing." I noted though that Silver said nothing to her about there being an arcane presence.

"Eat," Silver ordered. "It might not be soon, but there will be a fight coming."

A fight I would be useless in as restricted as I was. I debated contacting the TIO. We were going to be in over our heads if this did in fact turn into a fight. Someone needed to get to those people, but Silver was right and that we were in no position to act quickly. I could only hope that nothing happened to them while we figured this out.

14

It had been several days where time just seemed to crawl. As I walked toward the dining hall, I stretched. Even with spending time helping Marzena and working with Amanda, I had finished copying the entire library. I would still spend time in there, continuing my pattern so it would not seem suspicious. I had become friendly with a couple of the scholars and they seemed more than happy to answer any questions I might have.

The biggest problem I faced now was that each day I saw less and less of Silver. Soon enough I would begin to expect him not to return at all in the evenings. With the little time he gave me, I did what I could so he could calm down and rest, but he would never share what was going on.

Though I had found brushing his hair soothing - it was something that benefitted both of us. The first few times he seemed uneasy about the idea, but caved quickly. Last night he had even brought me his brush.

A small group of paladins who I found to be friendly approached. I forced a smile and nodded to them as they passed by. I turned and watched them walk away and toyed with one of the small braids hanging off the side of my loose bun. At least Silver still insisted on doing my hair in the mornings. Odd how I found it annoying before and now...

I shook my head of the thought. Why was I even here? If anything, I was likely putting more strain on my partner. Would this have been easier if I had not accompanied him?

My appetite had been lacking before and now it was certainly gone. Taking a deep breath, I decided a walk around the area would be better than another scrutinized meal. People could yell at me later for skipping dinner.

As the sun started to sink behind the mountains, I decided I had wandered long enough. I glanced up at the practice hall that I was walking past. Unfortunately, it was locked and I was not about to enter without permission.

The hairs on the back of my neck stood up and I spun around, searching the area. Someone was watching me. Or following as I caught sight of a paladin and a seeker heading toward me.

Realizing I was alone out here, I walked faster, wanting to get back to where there were others around.

Another paladin stepped into my path in front of me. "If it isn't the little fairy girl. Out for an evening stroll?" He gave me a toothy grin. It came across more like he was baring his teeth at me.

I clenched my jaw at the term he used and glanced behind me as I heard their pace increase - they were closing the distance quickly. I stepped toward a remaining opening, walking faster to get away from the group.

The paladin ahead of me ran to block my path. "What's the hurry? With the way you're running away, I'm starting to think you don't like us."

I raised my hands and took a step back, checking on where the other paladin and the seeker were. "Please, I just want to be left alone." If only I could teleport, this would not be a problem.

"I bet if that pointy-eared freak that brought you was here you wouldn't. He's not a real paladin you know," one of the men behind me said.

Biting the inside of my cheek to keep from responding to the jab at Silver, I pinpointed the openings and ran for the closest one. If I could get to a busier area, there was a high probability that they would leave me alone.

A hand grabbed my upper arm before I could get through. The paladin that had come at me from the front squeezed hard and yanked me back.

The sudden switch from going forward to backward caused me to lose my balance and I fell hard on my hip. I managed to catch myself before my head hit the ground. I glared at the man who had grabbed me.

He knelt down and reached for Silver's necklace that I wore. A gold-white bolt flashed brightly from the sun pendant just before he could grab it, sending him flying back.

Someone kicked my back. "Think you're so smart."

I pushed myself to get up and was rewarded with another kick. My power... if only I could use some spells to get out of this. The shrunken staff attached to my thigh would have to suffice. Unfortunately, it was sandwiched between me and the ground at the moment.

The paladin who had gotten shocked by the necklace came over and grabbed my hair, pulling me up in the process. "What in the Hells was that?! Huh?"

I cringed as he grabbed a fistful of my hair which pushed a number of hair pins painfully into my head. This was going to hurt no matter what I did. Better to go down fighting. I jammed two fingers into the base of his throat. The second his hand loosened, I shoved him back, scrambling past.

The two who were behind me immediately reached for me.

I spun to face them, dropping low to kick out, knocking the feet out from underneath the seeker who was closest. As I drew my shrunken staff from its holster, the second paladin fell forward as if hit from behind. *Silver?*

Marzena stood there with her sword drawn. She flexed her left arm, causing her shield to reappear on it. "Boys, you seemed to have forgotten how to treat a guest. Guess I'll have to remind you." She grinned broadly, eyeing both paladins and the seeker.

"She started it! She called us over here," the seeker said, his words practically tripping over each other.

The weapons master spun the sword in her hand - a move I had seen Silver do. "Do you really think I'm stupid enough to fall for that?" she asked, her voice steady.

The next thing I knew I was on the ground again and the men were gone. Marzena still stood where she had been. Had I blacked out for a moment? A number of freshly sore spots told me I had likely gotten hit in their escape.

My friend sheathed her sword and came over, kneeling down in front of me. "Come on, let's get you cleaned up a bit - see how bad the damage is." She got under my arm and helped me up.

"I'm fine. I can walk," I argued, sliding my shrunken staff back into its holster. The world spun a bit faster than I cared for, but I could work through it.

She gave me a toothy grin and lowered her voice. "But it's much easier to talk quietly this way. I certainly would have loved to see what you could have done if you didn't have to behave."

I rolled my eyes and let her escort me to the training grounds. "My first instinct would have been to run."

I SAT with my arms folded, glaring at the wall across from me as Marzena dabbed lightly at my lip with a damp cloth.

She had brought me into the indoor training grounds and to the small infirmary in the back. Outside of the occasional direction from her, there had been only silence.

It gave me time to sit and contemplate how much this was going to complicate things for Silver now. If I had been able to run without fighting back, they would likely not have told anyone about the altercation. About my arcane abilities would have been another story. Granted, I had no idea if they would tell anyone. For some reason I assumed they would report it.

Fighting back, however, would show me as aggressive and the Elders would use that against nullifying the arrangement. I closed my eyes. Either way I was in the wrong and set up to be so.

"Hey," Marzena said softly.

I opened my eyes and she had put the damp cloth aside and knelt in front of me.

She took my head in both hands. "They will pay for this." Her slim, gentle fingers brushed my bangs back. "I'm a bit torn. I should heal this before your intended sees you, but I know it drains you."

"It's too late for that," Silver said, pushing the door open and striding in. He folded his arms, staring both of us down. His braid was not sitting over his right shoulder.

Upon noticing that, I slid away from Marzena and got up.

"Sit down," Silver ordered.

"No," I said firmly.

"This is not the time to argue with me," he growled.

I scrunched up my face at him and drew a line over my right shoulder. "I'm not listening to you until you've got your head in the right place."

Marzena snickered behind me.

My partner put his hand on the right side of his neck and then sighed, pulling his braid back over where it belonged. He turned his attention behind me. "This isn't funny, Marzi."

"What happened with Kela isn't. The fact she's so observant and will call you out is." Marzena came over to into my view.

I returned to my seat, sore and tired. "It was my fault."

Both of them argued loudly against my statement at the same time.

I held up my hand for them to quiet and was somewhat surprised when they both did. "I shouldn't have wandered to an area by myself."

"Kela, what are you thinking? They cornered and attacked you. I saw the whole thing. So did a couple of others. How do you think he found out?" She tilted her head toward Silver.

My partner sighed and sat down next to me, wrapping his arm around my shoulders. "I'll admit, I was surprised when Amanda was the one who pulled me out of the meeting and told me."

"The two of them have become friends while you've been occupied." Marzena turned to look at me.

I shrugged. "I've just been working with her when she asks."

Silver moved and knelt down in front of me. He cupped my face in his hands, running his thumbs gently over my cheeks. He touched a sore spot and I cringed. "Sorry. Let's get you back to the room before I heal this. You'll want to get cleaned up at the same time and rest." He kissed my forehead.

For some reason, I did not want to move. I knew he was not using his power, but that one motion helped settle my mind. I feared the moment he backed away, the stress that had melted would return. And likely with a vengeance.

When he finally backed up, I simply felt exhausted. I stood up stiffly, my body protesting the movement.

Suddenly I found myself in Silver's arms. "Put me down," I ordered.

"Make me." He gave me a lopsided grin, but it was too gentle to be his usual mischievous one.

Marzena interrupted before I could continue to argue with him. "Kela, it's a long way back to the guest rooms and you're hurt. You can give him a hard time later."

I folded my arms and frowned. "Fine."

Silver interrogated Marzena about what happened as they walked through the indoor part of the training grounds. No sooner had we stepped outside when both stopped. I looked over to see that the Elder who had asked me to wear the seeker uniform was coming our way with another paladin. I searched my memory for a name.

I groaned and tapped Silver so he could put me down. He held me tighter in response.

"Elder Bisset," Marzena greeted. "What brings you all the way out here?"

"I had heard there was an incident." His words were gentle, but I remained wary. Valere came closer to me. "The men are currently being confined to their rooms. We'll question them when they sober up."

I bit my lower lip and quickly let go when I felt the scab tear and tasted blood. There had been no smell of alcohol. I knew I would have picked up on it. Especially off the one who grabbed my hair.

"Perhaps if you had been wearing the uniform..." Valere trailed off, rubbing his chin in thought.

"No," Silver barked. "I won't allow it. There is no reason for her to be uncomfortable while she's here. And there is no excusing their behavior. Drunk or no. Uniform or no. They should never have assaulted her in the first place. If you'll excuse us, I need to get her back so I can tend to her injuries."

"Elder Bisset, it's late. We can go over this in the morning after Kela has recovered," Marzena interjected. "I will have a full statement written up for you tonight."

"See that you do." Valere paused and looked between the three of us before turning his attention to Silver. "Perhaps it would be best if you sent her home." Then he spun on his heel and left.

After a minute, Marzena commented, "For an old guy, he can move quick when he feels like it."

"Let's get her back," Silver said, his voice quiet.

15

THE NEXT MORNING, the sun had risen and Silver was still curled up against my back. I had woken him when I heard the tones to call people for morning prayers, but he refused to budge. I had tried to get up to prompt him, but he tightened his arm around my waist and would not let me out of bed.

For the life of me, I could not understand why he insisted on being affectionate when it was just the two of us. If he had wanted to skip morning prayers, he could have just said so and let me go about my day.

I made another attempt to get out of bed, only to be dragged back against my partner. "It's getting late."

"Don't care," he mumbled, nuzzling my hair.

"Silver..." I warned.

"Just a little longer. I need to know you're here and safe." He curled tighter around me which I had not thought possible.

"You know I'm here and safe. Now let me up." I frowned and folded my arms the best I could. His necklace had also been trying to convince me to stay put, but yesterday's events still bothered me. There was no proof that the three men had not been acting on their own, but something with how Valere spoke had me considering the idea that they were under orders.

Loud banging on the door caused me to jump. I tried to twist and turn to face it, but Silver still had me mostly pinned.

He growled and let go, getting out of bed. I scrambled to follow, making it just in time to hide behind the door as he yanked it open.

Silver folded his arms over his bare chest and glared at the person standing on the other side. "What?" he demanded.

"You missed morning prayers," a male voice replied. It was one I had heard, but not recently. One of the Elders from when we first arrived?

"I can perform them just as easily in my room," Silver shot back.

"You're also late for the morning meeting." He started getting louder. I was in a poor place if a shouting match was about to begin.

Silver gripped the door tighter, his knuckles turning white. "My intended was assaulted yesterday, and you're concerned about a meeting that is nothing but a waste of my time? I'm spending my time where it is most needed. Or would be if you'd leave."

"Ah, yes, the incident," he sounded distasteful of those words. "We do need to discuss that as well. Get dressed and be at the Court in an hour. Make sure your guest does not go anywhere unattended until we get this resolved. In fact, it would be best if she remained here."

As my partner bared his teeth at the man on the other side of the door, I stepped around to be in full view. "It's a bit difficult to give my statement if I'm stuck here," I said calmly.

The Elder sneered at me. "There is no need. You are unaware of our procedures. He will speak for you." He jutted his chin at Silver.

I narrowed my eyes at the Elder before glancing up at my partner. No matter what, I was not going to be allowed to share my story. Unfortunately, I was in no position to argue how they did things. At least I knew Silver would not betray me.

"Marzena won't mind you tagging along. I'll be at the Court when I'm damn well ready," Silver said and slammed the door shut. He headed toward where his uniform was hung up, ignoring the banging on the door.

I looked at the door and then at my partner before going over to him. "I don't understand."

Silver growled. "Neither do I, but the threat is there. Either you stay here or with someone at all times or your safety isn't guaranteed."

I frowned and crossed my arms. "I can take care of myself."

He spun back around to look at me. "And what if Marzena hadn't happened to have been in the area? That's not something I want to find out."

This was not something I wanted to back down on, but I was fighting against his necklace pushing to accept. "I would have won that fight. I refuse to be a prisoner."

"At what cost?" Silver grabbed my head with both hands, staring down at me. "We both know what could have happened if you under-estimated your opponent." He mouthed the words "Mystic Port."

I sighed. That unconscious defense. There would have been no hiding that they had been killed by magic in that case. Damn, he had cornered me with a logical reason. The memory of the charred corpse of the Troll was not one I wanted to remember, and I closed my eyes, trying to push it away.

"Can you at least listen to me for now?" Silver brushed my bangs back. "I don't want anything to happen to you. Not when there is something I can do to prevent it."

"Fine." There was little point in fighting with him further on this. Even I could sense the threat as well. "Though I won't listen for long."

Silver kissed me. "That's the best I can ask for right now. I guess now that we're up we should get ready for the day."

***

For a few days following the incident, Silver started coming back barely in time to rest so I had no time to talk to him. The routine had become that he would return smelling of alcohol, I would help ground him, and he would turn in. More than once I would spend the next couple of hours on the balcony trying to sort myself out from his necklace. As the pattern continued, I realized I could no longer blame it for the empty feeling.

Never did he speak of anything to do with the arrangement or the corruption we had uncovered. Anytime I asked about what resolution they had come to after the attack, he would growl and storm away.

I took a long walk around the grounds, having no desire to be cooped up in the room right now - orders be damned. Perhaps Valere was right and I should just go home - my presence was only making things worse. I could find out tomorrow when the ferry would next return to the mainland. At least then I would be free to contact some-one. I needed to get word out about the people being held on the island. That had continued to weigh heavier on my mind the longer it took to get the news out to someone. *What I should do?*

Sighing, I shook my head and returned to the suite. I told Silver I would stay with him and I needed to keep to my promise. It would all work out and then everything could go back to normal.

I began to wonder what normal would look like.

As soon as I entered the suite, I put my phone and my watch on their chargers. It was less that they needed to charge and more as a place to keep them in the room. I headed for the vanity, reaching behind my head to start digging the hairpins out.

"Let me," Silver said softly.

I jumped at the sound of his voice, turning quickly. "I didn't know you were back."

Silver smiled, but it seemed forced. "I'm sorry I haven't been coming back until late. It hasn't been fair to you. I guess I can't be too mad at you for being out on your own." He brushed my bangs back.

At least he had not smelled of alcohol this time.

"Why?" I asked quietly.

"Why what?"

"Why have you been coming back so late?"

Silver turned me so I faced the mirror. As he pulled the hairpins out of my hair one at a time, he said, "I've needed to think."

"And?"

He shook his head. "Let me have this time, Kela. Just us. Nothing else."

I looked down at my hands. "You don't have to do this alone."

Silver wrapped his arms around me from behind, resting his head on my shoulder for a moment. "Shh... just us right now. Nothing else."

I sighed. Perhaps tomorrow he would be more willing to talk. There was little I could do until he told me what he needed. When I looked at him in the mirror, he appeared worn out. He also had his hair down. I never saw it out of his customary braid this early in the evening. I had no idea what to make of it.

"What do you need?" I asked. There had to be a question that would get him talking.

There was that forced small smile again. "Just to spend time with my intended. I'll never be able to make up for the time lost, but if you would indulge me this evening, I would be honored."

I raised an eyebrow at him in the mirror, but he was too focused on gently getting my hair out of its confines. As soon as the last of it was freed, he let my hair cascade down my back. I had not realized the updo had added to my tension.

Silver slid a stool over and signaled for me to sit.

Seeing no issues with it, I took a seat.

His fingers dug into my scalp and I closed my eyes, leaning back, letting him help me unwind. If this was what constituted his request, then who was I to argue?

Eventually his fingers moved, working on the knots in my neck and shoulders. It had been a long time since he last insisted on doing this. The thought that there was something serious going on came and went.

"I should have done this for you more often. You're too good at hiding how tense you are," Silver said, his voice gentle.

"Hm..." Any other thought was gone at the moment.

He moved from my shoulders and neck to working any tension out of my arms and hands. It was lulling. Occasionally he would push to stretch the line between my neck and arm. It was odd enough to keep me in the present.

That he had not done before. It had been so long, perhaps it was something new he had learned somewhere along the line.

"Come on," he said, tugging on my hand.

I blinked, half-awake, and followed him out onto the balcony. The sun had sunk below the horizon enough that the stars shone brightly before us. We were on the side of the building away from the rest of the Central Seat, which gave a spectacular view. I leaned over the railing and watched the ocean waves crashing below us.

Silver laughed. "I love that child-like curiosity of yours."

"Who are you calling childish?" I faced him and frowned, crossing my arms.

"I said 'child-like' not childish." He brushed my hair back. "Come sit with me. Let's enjoy what we can of the evening."

I nestled up against him on the couch that looked out over the dark waters, wanting the warmth he produced. Nighttime here got a little chillier than I was comfortable with.

There were just so many questions, but given how he acted after I returned, this was not a time that he would respond well to words, so I stayed silent.

As he stroked the side of my neck gently with the backs of his fingers, I closed my eyes. The stress of everything had gotten to both of us. Neither of us would be able to think clearly if we did not step away for a moment.

"Kela," Silver said softly.

I jumped. I must have dozed off. "I'm sorry. What time is it?"

"It's okay. You needed it." He stood up, taking both of my hands and tugging me to my feet. He led us over to the edge of the balcony. "I'm not sure on the exact time, but the sky will begin to lighten soon. Even in the dark the view is beautiful." My partner looked up, turning in the direction of the moon.

I hummed in agreement. Then I realized that meant we had spent most of the night out here. Surely, he had not been awake the whole time. He would not have time to rest before morning prayers. Not that he had been attending the group ones lately.

Silver leaned over and kissed me, stopping my thoughts before they made it out of my mouth. Then he picked up his sun pendant that hung around my neck. "I pray that the God of the Sun keeps you safe and his brilliant light guides your path," he whispered, tucking it down my shirt. Then he said at his normal volume, "You can't be here."

"Silver?" I reached up and wiped a tear that had slid down his cheek.

He kissed me hard. It made me think of the time on the pirate ship when he was uncertain if I would make it out back out of the system alive.

Before I could pull back to ask, I was falling. The balcony I had been on was now above me and getting farther away. Silver watched, his face unreadable. His loose hair seemed to be waving. *Why?*

As I hit the water, a soft golden-white light covered my skin. I bounced lightly off the jagged rocks before coming to my senses. I fought hard to swim back to the surface, my lungs burning at the lack of air.

I fought through the panic, trying to determine which direction was up. Before I got dizzy from the lack of oxygen, I created a bubble of air around my head. It would give me a couple of minutes at least.

The spell also helped me float. I followed the direction I was heading, hoping that was up.

When I finally broke the surface, I found I had drifted out a ways. I could still see the lights of the Central Seat, but I would be in serious trouble if I could not make it back to shore soon. My only saving grace at the moment was that I was still in warmer waters, but that would not help for long.

As I got closer, there was a bustle of activity.

"Find her! Find her!" I heard various people yell in from the shore.

I swam away toward the closest area that was dark, trying to keep my movements above water to a minimum. I let the tide help push me toward land.

The sky had begun to lighten by the time I reached a place to anchor myself to. I ended up further north than I planned, but it put me under the dock and I made my way to the ferry.

A pair of paladins were loading boxes. I hung in the water under the dock, keeping in the shadows.

"Have they found her yet?" one man asked.

"No. That's all jagged rocks below where he threw her. She's dead or soon to be."

"Damn Elf can't even make killing the heretic easy."

"Eh, he did it."

I covered my mouth to stop any noise that might come out and sank down into the water. Silver's actions this evening was all so...

I bit the inside of my cheek hard. Survival first, then I could think through what happened.

Once the men were out of sight, I climbed up onto the ferry, keeping to the side away from shore. I used my power to dry myself off and escaped down into the ship. There had to be some place to hide.

First step: get to the mainland.

16

AFTER NEARLY GETTING SPOTTED a few times during the trip, I slipped out of my hiding spot between boxes below deck with my invisibility spell in place. I figured it was better to take my chances above deck. I could also see if it was possible to depart before we docked.

As the mainland came into view, I snuck along the outer edge of the ship. Dawn had broken a full hour before we left which was going to make this far more tedious to get off without being seen. Though with any luck, the sun shining brightly off the water would help hide my movements when I left.

I could not risk getting off at the docks. I kept an eye on land as we approached, shifting to find the best spot to leave from. Once we got close enough, I would teleport to where I could see. It was either that or swim and I dared not attempt that in these busy waters.

As I moved past where the wind had been blocked, I shivered. Why was it so cold?

"Hey, did you hear something?" one of the men asked.

Someone else snorted. "Probably just a seal."

I covered my mouth. Damn, I had let my guard down. Even with my invisibility spell I could not afford to be lazy.

"You sure? What are the chances the girl survived? She could've escaped onboard," the first voice asked. I heard someone moving around near me.

The second man laughed loudly. "Did you see the height he threw her from? If the fall and the rocks below the water didn't kill her, the tide would've dragged her out to sea. She was a scrawny little thing. Probably didn't even know how to swim. Better that she be fish food than for us to have to clean up the mess. That pointy-eared freak at least had the decency to do that for us."

I did not dare stay any longer to listen to their conversation. I saw a quiet beach and teleported. Unfortunately, my targeting from a moving ship was off and I landed in the water. I hoped it went unnoticed by the men in the ferry. *Maybe they will assume it was another seal.*

For now, I needed to get to shore and call for help. I casted another bubble of air and kept up my invisibility spell, staying beneath the surface of the water for the moment. Biding my time until I thought the ferry would be out of sight.

It was getting tiring to keep up everything and I dropped my spells the second I found a rocky outcropping to hide behind. I was still in the water, but I was no longer swimming and trying to keep a couple of spells going.

The ferry was nowhere in sight and I rested holding onto the rock. I struggled to catch my breath and I wanted nothing more to do than sleep right now, but that option was not open to me yet.

My mind ran through thoughts while I was not distracted by running and hiding. What happened? Why had Silver turned on me? Had he just been using me?

I shook my head. Survival first. I was not out of danger yet. I needed get out of the water, dry off, find food, and contact the TIO.

Contact. I should be close enough now. I turned my wrist up and stared at the spot where my watch should have been. I lowered my head, resting my face against the hard surface, and closed my eyes for a moment to keep myself calm and not give into frustration. I had forgotten I had taken it off when I got into the suite last night. My phone was with it. That task was not going to be so easy.

I swam the rest of the way to shore and hauled myself out of the water. Finding a quiet spot to sit, I took my shoes off and wrung out my socks. At least I had still been wearing those when Silver threw me away. I thought about using my magic to dry myself off again, but that would only tire me further and I had no idea how far I was from the city. I mentally added a long hot shower to the list of things to do when I was safe. A list I wondered if I would ever actually get to.

Once I got to the roadways, I found a path and started walking barefoot to the city, allowing my socks and shoes to dry while I followed the street signs. I patted my pocket as I considered food. I had not been carrying my wallet most of the time I had been at the Central Seat. I paused and hung my head back. It seemed I was going to have to resort to old habits to make it through.

———

BY THE TIME I made it to the city, it was early evening. Within a couple of hours, I had managed to steal food from various restaurants and currently sat on a ledge overlooking an alleyway nibbling away at my ill-gotten gains. I remained unconcerned about being chased down for it - a little here and there would go unnoticed over trying to get a single meal from some place.

The sun had set and once I finished, I curled up for a minute in the oversized black hooded sweatshirt I had managed to snag as well. All that was left on my list was to contact the TIO.

There was no branch nearby. Perhaps if I called? I needed to find a phone number for them. I remembered passing a library on the way here.

I hustled back that way, hoping they were still open. With being in Human Territory, it was a slim chance, but one I had to take. I moved through the streets as fast as I could without drawing attention. I turned a corner when the sight of familiar white clerical garb caught my attention. I fell back and pulled my hood up to hide my face as much as possible. My calf-length hair was already wound around my neck under the sweatshirt.

Was the Central Seat looking for me?

The two male paladins continued on by laughing and joking. Their voices were indistinct among the bustle of the street. Those were two that had been friendly with me, but I would not take the chance. Not after having Silver turn on me.

After they passed, I continued on my way. I got to the doors of the library just as the lights turned off. "No..."

Glancing at their hours, they were closed tomorrow. Could I wait that long? What would I need to survive on my own for two days? It had been decades since I last had to do this. I remained unsure of my ability to do so.

"Is there something I can help you with?" a female voice came from behind me.

I spun on my heel. "Sorry, I guess I didn't make it in time. I just needed to look up a phone number for someone to come pick me up."

She eyed me carefully for a moment. "If I had the code, I'd go back in and get it for you. Are you in trouble, miss?"

I forced a smile. "It's okay, I'll manage."

The woman returned the smile, though it seemed sad. "Why don't you contact the local law enforcement? They should be able to get you in touch."

I bit my lower lip for a moment. "Thank you. Which way?" There was no reason to be rude.

She pointed opposite of the direction I just came. "Go two blocks that way and then take a right. You can't miss it."

I bowed to her and headed in the direction she stated. I had no idea if I could trust them. I was without identification and if they had any ties to the Central Seat, I was only letting them know I was still alive. But I had to contact the TIO. Was it worth the risk? I could make that judgement when I got there.

At the right hand turn I stopped, spotting the two paladins from earlier. They were outside talking to an officer, laughing and joking as if they were friends. That option was out.

I took a left and double-backed. I could not risk it. If I was presumed dead, why were they here?

I passed a cafe with a number of computers open. I looked up and down the street. Going in without being able to buy anything would raise suspicion. It seemed now I was on the hunt for money.

Making note of the location, I set off. I could deal with getting in trouble for stealing later. A little bit of food was easy enough to pass off, but money was another matter.

The crowds were thinning out as the hour grew late. My options for picking pockets had become slim. Too many carried only cards these days and not physical bills and coins.

I could work with a card, but that would leave a trace. Cash was easier to conceal my movements. The conundrum of needing to be found and needing to hide.

Eventually the streets emptied, and I found myself without any money. This had been much easier when I was a small child.

I needed to find a place to rest. I had no idea how long I would be stuck here. If only I knew where the closest TIO branch was, I could head for that. For now, I needed to keep up the basics. At least I had managed to find food and something to hide my identity better.

1 7

THE NEXT DAY I had better luck, snagging some money from a coffee cart while the employee was busy chatting up his customers who were taking a break from the rain under his canopy. If I was careful, the amount I took would last me a few days. I vowed to myself to come back to repay it and then some when I was in the position to do so.

I kept my hood up and made my way back to the cafe I had seen. It would satisfy food and contact. Unfortunately, I had not been able to satisfy rest last night. And with needing to feel clean, the usage of my power to do so left me even more drained.

Sitting at a terminal with my hot tea and small pastry, I logged in, quickly navigating to the TIO's page. I found an area phone number and scribbled it down on a napkin.

The pastry was gone before I had finished that task, my tea halfway there. At least I did not feel as cold now. Even with it being summer, I could not warm up last night.

I paused. How could I use the information? I had not seen a public phone yet. The only ones I could remember were down by the docks and those were questionable if they were even working. Not to mention the docks were not a place I wanted to be anywhere near right now. It would be too easy to be spotted there.

No, it was an opportunity I should consider despite the risks.

Though borrowing someone's phone was likely a better option, though possibly more tedious to do. I would not be able to hold onto it long with the location chips inside.

A pair of paladins walking by the window cut the idea of attempting it short. I shrank down, keeping an eye on them over the top of the screen. They had stopped under the overhang to get out of the rain. These two were different from the ones yesterday. I did not recognize them.

Dammit, I was stuck for the moment and this was my chance to contact someone. There had to be another way. I stared at the screen in front of me. I was not a member of the cyber team, but I should be able to look up information. I started searching for Lockonis. There had to be a way to get ahold of her directly. If I failed at that, I would search for Lexi next - she would be able to get me in touch with Lockonis.

The paladins stuck around as the downpour continued. As long as they stayed outside, I would continue in here.

No matter the search strings, nothing was turning up. I tugged on my bangs hidden beneath my hood. Lockonis, TIO, warmage... what else? Should I switch to trying to get a hold of Lexi?

Suddenly a black box opened on my screen. Text scrolled across it. "You've got some nerve searching for me. I don't want to fry some cafe's computer so knock it off."

"Lockonis?" I typed back. "It's Ketayl. I need help."

"Don't lie to me."

I looked around the cafe quickly, spotting a camera in the corner above the counter. "There's a camera here. I can't take my hood off for long. There are people looking for me." If they were actually looking for me, I remained uncertain, but I was not taking any chances.

There was a short pause before she responded, "Do it."

I eyed the window where the paladins still stood facing the street. I turned to the camera and pulled my hood down. Movement on the screen caught my attention and I pulled my hood back up.

"Shit, kid. We were told you were dead."

My hands shook as they hovered over the keyboard. "He tried." That was all I could manage.

The cursor blinked and blinked and blinked.

The woman behind the counter stepped outside and spoke with the paladins. She did not look happy about something.

"Come on. Come on. Lockonis, say something," I whispered at the screen, tapping the table rapidly with the tips of my fingers, willing the cursor to give me another message.

The paladins came in after the person at the counter gave them a hard time.

"I have to go," I typed and logged out of the computer. I hustled out the door while they had their backs turned ordering something.

I hurried down the street in the rain. I had gotten completely soaked within the first few seconds of being outside.

I stopped when I saw another pair of paladins up ahead. Even with the crowds, the main streets were unsafe. I ducked down the first alley, taking a direction away from both sets of paladins. How many were looking for me? They should have given up by now.

Even the TIO thought I was dead. With no further response from Lockonis, I had little hope of being rescued. I would have to try again, but when would depend on how soon the paladins departed.

While searching for a place to hide for the day, I entertained the idea of returning to the island to at least get my wallet. I knew it was a foolhardy idea at best, and I was unsure if I was prepared to face Silver. Survival had been foremost on my mind and it needed to stay there.

I reached a park and wound my way through the trails with the densest flora before stepping off the path. No one was out here in the rain and I took my hood off, pulling my hair out from where I had coiled it up. I could at least imagine the warm summer rain as a shower.

After standing there for a few minutes, I tucked my hair back under the sweatshirt and pulled the hood up. I shifted uncomfortably as my wet hair settled. I would have left it out, but my dark auburn hair would have been a flag.

I had gotten back to the alleys, preparing to gather food again when the hairs on the back of my neck stood up as if someone was watching me. I turned to find a Human man smirking as he stalked toward me.

He said nothing as he approached and I turned to continue on my way, hurrying.

The next thing I knew, I was slammed up against a wall with a knife pointed at my throat. "Now, where would a pretty thing like you keep your money?"

This was the last thing I needed. Sneering, I grabbed his wrist and shoved it away, slamming the butt of his knife into his face.

"Ow! Son of a—"

I kicked my assailant, sending him back into the opposite wall. He dropped the knife and it slid, falling through a gutter. I took off running.

He tackled me and I hit the ground hard. I kicked at him until I got both legs out from underneath him and shot to my feet. My hood had fallen off in the process.

The man stood up, glaring me down. "Damn girls thinking they can fight," he muttered. "And a damn fairy on top of it." He swung a fist.

I dodged the first punch and the next. After a couple more swings from him, I grabbed his arm and slamming a ball of conjured electricity into his stomach. I had no desire to continue this confrontation.

He shuddered and dropped. When he stayed down with no sign of waking, I knelt down and searched him. I found a wallet fat with money.

I took the bills and dropped the wallet on him. "Thanks." Then I jogged away, needing to put distance between me and him before he came around. I put my hand on the wall to steady myself as the adrenaline rush wore off. Using my power was coming at a higher cost than normal. I shook my head to clear the last of the dizziness and pulled my hood back up. I needed more distance.

At least now I could go for a while. My first stop was to repay what I had taken. I knew I should hold onto all of it until I was in a better position, but it bothered me too much to leave it.

THE PALADINS HAD BEEN LURKING around the area of the cafe again, so I dared not attempt it. I had hoped they would give up, but the cafe closed about the same time I figured it safe. Perhaps I had waited too long after I had last spotted a pair.

Taking a deep breath, I reminded myself that I could try again tomorrow. If I was lucky, I could get in well before any paladins arrived. There was also the library as well. The extra time gave me a chance to consider if they were actually looking for me or not. All of them seemed more interested in the crowds of people rather than searching. And after having been around them for almost two weeks, I knew they were generally not a subtle lot.

Not that this train of thought would do me any good. Either way, if they found me, I was in trouble.

I wandered for a few hours, hoping to wear myself out enough to rest. I spent too much time jumping at shadows. Even the view of the night sky over the ocean could not help settle me. At this rate, dawn would be here before I had located a quiet corner to hide in for at least an hour or two.

Finding a dark doorway in a back alley, I huddled into my over-sized sweatshirt. The attack earlier likely only added to my paranoia.

I rubbed my face. Perhaps it would be safer to find a place to rest during the day.

No, I had been attacked in broad daylight.

"This is getting me nowhere," I muttered to no one. For now, I could go a few days without rest.

I had been there long enough for the sky to lighten to predawn and for my butt to have gotten numb from the hard surface when a large dog entering the area caught my attention. Its nose was to the ground, searching for something.

The black, pointy-eared dog made me think of my sister's. She was likely going to kill me if I ever made it out of this. The short laugh I let out sounded strained even to my ears and my eyes watered at the thought.

The dog turned and trotted over to me. I backed up, bringing my knees to my chest when the wall behind me stopped my progress. It did not seem aggressive, but I had no idea and tried to make myself smaller.

It sniffed, whined, and then wormed its way onto my lap, using its head to get between my torso and my legs.

"Hey, you're heavy," I whispered and sighed in relief. At least it was friendly. My hand reflexively went to the soft fur on its head, scratching gently behind the ears. The motion was soothing. Maybe this would be enough.

A minute later footsteps echoed through the alley. Whoever it was, they were running. I used my invisibility spell and tried to push the dog off of my lap, but it would not budge.

"Dammit! Don't take off like that," a female voice said. It sounded familiar, but I had to be imagining things. "Would you get over here? We have work to do. I swear I'm going to give that girl an earful about your lack of training when we get back."

A flashlight shone in my direction and I froze. The dog was still on me. While I was invisible, a floating dog was going to be suspicious.

The dog put both paws against my chest. If I had not had my back to a wall, I would have fallen over.

"Riva?" The woman came closer. A familiar raven-haired half-Elf moved into view under the light in the alley.

No, that could not be Savanas. Savanas was in Ocean's Edge. So was Riva, who was my sister's dog.

Another dog of similar breed came over, sniffing at me. It barked once before head butting me lightly in the shoulder.

"Ket?" she asked softly. "Are you there?" She stepped closer to where I sat surrounded by the two dogs. She reached in my direction.

As soon as she touched me, my concentration broke and my invisibility spell dissipated. I stared at my friend wide eyed, uncertain how she was here. I shook and tried to curl into the corner more, thinking that this was simply a trick of my mind. I must have fallen asleep. "*I need to wake up. It's not safe to rest*," I muttered in my dialect of common, willing myself to consciousness.

Savanas pushed between the dogs, pulling me into a hug. "Thank the Gods you're alive." She backed up and shown the light in my face, causing me to wince and turn away. "You've taken a beating though."

I wrapped my arms around Riva and buried my face in her fur. She whined. Maybe this was not a dream.

"I know, I know. I just need to call in and then we'll go." Savanas stepped away, pulling her phone out. "We found her. I'm getting her out now."

I could not hear whoever she was talking to.

Savanas came back over and knelt next to me. "Are you okay to walk?"

I nodded.

"Come on," she said, shooing Riva off my lap and helping me to my feet.

I swayed and leaned against her. "Why are you here?" I asked, my voice cracking.

My friend laughed, getting an arm around me. "To find you, obviously. You know my specialty is in urban areas, right? After you lost my trio in Mystic Port, I figured it was better if I was on the ground this time. You've given Darius and whoever else he's been working with Hells of a time tracking you through the camera network though."

I hung my head. "Didn't think anyone was coming," I said softly. My chest tightened and my eyes watered.

"We'll talk about this later. Right now we need to get you somewhere safe. When was the last time you ate?"

"Yesterday morning, I think. When I reached Lockonis. It's morning again, right?" Even with the sky lightening, I remained unsure until it broke the horizon.

"Yeah, pretty damn early in the morning. When was the last time you slept?"

I opened my mouth to answer and closed it. "I don't know. Before I left the Central Seat."

We walked for a few blocks in silence before we stopped. Then I realized we stood in front of a car.

"Get in," Savanas ordered gently, opening the door.

"Where are we going?"

"A safe place. One with actual food and a bed."

⸻

WHILE SAVANAS ORGANIZED her report and called in again, I took a shower. I had long since finished cleaning and now simply stood under the hot spray. Riva lay curled up in the bathroom against the door.

Now that survival was not needing to be at the forefront of my mind, everything else started coming forward. Had Silver just been using me? Had everything been a lie?

But Silver never lied.

It did not mean he could not. All he said was that I could not be there.

And there was the barrier that had protected me from the fall and the rocks. I knew it had been his magic. He also knew I could swim. However, he would not have known if I was strong enough to be out in the ocean like that.

I leaned against the wall and picked up the sun pendant which still hung around my neck. Had he cast that spell or had the protective barrier come from it? If he was getting rid of me, he would have taken his necklace back, right? But he could have viewed my having worn it as having tainted it and decided to get rid of it at the same time.

Riva stuck her head into the shower and whined, breaking my debate.

"Hey, don't do that. You'll get all wet." I tried to shoo her out.

Black eyes stared up at me and she whined again.

"Okay, okay. I'll get out," I replied. Riva could be pushy. The fact that she would only follow me around when I visited Kitteren annoyed my sister to no end.

I wrapped one towel around me while I dried my hair with another. I stopped and looked at my hair in the towel. Why had Silver spent so much time taking my hair down? Why had he wanted time for just us? Was it to lull me into a false sense of security?

Riva pawed at the door.

I sighed and opened it. With her thick black coat, it was probably too warm in here for her.

I had started contemplating my hair again when Savanas came in carrying a bundle of clothes. "Kitteren sent me with these. She said they were yours." Then she stopped and looked at me.

I turned my face down and away from her. "Thank you," I managed to get out.

"Hey," Savanas said, turning for me to look at her. "Silver is going to answer for this."

"I..." I shook my head. My thoughts were too jumbled to speak.

She gave me a sad smile. "Get dressed and then we'll talk. Now that you're clean I want to tend to that scrape on your face. Do you have any others I should worry about?" She reached over and prodded a fading bruise on my upper arm that I had gotten from the paladin who had grabbed me.

I turned and looked in the mirror to see what she had referred to. My left cheek was all scratched up and bruised. It must have been when the man in the alley had tackled me. I touched it and hissed. How had I not noticed it before now?

"You didn't know?"

"It must have been from when someone tried to mug me earlier... yesterday." Why could I not keep track of the days?

Savanas sighed. "Darius said they were having a hard time following you. The team must have missed that altercation. Now get dressed. You don't want to be on a video conference call in a towel, do you?"

I sighed and waved for her to leave me be. I grabbed the bundle and got dressed as fast as I could manage. I did not recognize these clothes, but knowing Kitteren it was something she had at her house set aside for me.

"Ket, can you answer me one question?" Savanas sounded like she was right outside the door.

"Hm?"

"What happened to the mugger?"

I hesitated a moment, but eventually the truth would come out. *I might as well own up to it.* "I took his money and left him in the alley."

Savanas snorted and laughed loudly. "Sounds fair."

As soon as I exited the bathroom, Savanas pointed me toward the couch. She already had medical supplies out.

I stopped, unused to seeing it. I had gotten so used to Silver healing me that I had not needed to use other means to deal with injuries. I took a deep breath and sat down, holding as still as I could. Occasionally I hissed as she cleaned the scrape.

"It's not bad," she said softly as she gently put ointment on. "Nothing that will leave a mark, but I'd rather it be covered for now. I'm not that great of a medic. I'm starting to wish I had brought Brad with me."

"I'll be fine," I said flatly.

Emerald green eyes stared at me. Then she turned away to get a bandage. "Once I finish with this, we should start that call. They've been harassing me to get you on so you can tell us what happened. Are you ready for that?"

I looked down at my hands. "I'm not even sure what happened."

"Hey, I'm right here. And those two," she said, pointing at the dogs, "aren't going to let anything happen to you either. I'll make arrangements to get you home after you've gotten some rest."

"I'm not leaving," I said firmly, narrowing my eyes as I stared straight ahead.

"What?"

"I'm going back to the island. There's something going on with the paladins and there's a small settlement of people being held against their will further south." I planned on getting answers to all of it.

"Okay, we're getting on that call now." Savanas put the bandage on first and then grabbed her tablet, setting it up on the table.

It took a minute before the call connected. Lockonis and Vince were both on the screen.

"Thank the Gods. Ket, what happened?" Lockonis asked.

"Silver threw me off a balcony," I said flatly.

The three stared at me.

"Care to elaborate?" Vince asked.

I took a deep breath before explaining, "I don't know what's going on, sir. We were looking into corruption within the Order and I found a small settlement - mostly tents, but a few slightly more permanent structures - further south with strong arcane signatures. They were offloading people and cargo. The people appeared to be there against their will. Armed guards."

They sat there in silence for a moment.

"And apparently someone tried to mug her," Savanas said, pointing at her left cheek. "Ket, you've been awake for days. Maybe you should rest before getting too detailed." She was looking at the screen as she spoke.

"I'm fine," I answered. They did not need to know I was hardly resting before all of this.

"Ket," Lockonis said, her voice oddly gentle. "Go get some rest. We'll arrange for you to get home safely, though I think you're going to have to make a stop in Ocean's Edge."

"I'm not leaving," I said firmly. "I'm going back."

At once both women began talking, trying to convince me it was foolish.

"Stop," Vince said, his voice even. "I won't deny her the answers she seeks. However, you will wait for my okay. I intend to send a team with you."

I nodded.

"Ket," Lockonis said, "Did Silver say anything to you?"

"The last things he said to me was a prayer and then that I couldn't be there." I needed to stay to the facts. Trying to make sense of it would only push me closer to breaking and the job was not done yet.

Lockonis turned to Vince. "When Silver was on that call, he

specifically said that he got rid of her. It was whoever was with him that claimed her death."

"He's usually particular about his words when he's trying not to lie," I said. "I don't know where the barrier came from when I hit the water and he knows I can swim." Was I defending him? Why? He would have told me if he was trying to help me escape, right?

Savanas hummed for a moment. "Ket's right. We don't know enough about what is going on yet to determine if Silver was trying to kill her or save her. I noticed she's still wearing his necklace."

"Yeah, and it's that damn thing that makes scrying impossible apparently," Lockonis said.

I sat up straighter and pulled it out from under my shirt. I had considered taking it off, but I had no idea if it was what had protected me from the fall.

I still planned on throwing it at Silver when I got the chance. Whether it was before or after he explained himself, I had not yet determined. I tucked the necklace back under my shirt.

"Go get some rest while we get a team together," Vince said and ended the call.

I got up slowly. Suddenly everything ached.

Savanas helped me up. "Come on. You're going to need to be at full strength."

1 8

A WEIGHT RESTING on me was what woke me up from my nightmare. I shifted to see Riva making herself comfortable. "Hey," I said softly, running my hand over the soft fur on her head and scratching lightly behind a pointed ear. Where was I that my sister's dog was here? I did not remember being in Ocean's Edge.

Then I remembered that my attempt to contact the TIO had been successful. I was with Savanas at some house. I never even asked what this place was.

I was about to tell Riva she was heavy, but her presence was calming. She rested her head on my chest. It was enough to make the vivid images of Silver watching me fall over and over fade.

Now that I was awake, I could take stock of my situation. It looked like a bedroom. I could not remember making it to bed.

There was little I could do with Riva laying on me. She would do this often when I visited Kitteren and I found that until she was ready to let me up, she was not going anywhere no matter how hard I tried to get out from underneath her.

While I looked around the small, undecorated bedroom, Roh showed up and sat in the doorway. Compared to Riva's all black coat, Roh had a mix of black and tan, but they appeared to be of the same breed. He tilted his head and I laughed lightly. His pointed ears had made the gesture far more amusing.

Roh came in and put his head on the bed next to me. Now I had both hands full petting them. "Is it just the two of you? Where's Savanas?"

The only answer I got was Roh jumping up on the bed to lay down next to me. He turned his head to rest it on my unoccupied shoulder.

We were like that long enough that I found it to be getting too warm.

Both of their heads perked up a minute before I heard a door open elsewhere. The sound of plastic bags being put down preceded someone coming down the hall.

I tried to get out from under Riva, but she would not budge. I had no idea if it was friend or foe. Frantically I attempted to push her off me.

Savanas poked her head in. "Oh, you're finally awake. Feeling better?"

I let out the breath I had not realized I had been holding. "Yeah. Sorry."

She came in and shooed Roh out of the way so she could sit down. "I can only imagine what you went through. It's been over a day. Sorry I was out when you woke - we needed groceries."

I tried to shift into a reclining position only to have Riva smack me in the face with her paw. "Hey!"

"You're a brat," Savanas chided her. "Come on. Ket needs to get up and eat something." She tugged at her collar.

Riva hesitated for a moment before finally moving off me.

Savanas eyed me for a moment. "Actually, first you should clean up and change. There are more clothes in the dresser for you."

I pulled at the collar of my shirt. "Sorry. It got rather warm with the two of them."

She laughed. "I know. Riva hasn't flown before and she was on top of me for the first couple of hours of the flight. Take your time." Then she left.

I sighed and set about my tasks. Roh had left with Savanas, but Riva kept me in sight. It took longer than I wanted, but eventually I was making my way back down the hall. The house was small and had only furniture - no decorations.

Savanas glanced over at me as I entered the main room. It was open between the common, kitchen, and dining areas. "I haven't been able to get much information about the paladins roaming around town. It seems like it's a common enough occurrence to see them out and about in pairs. Guess preaching or whatever it is they do normally. I got snubbed pretty hard for being a half-breed."

"You don't think they were looking for me?" Now I felt like a fool with how I had been running, but if they had found me...

Savanas shrugged. "Can't say, but they probably think you're dead if they haven't caught sight of you for a few days. I want you to stay here just to be on the safe side though." She got up and headed for the kitchen.

I nodded, looking down at my hands. "How are they doing getting a team together?"

"Hm?" She paused and turned to look at me for a moment. "They're still working on it. It's not just people but equipment and supplies as well. If there are two or possibly even more settlements on that island, they want to get them all at the same time - make sure no one can escape. I can only imagine the scrying and satellite surveillance they have going on at the moment."

I fingered the bracelet I still wore. The one Silver had made for me so I could copy the library at the Central Seat. No, that thought was not quite right. I stared down at the other gift he had left me with, not wanting to delve too deeply into that train of thought. "I don't know if I have anything useful, but I did finish copying their library as well as the Sutton vault."

Savanas hummed for a moment, stirring something in a pot. Whatever it was smelled amazing. I had forgotten she liked to cook. "I'm not sure what use it would be either at the moment."

"Maybe there would be something if I could get into the other vaults."

My friend frowned. "By the time you can, we'll be moving to take the Central Seat down. They want Silver taken into custody along with the Elders. They pissed off the wrong people with that call."

I took a deep breath. It was easy to understand why, but... "Do you think he meant to kill me?" Why did the whole idea feel wrong? Maybe she had a better perspective.

Savanas folded her arms and leaned back against the counter. "I don't know. Would there be a reason to fake your death?"

I sighed and rested my head on my arms on the table. Why was I still so tired? "I wish I could answer that. Silver said little if anything about what was going on. I don't think they knew I was an Arcanist, but I wouldn't rule it out. I still can't figure out if he was trying to kill me or get me out of there."

"Okay, enough speculation. You need to eat," Savanas said as she ladled soup into a bowl.

Once she put it down, I stared at it.

She let out an exasperated sigh. "Eat, Ket. I swear to the Gods I'll force-feed you if I have to. You've lost a lot of weight."

I hesitated, picking up the spoon, but my appetite was simply gone. It smelled delicious, but that did nothing to solve the problem.

Savanas sighed and sat down next to me. "Look, I understand that you're conflicted if he's betrayed you or not, but if you want a chance to take a swing at your former partner, you need your strength."

"I should hit him?" My brain was not processing her words correctly. Surely, she had not meant that literally.

She gave me a wry grin. "I would no matter which way it falls. He threw you off a balcony. That's reason enough."

THE NEXT MORNING I had been sitting in the common room reading when a knock on the door startled me and I jumped, immediately calling raw arcane energy to my hands.

Savanas frowned at me and pointed at the couch. Both dogs circled me once before Roh led the way and Riva nudged me in that direction with her head.

I hesitated, but did as I was told. I had to remind myself that here was safe. Riva sprawled across my lap the moment I sat down.

Once I was settled, my friend opened the door. "I was wondering when you guys would start showing up." She moved out of the way for whoever it was.

"Would've beat ya here if we hadn't needed to wrap somethin' up. I'm the first, but the others are comin'," a familiar female voice replied. It was not someone I had spoken to in a long time though. "Where's the lass?" the Dwarf asked as she came in.

Savanas nodded in my direction. "She's a little jumpy."

"Fan?" I asked softly, pulling the name from memory. I had not been in good shape the last time I saw her either.

"Aye, ain't seen ya since Mystic Port. Hear you've been gettin' yerself into plenty of trouble since." She came over and ruffled my bangs before sitting down on the coffee table across from me. "Let's have a look at that scrape. Savvy says it dun look too bad."

Savanas put the medical kit on the coffee table near Fan. "Darius was able to find a recording of the mugging. She hit the pavement face first."

Fan pulled the gauze taped to my left cheek off gently. "That'll hurt. Gonna agree it doesn't look bad. Healin' nicely now that it's been treated. I'd finish it off with magic, but lass, you about gave me a heart attack the last time." Her hand hovered a few inches from my face.

"I haven't taken anything. It's the mixture of medicines and magic that's the problem," I stated, staring straight ahead. If I wanted to be a part of this operation, I needed to be at full. Consequences be damned.

The Dwarven woman shook her head. "Not riskin' it. There's no damage to the bone, but..." She sighed and sat back. "I'm not comfortable doin' it. Not after readin' yer file and knowin' the crap you just went through - yer body won't take well to magic right now. It'll be gone in a week anyway. Best to keep it covered." She dug through the kit, pulling items from it.

I sat still with my arms crossed, staring straight ahead, frowning. The tension hung heavily in the room as the silence stretched out.

When Fan finished, she packed the kit back up. "I best get arrangements made before the rest get here. A couple will be tomorrow. Mackie and the remainin' are goin' to need another day or two."

Savanas nodded. "I've got to check the ETAs on the rest. Thanks for coming by. Like I told Ket: I'm not a good medic."

"Bah!" Fan stood up and smiled. "I needed to see for myself that the lass here was alive and kickin'. And by that face of hers, she be lookin' to be doin' some hurtin' back."

I scrunched up my nose at the two and refused to look at either of them. The movement made the tape holding the fresh gauze to my cheek pull awkwardly.

My friend sighed. "I know I'd be too if I was in her position. I'll get a meeting set up when I've gotten more information."

They exchanged a few more pleasantries before Fan left. I remained where I was.

"Ket..." Savanas warned softly. Then she sat down next to me.

"You need time to recover. Not just from the cuts and bruises, but also from the days of no rest and a lack of decent nourishment."

I sighed and ran a hand over my hair, tugging on my bangs. "I need to do something."

"Well, first you can help me make lunch and then I'm certain we can figure out something. You still have reports to file after all and plenty of calls to make. If Kitteren messages me one more time I'm going to throttle her when I get back." Savanas moved toward the kitchen.

I made a face and got up to follow. I had been granted some time before needing to submit my reports, but I should get it over with. Especially where the teams were going to need the information I held. The calls I intended to keep short.

THE NEXT FEW days were painful. Savanas refused to let me leave the house and reading through the information I collected from the library at the Central Seat was worse than having nothing to do.

She also insisted I ate more frequently. It seemed every time I looked up, there was another snack waiting for me.

I frowned as the sun pendant still hanging around my neck shifted awkwardly and moved it to a more comfortable position. Because it blocked me and my surrounding area from scrying, it had been strongly recommended that I continue to wear it. I knew an order when I heard one. Logically, the necklace was beneficial to not only me, but the rest of the team. I kept reminding myself that it was not just me at stake to not give into the desire to be rid of it.

People had been showing up a few at a time and I doubted that I had met everyone involved. Some of them I recognized from Mystic Port, others were unknown to me. They came and went, saying little while they were here. Savanas often went to them, leaving the dogs to keep me company. I tried to sneak out to get fresh air a few times and they would not allow me anywhere near the doors.

However, I had been able to pick up on some information: they were planning to send three teams out. One to each of the settlements and the third would remain at sea, either to catch anyone trying to escape or help out a particular team.

Where I was going to be and what they would allow me to do, I did not know. I voiced repeatedly that I wanted to head for the Central Seat. Part of me worried for the people I knew over there. They may not care whether I was alive or dead, but...

I tugged on my bangs. The magically projected book I had been reading had lost my attention long ago.

"I've told you to stop that a thousand times," Savanas chided.

"I need to know what's going on," I snapped. I covered my mouth with my hands. "Sorry."

She shrugged, never looking up from the magazine she was reading. "You've been cooped up. I'd be worse if I was in your position."

I sent the book away back into the bracelet. "When are we going?"

"Soon. I'm waiting for the other boat to get here." Her calm demeanor irritated me to no end.

I needed to keep a level head though. "I know about the three boats. Can you tell me more?"

Savanas stopped and looked at me like I had lost it.

Perhaps I had.

She sighed and put the magazine down. "Sorry, I guess I forgot I needed to relay it. As soon as the second boat is here, we're going to take the Central Seat's ferry. The Highlands team will accompany us."

"Are we going to the Central Seat?" Mentally I prayed she said yes. Technically I would be better suited for the other settlement against arcane casters, but I knew the grounds at the Central Seat.

"Yes. They won't think anything of their own ferry returning. The others will already be staged out on the water." Savanas glanced out at the clouded sky - it had been raining all day again. "You need to get out of here before then though."

"You're not sending me home," I said firmly, preparing for an argument.

She rolled her eyes. "That's not what I meant. You'll be uncontrollable if I don't get you out of this house for a bit."

I frowned at her words, but I had been practically climbing the walls.

She crossed her arms and tilted her head in the direction of the bedrooms. "Go get your sweatshirt on. The least I can do is treat you for putting up with all of this."

I hurried for the oversized black hooded sweatshirt. I could not miss this opportunity.

Savanas was waiting for me at the door when I returned. "Ready?"

I nodded. The dogs both seemed content to remain lying about: one on the couch and the other in a chair.

She drove us into town. I had pulled my hood up and sat back. It was nice seeing something other than the same boring walls of the house.

"Ket, you don't have to do this, you know. It's hard watching people who you've worked with get taken into custody," Savanas said after a bit, her voice gentle.

"I'm going," I said flatly. Silver had not just been someone I worked with. He had been the person I trusted the most.

"Geez, you two are a handful," she muttered.

"What?" I was unsure if I had heard her right.

She sat up straighter. Perhaps she had not meant to say that out loud. "You and Kitteren. I think you might have her beat on stubbornness."

I folded my arms and sunk back against my seat, frowning. Something white caught my attention. A pair of paladins walked down the street. I pulled my hood lower and looked down.

"Easy, Ket. I'm right here," Savanas said, her voice soft. "They likely won't see you through the windows."

With the traffic, we inched by them. I glanced at the two, but they seemed more interested in the people passing by on the sidewalk.

"Do you know them?" she asked while I watched them.

It was enough to pull my attention away and I shook my head. "Not enough to know their names. They were indifferent to my being there."

Savanas made a face and then shrugged. "I wouldn't worry about them then. They're too busy spreading the good word it seems. I don't know how the Order even survives being so separated from the mainland."

I bit my lower lip, considering how they operated. "Maybe money from the churches they have all over. I don't know much about their cash flow."

She raised an eyebrow at me. "You're probably right. Add to that whatever is going on in the other settlement. I doubt they are unaware."

Silence fell between us for a bit. I spent the time staring aimlessly out the window, attempting to ignore the internal debate about why

Silver acted the way he had. It was ongoing and I had grown tired of it.

Savanas parked away from the bustle of the center of town, finding a quiet side street. "Before you get out of the car," she said sternly, "I need to know what's going on in that head of yours."

I bit my lower lip. I could lie. She would likely not know, but was it worth it? I decided on vague. "Mostly just driving myself crazy."

She sighed. "You're holding onto far more than you can carry. I can share that burden, but you need to talk to me."

I took a shuddering breath. Talking would cause the dam to break. "I'll deal with it after the job is done."

"Will you though? Ket, you're notorious for ignoring yourself. Even I know that," she pointed out.

I pinched the bridge of my nose. "Can we save the psycho-analysis for later? I'm sure you need to get back to planning."

Savanas scrunched up her face and shoved the door open. Aggravating my friend at the moment was not the wisest of decisions, especially where she could pull me from the assignment, but I could not afford to go down that path right now. I needed to get this over with first. Then I could pick apart the emotional turmoil I kept under tight wrap.

19

Savanas and I watched the ferry slowly pull in. We were hidden on the neighboring ship, waiting. The team from the Northern Isles had created a blockade and stopped anyone from coming down the dock. Riva and Roh were somewhere on the pier, but I could not spot them. We needed to secure the boat itself. Knowing the crew was always so few, the two of us would suffice.

"Let's go," Savanas said quietly as the engines of the ferry started winding down. She had both of her swords drawn as she led the way.

"They're mine," I said before teleporting ahead of her as soon as I recognized the pair of paladins and the one seeker coming down the ramp as the ones who attacked me previously. Their attention was elsewhere until I was right in front of them on the dock.

"Did you miss me?" I asked. Behind me I heard Savanas running and cursing.

The seeker immediately reached out to grab me. I danced away from him, bouncing lightly on the balls of my feet for a moment before spinning a kick to his head. He fell, but I knew he would get back up soon. A mass of black fur appeared and stood over the downed man, growling at him.

Roh stood to my side, also growling, his teeth bared at the two paladins.

The quick altercation with the seeker was enough time for the paladins to have drawn their weapons. "Guess we do get a chance to kill you. We would've done it right the first time."

Savanas slid in front of me. "You and I need to talk later."

I shrugged and teleported behind the paladins.

"What in the Hells?" one asked as they both turned.

I touched them with the quickly conjured electricity in my hands, dropping both.

Savanas held one of her blades at the throat of the seeker who was starting to get up. Other TIO agents were heading down the dock to us.

"They... they were right. You are an arcane caster," the seeker stuttered.

I folded my arms and smirked at him. "Too bad the last time I was behaving. You wouldn't have even landed a hit." I drew raw arcane energy to my hands.

"Enough," Savanas warned, staring me down. "You made your point."

Riva had abandoned her position to rub up against my legs, whining.

"Fiesty, aren't ya?" Fan said, waving me over to her while the others took care of the three we captured.

While I stood next to Fan, Savanas gave orders. I was pushing it with my behavior. As she started organizing people to clear the small vessel, I made my way up onto the ferry. It would be harder for them to remove me from this operation if I was already onboard.

A strong, slim hand grabbed my shoulder. "Oh no you don't. Lockonis will fry me alive if anything happens to you," Savanas said, signaling that she wanted to get ahead of me.

I sighed and stepped back. My allowance to even be here was tenuous at best. Once we were out on the water I could ignore orders. At least the dogs were busy nipping at the prisoners instead of herding me.

Savanas led the two of us down into the ferry to make sure it was clear. She rounded a corner ahead of me and stopped, bringing her swords to bear.

Damn, someone had stayed onboard.

Before I could get there, a familiar figure, wielding a sword and shield engaged Savanas. Her honey-blonde hair swung wildly in a ponytail behind her.

"Stop!" I called out when I recognized Marzena. I ran to try to get between them, knowing that was likely the worst idea I had had lately.

They separated and stilled. Savanas stayed at the ready, but Marzena's arms dropped as she stared at me.

"You're alive," the female paladin whispered. She dropped her weapons and rushed at me, pulling me into a tight hug before Savanas could get between us. "Sun's grace, you're alive." She wore a short-sleeved shirt and jeans - a far cry from the paladin uniform I normally saw her in.

"What are you doing here?" I asked, managing to pull back from her.

"I should be asking you that." She noticed Savanas still not standing down. "Who is she?"

"TIO," Savanas said flatly. "Give me one good reason not to run you through."

Marzena held up her hands defensively. "Well, that makes this easier since I was coming to find both Kela and the TIO."

"What's going on?" I asked. I knew I sounded desperate and I was. If Marzena was here looking for us, what was the situation back at the Central Seat?

"Not now, Ket. We need to get back out on the water. The rest of our team should be here shortly," Savanas chided.

I nodded - time was ticking by and it would take a couple of hours to get there.

"I'm going with you," Marzena said firmly.

"Why should I let you?" my raven-haired friend challenged. "Why should I believe anyone coming off that damn island after what happened to Ket?!"

"Savanas," I said softly, "You can trust her. She's the weapons master. If she wanted to, she could have easily attacked me barehanded."

My half-Elven friend glared at the paladin for several more seconds. Finally, she sheathed her swords. "Alright. We could use another person who knows the grounds."

The rest of the team arrived to refuel and got us back out on the water as quickly as possible. I had left Savanas to interrogate Marzena. I was not yet ready to hear what Silver reasoned for his actions. All I caught was that he had sent her to contact the TIO.

After a while a Dwarven woman came out onto the deck. Riva had been curled up at my feet the whole ride so far.

I forced a smile at her. "Hi, Fan."

"Hi yerself, lass."

I sighed. "Sorry I haven't thanked you for coming before now."

"Bah!" she waved my apology off, "Told ya when ya needed help to let us know. This situation is a right mess."

I leaned on the railing. "I don't even know what to think."

"Well, my thoughts are yer boy was an asshole for what he did. Never would have thought he could do that from when I last met him." She came and stood next to me.

"And no one knows all of it," I muttered to myself. The care he showed, the healing touches, the kisses... I would keep the shame that he used me hidden.

Riva whined and nudged my leg with her nose.

A hand touched my elbow. "Lass, I would love more than anythin' for you to let it out, but the job ain't done yet. Just a little longer, okay? Ya held it this long and I be thinkin' yer gonna need it to see you through."

I turned to her in surprise. Then I realized I had started crying and quickly rubbed my face to get rid of the evidence. "Sorry."

"Nothin' to be sorry for," Fan said softly. She turned. "I just hope ya ain't here to defend the bastard."

I turned to see Marzena standing in the doorway.

"No, because I haven't forgiven him yet," the female paladin said. "And seeing as he made her cry, I'm not about to anytime soon."

I turned away. I wished no one had seen that lapse.

"Kela," Marzena said softly, "Please understand that I intend to save my brother from himself. After that... well, I don't know."

I nodded.

"Actually, I have one question." Marzena came up on my other side, leaning on the railing. "Am I supposed to call you Ket?"

I laughed lightly. I had no idea why I found that amusing.

"The lass' name is Ketayl. Dunno where Kela came from," Fan commented.

"It's what Silver used to use when it was just the two of us. He was worried the Central Seat would recognize my name." I had no intention of delving further into the topic.

"Ah," Marzena said. "I don't know if they knew it or not, but it was wise choice. I know they were upset when he resigned. I was too, but for a different reason."

I clenched my jaw and closed my eyes. I could not handle a conversation about Silver right now. "Excuse me." I hurried off the deck.

Riva was on my heels.

"Kela... Ket, wait!" Marzena called, but I refused to stop.

I had a job to finish first. Then I could sort through the emotional mess.

SAVANAS FOUND me after a while below deck with Riva on my lap. "We're almost there. Let's head up."

Riva let me up without prompting and I nodded before silently following her.

"Are you sure you're ready for this?" she asked as we got out on deck. "This isn't your fight. You can stay with Mackie on the ferry."

I threw a sidelong glare at her. Would she honestly make me repeat myself?

She put her hands up. "Okay. I'm not going to get in your way. Just don't get in over your head."

The water was far less demanding to look at - it was not evaluating and judging me. "It's the only thing I know how to do apparently."

Savanas let out a short laugh. "Yeah, yeah it does. At least... what in the Hells?" She hurried to the bow to get a better look at the commotion on shore.

"It looks like they be fightin' amongst themselves," Fan said.

The scene looked like utter chaos. Heavily armored combatants entangled with no ability from here to make out which side was which. Not with them all wearing the same gear. The sun shown as brightly off their armor as it did off the water.

Marzena punched the railing. "That damn bastard. He sent me away to keep me out of the fighting."

"You knew it was going to come to this?" Savanas asked, her tone both accusing and demanding.

"Not this specifically, no." Marzena waved a hand toward the chaos on the shore. "Things were getting tense, but... ugh!" She paced, running a hand over her hair. "The Order had mostly split into two before Silver and Kela had even arrived - those of us who kept our oaths and those who pledged themselves to the Elders. That bastard went ahead and confronted them about the corruption without me."

"Fan, tell Mackie to be ready to take the ferry back out right off. No one leaves the island unless I say so," Savanas ordered, crossing her arms and staring at the chaos on shore.

"Aye. Think she already figured you wanted it to remain off-shore." Fan left to go relay the message.

"And you," Savanas said, pointing at me. "Don't you even think about teleporting over there ahead of us."

I crossed my arms, frowning. "It's tough to target while moving and I don't feel like ending up in the water again." Granted, I could go for any point on the grounds I remembered. It would likely work better than trying to spot a place on the dock. The energy required though would put me at a disadvantage if it turned into a prolonged fight.

"Good. That's one less thing I have to worry about."

I sighed and waited, idly listening to Savanas giving orders to the others. If I disobeyed her now, she would figure out a way to keep me from reaching shore. The dock rapidly approached and the battle shifted in our direction. I saw a familiar set of unique armor among the rest.

Silver was wearing his heavily textured, mostly black armor from the TIO. He was in the middle of the fighting by the dock, but I would never be able to tell the rest of the paladins apart with them all wearing similar full plate.

"Hey, Savvy," Fan said softly when she returned. "Should we really be gettin' in the middle of this? It's a bleedin' civil war by the looks of it."

Savanas crossed her arms, staring at the ongoing battle. "Techni-cally, no. The chaos may work to our advantage though. I'll make the call when we get on the ground and find out what's going on. With any luck we can wait it out."

"You're not going to stop me from defending my brothers and sisters, are you?" Marzena challenged.

"No, I can't order you around. I'd like to say I can order her around, but I know she won't listen." Savanas thumbed at me. "Just please don't try to get yourself killed."

Instead of answering, I ran down to the side of the ferry closest to the dock as we came in. I got up on the railing and jumped off, using my power to soften the landing. It was not a teleport so she could not complain.

"DAMMIT, KET!" Savanas yelled. It was accompanied by barking.

I heard more people jumping down to the dock behind me as I took off running. Marzena and Savanas managed to catch up to run alongside me. Both women had their weapons drawn.

"Keep them off the dock until the ferry can get back out!" Savanas ordered.

"Be careful who you're attacking," Marzena shouted.

Savanas bared her teeth at the female paladin with us. "If they come after me, they get to meet their God."

A couple of paladins turned and ran toward us. Others followed.

I cast a quick flight spell to get ahead of the women running next to me. When I landed, I cast my shield spell to create a barricade across the dock. The time of hiding my power here was over.

The paladins ran into it and bounced off, falling down. I grunted, the force of the blows pushing me back a half step.

"Nice job, kid. How long can you keep that barrier going?" Savanas asked once she caught up.

"Not long. The more it gets hit..." I trailed off, needing to focus. So far no others had come charging at it after the two bounced off, but it was only a matter of time.

"Understood. On my signal, drop it." Savanas held up her hand. Her attention was behind me. She pushed the button on her earpiece, "Mackie, keep Roh and Riva with you."

"You've got to let me through. I need to help the others," Marzena said, her eyes pleaded with me.

"You can pass through this side," I said quietly, eyeing the paladins getting up and steeling myself for the onslaught to come.

As Marzena stepped through to take care of the two getting up, Savanas brought her hand down and I dropped the shield. The others moved in front of me to engage anyone attempting to get to the ferry.

I turned to see where it was, and it had already begun to pull away from the dock. We would not need to hold this position long. Would they keep pushing to take the dock after it had left though?

Returning to the fight at hand, even the TIO agents had little to do as the paladins and seekers were busy fighting each other. The agents had formed a line across and Marzena had not made it much past that. The battle was slowly shifting away from the dock and spreading out again.

I breathed a sigh of relief that this team would not have to fight. I needed to get through, but teleporting into the middle of all of the fighting was suicide. Out of habit, I looked for my partner.

Silver was working his way toward us, cutting down those who blocked his path and shoving others with his shield. As he got closer, I squeezed past a couple of agents and stormed toward him, my hands balls into fists.

Marzena fell back next to me. "Kela, it's not safe out here."

"It's not safe for you without armor either," I shot back, my eyes never leaving my target.

As soon as Silver was close enough, before he could get any words out, I swung at his face with everything I had. I shook my hand. I hoped it hurt him worse than it had me.

Marzena made some sort of noise, but what it had been a combination of, I knew not nor had I the time or inclination to figure it out.

Silver stared at me for a moment, touching his cheek lightly. "I deserve far more than that."

I stepped up next to him, looking over the battle scene before me. "What's going on here?"

He looked to where I assumed Marzena was before answering, "The Order has been split into two groups. Right now, we're trying to get to the Elders to take them into custody. They knew I was coming to confront them."

Savanas came up to us. "Ket, can you do that again?"

I glared at her.

"Guess I'll have to be content with the recordings." She held her hands up. "Look, we're supposed to take you," she pointed at Silver, "into custody along with the Elders. It seems in our best interest to help. The team can hold the dock and we'll keep the ferry out until this dies down."

"Can you also care for the wounded?" Silver asked. "The ones with the white strip of cloth tied around their left wrist are oath keepers. I don't want to see anyone else get hurt because of this."

Savanas looked at me with a weary expression. "Let me get Fan. Our resources in that area are limited." She stepped to the side and started relaying the request over her headset.

"Marzena," Silver said. "Can you help them?"

She scrunched up her face at him. "You just want me to stay out of the fight. You know I can best all of them."

"Please, Marzi. You're not prepared for battle," Silver pleaded, his voice soft.

While they argued, I walked toward the fighting. When the ferry left, the paladins seemed less interested in getting to the dock and had moved back to where there was more room to fight. I could not even tell which group was which. Did it really even matter at this point?

Someone grabbed my arm and I reflexively yanked it out.

"Kela, you can't fight them. You're good, but you're not even armed let alone armored," Marzena said. "I thought I lost my sister once already. Don't make me lose you again."

I rolled my eyes at the sentiment and huffed lightly. "I'm always armed. You need a path, right?"

"Kela... no, you need to stay out of this," Silver warned. "This isn't your fight."

That was a phrase I was tired of hearing. Ignoring him, I brought my hands up in front of me, about shoulder width apart before crossing them, creating a shockwave, knocking everyone down in about a fifty-yard cone. I took off running before they hit the ground.

A paladin stepped into my path on the outskirts of the affected area. I managed to dodge his swing, sliding under his sword arm.

"Guess I'll have to do what that Gods-damned fairy couldn't," he said as he spun around. I recognized him as the one who had wanted to deny me lunch that one day.

I grinned at the situation. I had no need to hold back now. I teleported behind him and slammed a ball of conjured electricity against the metal armor on his back. He dropped.

The scuffle was just long enough for Silver, Marzena, and Savanas to catch up.

"Which way?" I asked. Despite my time here, I did not know the grounds well enough to guess where they might be.

"They're likely holed up in the Court of the Elders," Silver said. He had already engaged with another paladin.

"It's going to take forever to get there through this," Marzena said, standing at the ready.

"Cover me," I ordered, not waiting for compliance before starting the spell.

"What?" the weapon's master asked.

"Just do it," I snapped while trying to concentrate. "I remember the place, but I need time."

Silver nodded to Marzena who was looking at me like I was crazy. Savanas shook her head.

Perhaps I was crazy to be helping Silver at all. I would deal with him personally later. Right now, he was useful.

This bridge was not as long as the last time I had to teleport more than just myself. The sounds of battle raging around me would not deter me from my task and I extended it quickly.

As soon as I was done, I ordered, "Hold onto each other." It took a moment, but they managed to free themselves from their fights. I grabbed Marzena's wrist since she was closest, teleporting us to the Court of the Elders. I crossed my eyes for a moment after arriving as the room spun. Teleporting multiple people always made me dizzy for a short time afterward, which was the downfall that I hoped would not be taken advantage of.

No one in the room seemed to know what to make of our sudden appearance. Amanda was here also.

"You said you killed her!" one of the Elders raged.

Silver stepped in front of me. "No, I said I got rid of her."

I rolled my eyes. Silver had thrown me off a balcony so he could play word games.

All of the Elders, including the typically gentle Valere were glaring at him. The same one shouted, "How dare you! Not only did you disobey a direct order, but you had brought that heretic to these holy grounds to begin with."

"Odd thing to say since you aid those seeking to learn necromancy," Silver said, walking closer to the Elders, leaving me in the middle of the room between Marzena and Savanas.

The room seemed to be collectively holding its breath.

"Stand down!" Silver ordered. "It's over. You will answer for your crimes."

"To you? Your hands are as dirty as ours," another who I did not know said, sneering at him.

"The TIO," Savanas said, stepping forward. With the focus on my presence, it seemed they had not paid attention to her.

"That's a lie. You know you have no jurisdiction here," Valere pointed out.

"When you ordered her dead, we did," Savanas said. "We don't take too kindly to someone harming one of our own."

"It was his hand," the Elder from before pointed at Silver.

"You're right, it was," Silver replied. "And I will accept the punishment for it as you will for giving the order."

A paladin off to the side was quietly casting something.

I brought my finger to my lips. "*Silence.*"

An iridescent band wrapped around the woman's mouth. She tugged at it, trying to get herself free.

Marzena engaged another on the other side who decided to attack. She easily blocked the attack with her sword before slamming her shield into him, sending him to the floor.

Everyone else stood in silence with their weapons at the ready. The other paladins present who were loyal to the Elders looked at each other.

Amanda stepped forward. "Are his claims true?"

"Why would you believe such nonsense?" Valere asked. "Elves are nothing but liars - they could never rightfully follow the path."

I raised an eyebrow at the Elder. Silver had not lied. I might be mad at my partner, but I knew that much from what little he said on the matter.

"What are you lot standing around for? Kill the mage," ordered the first Elder who spoke when we arrived.

"Kela, run!" Marzena called. She moved to engage the ones closest to her.

Silver had done the same. Savanas stepped between me and the ones heading in my direction, but there were too many for her and I ran to give us space and hopefully split the group.

With having teleported the four of us, my reserves were lower than I liked for what might turn into an extended fight. I needed to calm down and think through my tactics.

"If you're expecting a mage, you're going to be sorely mistaken," I said, mostly to myself, bringing my hands up, palms down. Violet bolts of arcane came up from the floor around me.

It caused the paladins and seekers who were unoccupied to slow and distracted the others. The ones heading toward me paused as the power circled around me. I knew it was little more than a light show, but it looked deadly and it was enough for Savanas to take one down.

I brought my hands together and then threw them out, creating a staff of arcane energy. I snatched it from where it hung in front of me, standing ready for the first fool to approach.

Two paladins broke off from the group to attack Savanas while the remaining three came my way. I was more concerned about my friend being overwhelmed than myself.

I quickly found myself fending off attacks from all sides as they managed to surround me. I struggled to keep up, never finding an opening to go on the offensive or break out. Teleporting around the room would wear me out too quickly. These were not the ones who shirked their training, but they also were not at Silver or Marzena's level. But three of them, even uncoordinated, kept me blocking sword strikes. They only defended with their shields, never attacking. That was the one saving grace for me.

One suddenly fell. Amanda stood behind him.

I could not give her much attention while I still had two more to fend off. She engaged the woman I had been fighting.

"You blind, traitorous fool! You deserve to be married to that fairy filth!" the paladin she fought yelled at her.

Refocusing my attention on the man remaining from the group, I dissipated my staff. I slammed an open palm against his shield, turning the raw arcane energy into electricity. The contact sent him to the floor, convulsing.

I turned in time to see the female paladin get her blade between the plates of Amanda's armor under her arm. As she pushed her blade in, I charged the woman, slamming into her to push her away.

Savanas got between us as we separated, one of her swords slicing the paladin's throat.

I took quick stock of how the other two were doing as I knelt down next to Amanda. Silver ran toward us and Marzena had just dropped her last opponent.

"Hey, look at me," I said, struggling to remain focused and not give into the rising panic.

Amanda smiled at me, but it seemed to take a lot of effort for her.

"Why?" I could not do anything. I was unable to heal her. I cursed myself for not having figured out an arcane means of doing so.

"You were genuinely kind to me. No one like that can be a heretic. You're not my enemy," Amanda said quietly.

Silver slid down next to me. "Give me room."

I stepped over Amanda to get out of the way as Marzena arrived, ignoring Silver. "Can you heal her?" I asked, fighting to keep my voice as neutral as possible.

Savanas stood over us at the ready.

"Marzi?" Silver looked up to her.

"I'll take care of her. Can you help me?" Marzena looked to Savanas.

"I saw the Elders leaving with some of their followers out the back. Go. I'll do what I can here and catch up," Savanas ordered, pointing in the direction they had gone.

I squeezed Amanda's hand before I stood up and followed Silver. I kept my eyes ahead as we ran down the hall.

"Kela, this isn't your fight," Silver said. "You shouldn't be here."

"You made that apparent," I replied flatly. "I choose what fights I get involved in. This was my fight before we even left the main office."

Silver let out a short laugh. "I really should know better by now."

"Just shut up. We need to end this," I snapped, not wanting to listen to him. He was useful as a fighter, I refused to deal with him beyond that at the moment.

He held a familiar metal object out to me.

I glared at him and tore my shrunken staff out of his hand, extending it immediately. I could have used it earlier.

We ran down the halls - the sound of our footsteps being the only thing to break the silence.

My partner slid to a stop as we approached a set of doors glowing blue. "Dammit, they sealed the Chamber."

Sneering at the barrier, I ran past him, conjuring a fireball in my hands and throwing it. The door exploded into a rain of splinters away from us.

Without stopping, I ran through the opening, sliding to a stop on the other side to take stock of the situation. The Elders were gathering their weapons and armor, most of the people they took with them were helping them prepare. A couple of seekers lay in heaps on either side of the door.

One of the paladins decided to rush me. I hit him with a strong blast of wind, sending him into two other paladins and one of the Elders. "I'm done with this," I snapped at the group.

"Kela, your eyes," Silver said quietly once he caught up to me.

"I'm done!" My voice boomed with my power. My vision had gotten blurry from the tears I struggled to hold back. I raised my staff and slammed one end down on the floor, creating a massive shockwave, knocking everyone back.

The shockwave threw all but Silver into walls and shattered windows. The Elders and paladins did not get up. Not a single one was even moving. Silver had been thrown a few yards, landing on his side and sliding.

My hair floated about me as I looked down at the men and women scattered about. One of them would eventually get up.

I waited. Still, no one was moving.

Silver shakily got to his knees. "Kela…"

So, he chose to be first. "Kela is dead. You killed her," I said calmly, my voice echoing with my power.

There was a long pause as he stared at me. Then he slowly rose to his feet.

"Ketayl, it's over. You can stand down," Silver said calmly. His sword and shield were away - he held his hands up defensively, walking over to me, taking each step carefully.

I pointed my staff at him. "It's not over."

Silver paused for a moment. "You can have at me later. Right now, we should secure the others before they become a threat. I am not your enemy."

This was not over. I was not done. I glared at him, my eyes watering, making my vision blurry. "You used me. You used me and then threw me away like garbage when I wasn't convenient anymore!"

His mouth opened and closed a few times before he said, "That's not it at all. I just need you to calm down and we can talk. I can explain—"

"I don't want to hear it!" I yelled, cutting him off. Charged at him, I brought my staff down for an overhead swing.

Silver's shield appeared on his arm in time to block it. The sound of metal hitting metal echoed through the room.

Shifting my stance, I switched to attack from below only to be blocked by his sword.

"Ketayl, knock it off. I don't want to hurt you!" he pleaded, shoving me away with both his sword and shield.

"You should have thought of that before!" I charged at him, sliding under his sword arm, shrinking my staff en route. I spun to extend it at his back.

Silver managed to block it with his shield, but I had caught the edge. If only I had been a split-second faster. "Please, stop! This isn't you."

I shoved him off-balance and swiped his legs out from underneath him. Before he hit the ground, I had shifted so I could aim for his head.

He brought his sword up to block and twisted, kicking my legs out from underneath me. "Gods help me, you need to stop," he said, scrambling to his feet, backing away from me.

Getting to my feet faster, I kept up my attacks and Silver continued to block, but I could not seem to break through his defenses.

After chasing him around the room for a bit something stung my left shoulder. My arm immediately started tingling. I glanced to the side.

Marzena and Fan stood flanking Savanas who held a thin rifle.

"Stay out of this!" I yelled at them, quickly yanking the dart out. I stopped using the arm that was quickly going numb, returning to attacking. I was not done yet.

Silver looked to the side and nodded, shifting to brace his shield with both arms, dropping his sword. I pressed against his shield with my staff, using all of my weight. I could wait him out.

"Ket, I'm sorry," Savanas said, her voice faint from the distance, before I felt a second sting on my neck.

I shook trying to press my attack, but my legs gave out and I remembered nothing else.

2 O

"YOU SHOULD LEAVE before she wakes up. Bad enough she's going to be pissed at me," Savanas said, her voice cutting through the haze. My body felt heavy - too heavy to move. Where was I? Why could I not remember what happened? We were chasing down the Elders and those loyal to them...

"I'll take her fury," Silver said quietly. "I'm not sure how much this was influencing her, but it doesn't matter. At least it let me take it off her this time."

"Heavens help me for even allowing you near her like this, but I've never seen her that out of control. She never said anything about your necklace influencing her," Savanas said sounded exasperated.

Silver's calloused fingers stroked my hair gently. "Likely she wasn't going to since it would only do it with me. I had caught her a few times when she wasn't able to separate herself from whatever it is that it puts out. I don't get anything from it, so I don't have a clear picture of what she struggled with."

Someone moved about the room, but until I heard Savanas speak, I could not tell who it was. She said, "It blocked the scryers from finding her, I know that much. It certainly made it a royal pain to find her. Though she was a lot more irritable and short than I had ever seen her before. At the time I chalked it up to the Hells she had been through, but now I'm wondering if that thing had something to do with it. I was surprised she was wearing it when I found her."

"I had a feeling it was what caused that phenomenon once I started sensing power from it. That's why I left it with her. I wish I could explain her behavior. Then at least I would know what to do." Silver's voice was strained.

"Seriously though. Couldn't you have found a better way to get her off the island? Something less traumatic to her? She's been through enough Hells since she first started going into the field - you didn't need to add to it," Savanas snapped.

Silver sighed, still stroking my hair. "In hindsight, probably. It was the only way I could think of to both get her off the island as well as satisfy the Elders so I could get into the inner circle. I was a fool to think I could do it all."

"What was so damn important that you'd risk everything?"

There was a long pause before Silver replied, "The truth. I want to say it was worth it, but the cost was much higher than I expected."

Savanas made a noise of agreement. "Though you should consider the fact that not only did we find necromancers in training, but also a slave trafficking ring - the others are tracing back how far it goes. That's not counting the mess here. That's a lot that you two uncovered."

Rough fingers stroked my hair. "Was it worth it though?"

My body had started to tingle beginning in my fingers and toes and slowly moving into my limbs.

"Time will tell, though at least you're not under arrest. One lesson you need to learn is to keep your partner in the loop," Savanas shot at him. "If you had told her maybe she wouldn't have lost it."

Silver sighed. "Whatever punishment awaits is nothing compared to what I've done."

Savanas growled. "You know what? Get out of here. Ket's not going to want to wake up to your crap."

Silence followed for several long seconds before Silver said, "Yes, ma'am."

There was another long pause as footsteps moved about. A weight landed on the side of the bed. "I swear that guy sometimes. How in the Hells do you put up with him?" Savanas muttered.

The tingling had kept growing in magnitude as it traveled and it shifted to pain and I hissed, curling up on my side, not sure what to do to alleviate it.

A smaller hand stroked my hair. "Sorry, kid. That stuff has a nasty side effect and I had to hit you with a double dose. It'll wear off soon."

Not soon enough, I thought as the sharp, poking pains intensified. I rolled and twisted, trying to find some relief.

Thin, strong hands held me still. "Stay still. Nothing's going to help until it wears off. That was meant to take down someone far bigger than you. Hells, the first dose alone should have dropped you almost instantly."

Once the after effects had run their course, I struggled to sit up.

My friend helped me. "I should have known letting you go was going to be a problem," she said flatly.

There was little point in arguing with her. A furry black face plopped itself on the bed next to me. Out of reflex, I started rubbing Riva's head.

"Silver seems to think there's a chance that his necklace was influencing you," Savanas said, her tone conversational.

I pinched the bridge of my nose. "It might have been. I'm honestly not certain." I went to hook the chain with a finger and could not find it. I patted the upper part of my chest, but it was gone. Was that what they had been talking about?

"He took it back."

"There goes my plan of throwing it at him," I muttered.

She looked me over. "Well, you seem to be in a better frame of mind. I think the theory is plausible."

I shook my head. "It doesn't matter." Whatever I had done had warranted getting tranquilized. It had to have been bad, but damned if I could remember much of anything.

"Well, you're probably not going to like this part, but given the situation, we aren't arresting Silver. He'll still have some sort of punishment to deal with, but I have no idea what that entails."

Riva crawled up onto my lap, sticking her face under my chin.

"Did we get the other settlement?" I asked while trying to figure out what to do with the large black dog on top of me.

"Yeah, the necromancers there were caught off-guard. That one was far easier than the landing here. Though now they have to figure out who the people they held captive are."

At least people would get to go home alive.

"Hey," Savanas said softly. "Sorry for having to tranquilize you. I was worried you were going to get hurt if I didn't."

"Not that I was going to kill Silver?" I had gotten the sense that I had attacked him, but it was still like trying to watch a grainy video through thick fog.

She looked at me like I was crazy. "Ket, it was like you had lost all reason. I mean, you were trying to overpower him physically. He would've ended up hurting you to get you to stop."

"Guess I got off lucky then," I muttered. Perhaps it was better this way.

"Wait, you don't remember what happened?"

I shook my head. "Not enough to piece it together."

Savanas frowned and crossed her arms. "Well, now I feel worse about tranquilizing you. Get some rest. I'll send Fan in to check on you when she's free."

AFTER A LONG LECTURE FROM FAN, I left. At least I had not been in the same room that I had shared with Silver. I would somehow need to collect my things. Perhaps I could ask someone to do it for me.

I had sought out Savanas so I could assist with collecting evidence. She sent me away, saying she did not need help. With nothing to do I walked along the shore, occasionally picking up a rock and throwing it. Riva and Roh played around me, sometimes coming closer, most of the time enjoying the wide-open area to run and chase each other.

Someone had been following me for the past few minutes. Probably to make sure I stayed away from the investigation. As if the two dogs were not enough.

"You're in a mood," Marzena said, her voice coming from behind me.

I growled low. So, she was the one who had been following me.

"Not that I could blame you. Mind if I walk with you?" She sounded far too cheerful for my current mood.

Frowning at myself, I shrugged. Marzena was not my enemy. "How's Amanda?" There had to be some good news somewhere.

"She lost a lot of blood. I don't know much more than that. I was able to stop the bleeding before help arrived, but..." She blew a breath through her bangs. "I'll go check on her again later. The healers threw me out the last time."

I closed my eyes. It was my fault that Amanda had gotten hurt.

"Hey," Marzena said, grabbing my shoulders, "you better not be blaming yourself."

"It's what I do." I shrugged her arms off of me, walking away from her. I wrapped my arms around my waist.

"Kela... Ket. Dammit, it's going to take me forever to switch." She hurried to walk beside me.

I shrugged. It was a name and nothing more.

She stepped in front of me and pulled me into a hug. "You can talk to me. Your pain hasn't been eased yet. And I'm so sorry I didn't realize how much I was upsetting you on the way here."

"Marzena, don't do this," I said, my voice breaking. My eyes had already started to water. She had said so little and yet I could not keep everything contained. The job was still unfinished.

"It's okay. Really. I'm not overly experienced at this comforting thing, but it's the least I can do. I know if I was in your position, I would have reacted the same way." She stroked my hair gently. "I didn't realize how much hair you had since I always saw you with it up. It's so pretty."

"We don't know if it was me or not," I said softly, trying to keep it together.

"What?" Marzena held me out at arm's length.

Taking a deep breath, I focused on the facts. "Silver's necklace... it could influence me. He had caught me before when it had taken over."

She raised an eyebrow at me, tilting her head and looking over my face. "You still seem like the same person."

I stepped away from her, leaning back on the short wall along the rocky shoreline. "It was only with him. I don't know if he imprinted on it or what. Silver doesn't know either."

Marzena tugged lightly at my collar, pulling it to the side. "And yet I see you're not wearing it."

"He took it back before I woke." I refused to look at her. I should give her a hard time about touching me, but I was too tired to care let alone fight.

"And yet you're still upset. I think it's safe to say these emotions are yours. Own them," Marzena said firmly.

I tilted my head, not understanding. Did she have some insight that I did not? She had not even known about the necklace affecting me before I mentioned it.

Marzena made a face at me. "Let yourself feel. Kela, even I could tell you kept tight rein on yourself. It's worse now. You can't move on like this."

"Last time that happened I got tranquilized." I frowned, rubbing the back of my neck. I had been ignoring the stiffness up until now. My left shoulder was also sore.

"And you just said you weren't sure it was you. I saw you - even I hadn't believed that you would be acting like that normally. You were completely different from when we parted at the Court."

I cringed, wishing she had not witnessed whatever it was I had done. "I don't really remember what happened. I've been trying to recall, but about the time we got to where the Elders were, it became a fog."

"Really? Hm..." Marzena pursed her lips, looking at the ground. "I guess I don't know enough about how you were being affected. I don't even know how on Terra you were casting as fast as you were, which gave me a huge appreciation for how much you had been holding back."

I sighed - it was only fair to tell her. "I'm an Arcanist. I'm genetically tied to the arcane."

Marzena stared at me with wide eyes. "I didn't know anyone could be."

I rubbed my arms. Now that I had nothing to do, the thoughts about what happened kept trying to take over.

"Would sparring with me help? I hate seeing you in pain like this."

I shook my head. "It's too dangerous. I don't want to accidentally hurt you."

Marzena threw her hands up. "Dammit, girl, just cry already. Silver was an ass. It's okay to be upset about that. Hells, I punched him when I found out what he did, and I still wasn't satisfied. I punched him quite a few times actually."

Her words made me laugh hard enough for my eyes to water. Then the tears started falling and I could not make them stop.

She pulled me into a hug and stroked my hair down my back,

doing nothing more than making soothing sounds. It felt like an eternity before I could get myself back under control.

"Sorry," I said quietly, backing away and wiping my face with my hands.

"Don't be. Actually, I should probably apologize," Marzena said, her cheeks had reddened slightly.

"Huh?" I was still attempting to rub the evidence off my face.

"I, uh... borrowed this after you dropped it." She held out my shrunken staff. "It looked like so much fun, I couldn't resist. I hope it's okay."

I took it and stared at it in my hand and then I started laughing. "It's fine. You're probably far better with it than I am."

"I, uh... hit myself extending it."

I cringed. "I wish I had warned you."

Marzena shrugged. "Come on. I'm starving." She grabbed my hand and dragged me along. At least I thought I might be able to eat something now.

2 1

THERE WAS a familiar silver-white haired paladin waiting for me on the dock as the ferry returned. I had spent the day down at the necromancers' encampment, looking through their records, trying to make heads or tails of what they had been doing.

Mostly I agreed to go down there in order to get away from Silver. He had been attempting to get me to speak with him over the past few days. Whenever I sensed him nearby, I left what I was doing. I would leave a task incomplete if necessary.

With Silver on the docks there was nowhere for me to go to get away from him. There was no one else onboard who he might possibly be waiting for. I glanced at the golden lines crisscrossing the grounds of the Central Seat - all of them the traces of me running from him.

I knew eventually I would have to talk to him, but I was still unprepared for that moment. I might never be ready. There was no way we were going to be able to continue working together. I bit my lower lip debating if I should teleport again.

The biggest problem was I really needed to get started on transferring the information I had collected into the TIO's database so that others could access it. Given the sheer amount of information, that was going to require a significant amount of arcane energy. Teleporting also had a high cost. It was one or the other. Pushing off getting the information transferred one more day would be fine.

While I debated, Marzena and Savanas both came down the dock. Avoiding Silver was one thing, but I could not this time without possibly upsetting one or both of the women.

Riva bumped my legs, whining softly.

I knelt down to pet her. "Sorry. I almost left you behind with that idea. It hasn't been easy keeping up with me these past few days, has it?"

She stuck her head under my chin again. The black dog had been my constant companion - she even stayed with me in my room, often snuggling while I rested. Not that I was able to rest much. Though she did have a knack for finding me after I teleported. It was going to be hard to part with her once she went back to Kitteren.

My fingers were buried in her thick fur without me realizing I had done it. "I guess I can't get out of this one."

Silver's eyes were locked on me as we pulled into the dock. I moved away from the windows to the other side of the ferry before taking a seat and hugging my bag to my chest. I would only have a few minutes out of his view, but hopefully it would be enough to come up with a plan.

While I thought through my options, Riva got her head between my arms and my bag.

Too soon Mackie poked her head into the room I was hiding in. "Hey, girl, we're good to go. Looks like there's some people waiting for you."

I forced a smile and scratched behind Riva's ears one more time. "Thanks." I stood up, still no plan in place. The only thing I had come up with was to try and pretend he was not there.

The three were still waiting for me at the bottom of the ramp. I took a deep breath and hiked my bag higher up my shoulder, attempting to appear as collected and confident as I could. Riva trotted ahead of me, likely happy to be back on land.

"What'd you find?" Savanas asked once I was close enough.

I bit my lower lip, thinking through the information. "Nothing more than I expected. Most were notes by the necromancers. There were records of the people in the encampment through the years and who they've dealt with for supplies." I hated the use of that term for the people they experimented on, but at this point, I could not think of a more delicate way to put it. "We may be able to use that information to track down slave traders."

Savanas frowned and crossed her arms, looking at the other two for a moment before turning her attention back to me. "Thanks for doing that. We're going to need your expertise on another matter that may help connect how in the Hells this all came to be."

I raised an eyebrow at her and looked to Marzena for a moment, still attempting to ignore Silver.

"We're unsealing all of the vaults," Marzena said. "But obviously some lines are refusing to cooperate and I'm not allowed to force them." She thumbed at Savanas.

"You blew through the same type of barrier with a fireball when we were chasing the Elders," Silver said, "As well as there is a small library only accessible to the Elders and heads of lines. I've read some of what is in there and it'll definitely help piece this together."

I scrunched up my face, clenching my jaw at the sound of his voice.

"Come on, Ketayl. This is work," he argued.

I crossed my arms and turned away from him. Riva started growling. I looked down to see her between me and him, her teeth bared.

"Riva, knock it off," Savanas ordered, "Silver, go take a walk. We'll finish up here."

There was a moment of no movement before he stormed off the dock.

Savanas pinched the bridge of her nose. "As much as I don't want to force you to have to deal with him, he has a point. This is work-related."

"I know, but..." I trailed off. "In any case, I can't use a fireball on the doors. I'll damage the interior of the vaults you need opened. I'm sure I can come up with something. No guarantee you'll be able to close those doors again though."

Marzena shook her head. "It would be just as well if they never closed. That includes the ones we've been given access to. I'm sure we can find a new use for those rooms. The scholars are always complaining about wanting more space or private study rooms."

"That means there's more information that will need to be copied. Think you could do it tonight?" Savanas asked.

I bit my lower lip and considered the request while trying to ignore Silver storming around on shore. "Give me an hour or two and

I can probably come up with something to open them, but depending on how many vaults there are and how big that other library is... it could easily take me a day or more to copy the information. I still haven't started getting any of it into our database."

"Well, you've been too busy running away from your partner," Savanas said flatly. "You two are going to have to work this out."

I scrunched up my nose at the idea. "I need to not be disturbed while doing it."

Savanas made a face at me and turned to Marzena. "Can you keep him occupied for her to get it done?"

"Depends on how long it's going to take," the weapon's master said. "He's getting desperate. Hells, he was out here waiting for the ferry to return for hours."

I had not thought he had been waiting anywhere near that long. I needed to focus on my task before the guilt of what I unintentionally put Silver through distracted me. I bit my lower lip, going through the variables I at least had a rough idea on. "Given the equipment we have, the connection, and how much information I can reasonably guess I'm going to have..." I trailed off, trying to math it out. "Three to four weeks at least. That's with working 16 to 18 hours a day, seven days a week. Provided I can keep up my arcane energy levels to continue at that pace."

"Oh Hells no. I can't afford to be away from Ocean's Edge that long," Savanas said.

"You're from Ocean's Edge?" Marzena asked, sounding surprised.

Savanas nodded. "I head the branch there. One of my guys, Brad, used to go to the church. Not sure if you know him."

"Oh, I know Brad!"

"We're getting off subject," Savanas said. "And you'd probably like to get home soon." She eyed me.

I nodded. "I could cut that time in half with even the media room at a branch that has one. Ghost Forest does." It was the closest one I knew of and visiting the people I knew there - both TIO and the werewolves - might not be such a bad idea.

Marzena held up her hand. "Ke-t," she tripped over which name to use again. "You can't be serious about working those kinds of hours nonstop."

Savanas made a face. "Unfortunately, she is. And the answer is no. The transfer can wait. You'll be coming back with me for a bit if only to settle your sister. You can use our media room, but no more than a few hours at most a day with days off. I'm not watching you burn yourself out."

I folded my arms and frowned. Riva touched my leg with her nose.

"Come on," Marzena said. "We can talk over dinner on how to get the vaults open."

"Yeah, sure." I followed them off the dock. Thankfully Silver was nowhere in sight.

———

"Are you sure this is going to work?" Marzena asked for the umpteenth time as we headed down into the vaults. We had gone over as much information during dinner as we could, limiting the unknown variables so I could create a spell to destroy the doors.

I pinched the bridge of my nose. "Theoretically, yes. Until I try it, I won't know for certain. I do want to look over the Sutton door before attempting it though."

"Oh? I thought we went over everything." She was toying with her ponytail.

"I'm curious about something. I'm not sure how to word it." At least not in a way without embarrassing myself.

"What?"

I debated telling her it was some complex arcane thing, but it would not hold for long. "I... I'm curious if Silver had actually given me permission. I don't know if he knew how easy it was as you explained it to me."

"Oh." Marzena wrung her hands. "Well, it can't hurt to try. I heard you went to visit Amanda before you left this morning."

I nodded, glancing at the name plates on the doors as we passed. "She was asleep when I stopped in."

My friend shook her head. "She might be stable, but I'm thinking of having her moved to a hospital on the mainland. There's only so much that can be done for her here. At least it seems no one is going to fight me on it."

That was not the best of news, but at least she was alive. In that there was hope still.

Upon reaching the door to the Sutton vault I tentatively reached out and touched it lightly with the tips of my fingers. At first, I could only sense the grain of the thick wooden door, but something much more subtle made itself known.

Magic, but not arcane. I had begun to realize that I could sense the divine if I was more or less touching the source. Perhaps a legacy from my biological father. From what I remembered, he was a strong divine caster.

Either way, I was not yet ready to reveal that information to anyone.

"Do you remember the words?" Marzena asked, her voice soft.

I nodded. Though I wanted to test a different theory about opening the door. I ran through the words in my head quickly, working my way through the magical lock. Suddenly the barrier released and the door unlocked.

Marzena and I looked at each other and shrugged. "Good to know *now* that I didn't have to say it out loud all the time. Someone could have told me that years ago. Looks like he gave you permission - or you're good at breaking into places."

"Probably the former, and sorry about that." Gently, I pushed the heavy door open. I had not expected to find Silver inside.

He looked up from where he sat at the desk reading one of Blaise Sutton's journals.

"I... um... I'll come back later." I backed away from the door.

Marzena moved behind me, grabbing my shoulders to hold me still. "No, we're testing this now."

"Testing what?" Silver asked, closing the journal and standing to face us.

She gripped my shoulders tighter when I tried to escape. "Her theory on opening the vaults. The Sutton vault is already copied so we won't have to worry if something goes awry."

Silver looked back at the journal he had been reading. "If you don't mind giving me a minute, there is something I would like to preserve for my own sake."

"Sure, take your time," Marzena said, pushing me into the vault. "Kela needs to examine the door anyway."

I tried to dig my feet into the floor to stop my forward movement, but she was stronger. "Really, this doesn't have to be done now."

"Nonsense. We're going to test this tonight that way we can get to work tomorrow," she said cheerfully with a broad smile on her face.

"Remember, we planned on the vaults first and then the Elder's library. On that, you'll have to show it to us, dear brother."

"Marzi, leave her be. She needs to concentrate," Silver admonished. "Come help me find all of the journals. I think I've located most of them." He picked up a brown leather bag that had been hidden on the other side of the desk.

I took a deep breath as she stepped away. Out of habit I began to turn to thank Silver, but stopped and returned to my task. The faster I completed this, the faster I got to leave.

They chatted about what they had read in the journals. Marzena teased him about being an unruly child. He reminded her she was no different. I remained silent and hoped I would be ignored.

There was little I could glean from the door itself. I bit my lower lip. I only hoped I could keep the spell contained to just what I wanted destroyed. Untested spells always made me nervous the first time or two.

"Kel... Ketayl," Silver said softly coming up behind me. "You're the best at this. There's no need to second guess yourself."

I stiffened up as he spoke to me, refusing to turn around.

"I'll be going now. I'll get these back to you when I'm done," Silver said solemnly and left.

After a few long moments Marzena spoke. "He's right. I may not understand what you were working on over dinner, but you obviously know what you're doing. I wouldn't trust anyone else."

My hands clenched into fists. Part of me wanted to refuse to do this. To just be used for something else. No, I needed to keep work separate. This needed to be done and the truth be known.

"I have an idea to settle things between you two, but it can wait until we're done copying the vaults at least. You can't keep going like this. Neither of you." There was no missing the concern in her voice.

I shook my head.

"Kela!" Marzena grabbed my shoulder and spun me around to face her. "I'm not asking you to forgive him or trust him or anything else. You need to do something before you explode. Running from him isn't working and damn him from ordering me to keep silent on the truth. He wants it to come from him, but he won't say it until you're willing to listen."

I defaulted to my usual response. "I'll deal with it when the job is done."

She frowned and crossed her arms. "Well, let's get this started then." She waved at the door.

Both of us moved out of the room, closing the door behind us. I put my hand on the old, thick wood once it locked. Raw arcane energy turned to fire, spreading from where my hand was outward until the entire door was nothing more than a pile of ash and scrap metal. However, the process took several minutes to complete.

Marzena waved the smoke away as she carefully stepped over the disintegrated door. She looked around the interior and whistled. "You did it. Everything in here is preserved. Not even a mark on the door-frame. Damn, you're good."

I fought down the heat rising to my face at her praise. "We have our entry then. I wouldn't want to risk turning up the intensity though to try and burn through faster."

Marzena nodded. "No use rushing it and damaging something. Alright, let's go get some rest - we'll be at this all day tomorrow."

"Hey, um..." I started and trailed off, unsure if I should broach the topic, but I was already this far. "Do you think maybe there will be something in one of the other vaults about your sister?"

She shrugged. "I wouldn't get my hopes up, but it's possible. I'll likely be going through the records anyway and if I happen across something, great, if not..." She trailed off and shrugged. "I'm okay with not knowing. I'm sure she escaped this life and found a happier one. Besides, I'm also going to have my hands full helping get the Order back in... order."

I scrunched up my nose at the thought. "No offense, but I'm glad that's not my job."

Marzena laughed. "It could be fun. Now that the old guard is gone we can reevaluate our traditions and get rid of stupid ones and maybe find something new." While we walked, she continued to talk about which traditions she would like to get rid of or change. Her positive attitude was infectious.

"DONE?" Marzena asked as I took my hand away from the last book in the vault.

I nodded. It was late, but we had completed getting through all of the vaults in two days. I pinched the bridge of my nose and shook my head. Riva bumped up against my legs and I grabbed the bookcase to steady myself.

A hand grabbed my shoulder lightly, helping me stay upright. "You okay?"

"Yeah, just tired and wasn't ready for her." I reached down and rubbed the black dog's head.

Marzena formed a thin line with her mouth. "And you wanted to pull that insane schedule for getting the information transferred."

"I never said I wanted to. It was the fastest I could calculate to get it done." I sighed, looking at the bracelet. "The use of arcane energy was more constant than I'm used to. I'll have to keep that in mind when I go to transfer to the database. I might just wait until I'm back at the main office."

"Either way, let's go - I'm starving," Marzena said, shooing me along. "The others will be over to this vault soon enough to collect the books and artifacts." She did not wait for me as she walked quickly out the door.

I tilted my head to the side - that was unusual for her. Was there something going on? She could have demanded we took a break sooner. Not to mention there was the Elder's library still. I was not looking forward to dealing with Silver for that.

Slowly I followed. By the time I reached the hallway, she was out of sight. It was a good thing I had been down here enough times to be able to navigate my own way out. By the time I got up to the main part of the library, the sun was in the process of setting. I knew it had gotten late, but not that late. We had been down there since just after breakfast. Silver had brought lunch down to us, but left quickly, only staying long enough to get an update from Marzena on our progress.

At least it was done. Well, that part anyway. I nodded to the TIO agents guarding the entrance as I passed them. The Order was still sorting itself out so since we were still here, they asked our agents to stand guard.

My footsteps echoed loudly through the otherwise empty building. Not even the scholars were being allowed in here until we completed our tasks.

"Can't you discuss this with her later? She's exhausted," Marzena said sharply.

I hesitated at the door, unsure what I was about to walk into.

"As much as I'd like to agree with you to hold this off, it's been long enough and they're going to need to be able to work together for the next part," Savanas said.

Taking a deep breath, I pushed through the door. With only having heard two voices, I had not expected to see three people. Silver stood with the two women, his arms crossed.

"At least wait until after she's had something to eat. She barely touched her lunch. There's no need to kill her appetite," Marzena argued, gesturing in my direction, but she had not turned to see me come out.

Silver's eyes slid over to where I had paused just outside the doors. "We're doing this now." He walked over to me.

"Dammit, I know it was my idea, but you need to listen to me." Marzena hurried to get over to us.

"What idea?" I asked, turning to her. It had not helped to ignore the stare Silver directed at me.

Marzena frowned and shook her head. "It can wait. You need to eat and rest. You haven't been doing much of either from what I can tell."

Savanas joined the group that had shifted over to me. She folded her arms and looked at the ground. "I still don't like this idea anyway. There's too many risks."

"Risks that I know full well and am willing to take," Silver snapped. "It's only my neck on the line here."

"What risks?" I asked, growing impatient. I had a long list of things to do and standing around listening to them talk was not on it.

The three of them fell silent, each looking to the others.

"Either someone comes out and says it or I'm leaving," I said. I was tired and wanted nothing more than to go back to my room. I would say to rest, but I knew I would be staring at the ceiling for most of the night again.

For someone who wanted to do this now, even Silver stood there in silence.

Marzena shifted uncomfortably before she said, "You should fight him."

"What?" With how quiet the word came out, I was unsure if anyone heard my question. What good would it do to fight with him?

She tugged on her ponytail. "There's nothing else I can think of. Just fight him - get it out of your system."

"It's too dangerous," I said quietly, remembering the image of

Silver looking at me from over his shield, the remnants of my fireball on the scorched floor around him. It had been the better part of a year since then, but I still could not forget what I had done.

"Dammit, Ketayl!" Silver snapped. "I know the risks. And you know that I know them. We can us the outdoor training grounds to get rid of any restrictions on you."

"And I can be there in case someone needs to intervene," Marzena added quickly.

I closed my eyes, thinking through the idea. I could argue and ignore and everything else, but this cycle would never end. "Alright, but no audience."

"Kela..." Marzena said softly.

I shook my head glaring at the ground since I was uncertain who to turn it to. "Silver knows the risks, but I can't guarantee your safety or anyone else's."

"Tomorrow afternoon then. Make sure you're rested," Silver said sharply and stormed off.

"Do you know what you just got yourself into?" Savanas asked. "I should call this off. The others are going to be upset if I let you do this."

"Yes, and you said yourself it's been long enough." The real question was if Silver understood what he was getting himself into. Not that I really cared to have this fight.

22

THE SUN BROKE THE HORIZON. I had been awake all night again. So much for getting enough rest. Riva laid with her head on my shoulder. She perked up as I shifted and licked my face.

"Hey, that one was slobbery," I admonished gently, wiping my face before rubbing her head.

After a few more minutes, I sighed and got up, setting about getting ready for the day. With as quiet as it was, perhaps I could get into the practice hall. I had not had the chance to go back since the first time I went with Marzena and Silver. The piano that had been enchanted to keep its tune still intrigued me.

There were plenty of tasks for me to do, but none that demanded my attention so early in the morning. I was also certain anyone I had to work with would appreciate not being woken up at this hour. Not to mention that I was still not ready to deal with Silver.

My room was on the ground floor and much smaller than the suite I had been in previously. I missed my quarters back at the main office. Even my room at my adopted parent's house would be preferable right now. The closest I was likely to get any time soon was crashing at my sister's house in Ocean's Edge.

That visit was going to be an earful. I could almost hear the lectures now.

I checked the hallway first to make sure I would be unseen

leaving and then hurried out. There would be little time before someone came looking for me. At least with the practice hall being set so far out, there would be minimal traffic there.

Using my invisibility spell through the areas where people were moving about, I made it to the practice hall without issue. The doors had been unlocked so that the TIO could check it and Marzena had elected to leave it that way. There were no visitors allowed to come to the island until the TIO had completed their business anyway. Marzena said she might keep the order longer than that.

There were other paladins and scholars working to make heads or tails of the chaos the Order went through, but it seemed the weapon's master had ended up being the leader of the group. Though she spent most of her time with me, she was often called upon to make a decision on something or other.

The practice hall was still rather dusty. Since my arcane abilities were known, I could use my power to clean the place quickly. I set about opening the windows.

As soon as that was done, I raised my hand to start the spell when a memory hit me. The day before all this started I had to stop an out of control enhanced version of the spell. I rolled my eyes and shook my head to clear the memory. Even that was not anywhere near some of the strangest things I had encountered since I started working for the TIO.

Especially not since I had met Silver.

I lowered my hand and looked to the ground. I expected to feel something, but I had grown numb to the world around me. Was this all I was? Just someone to be used?

But in truth, I had not stopped to consider what I wanted. The pattern would continue until I had, but I could not see a way out. Not with always being concerned about others. Placing myself first always felt wrong.

My phone rang loudly in the empty hall, startling me. I sighed and pulled it out of my back pocket, looking to see who it was. The name Lindale showed on my screen requesting a video call. I had spoken with my adopted mother along with several others after Savanas had found me.

What time is it there? It had to be late. With any luck, this would be short. I sighed and answered Mother's request. "Hi."

"Hi? Is that all I get?" she asked, pouting. "My daughter somehow survives unspeakable horrors and that is all I get for a greeting?"

Bards... I rolled my eyes at her dramatics and sat down on the bench with my back to the piano. At least that was free of dust. "I thought we had already been through that the last time we talked." I had gone through several video calls with different people to let them know that I was, in fact, alive. After the initial calls though, I had gone back into communications silence. Partly because I was on borrowed equipment. Mostly because I did not have the patience to deal with the long-distance coddling.

"I'm grateful you called after you got some rest, but I haven't heard from you since. Ketayl, what's going on? And where are you? Is that a piano behind you?"

She would pick up on that. "I'm at the Central Seat. This is... was their practice hall, but they haven't used it in a long time."

She narrowed her eyes at me through the video. "You're not in hiding again are you?"

"Mom..." I whined and then covered my mouth. "Sorry, I didn't mean to disrespect—"

"Ketayl," she cut me off. "We've had this conversation before also. I actually like hearing that better than your over-the-top formality. And I'm going to go out on a limb here and say you're hiding, not in hiding."

I rolled my eyes.

"How badly out of tune is it?" Mother pointed, but because it was video, I was uncertain what exactly she was pointing at.

"Is...?" I turned to the piano. "It was fine the last time I used it. Someone said it was enchanted to hold its tune."

She made a circling motion with her finger. "This isn't ideal, but get to it. You're in need of practice." The video shook a bit as she moved. "While you warm up, I'm going to switch this over to the computer. It'll be easier to send you things."

I frowned and turned to face the piano, putting my phone up where music sheets would normally go. Music lessons were preferable to coddling.

"Oh, don't give me that face, Ketayl. You seem to constantly forget that I know how you are. You need this to center yourself. You don't look like you've been getting enough rest," Mother observed.

While I gently lifted the cover from the keys, I scrunched up my face at her. I hesitantly pressed a key, cringing at how loud it was in the quiet room. The piano had not sounded so loud when I was last here with Marzena.

I sensed a familiar presence, but ignored him. Soon enough Silver would grow bored and leave.

Mother hummed for a moment while I heard her type. "I might need to find out about that enchantment - it would certainly save me some time on upkeep. Have they spoken with you about what you're going to do after you return?"

I shook my head while I worked through some basic drills. "I assume I'm still making a stop in Ocean's Edge to appease Kitteren."

Mother made a noise of agreement and the video shifted suddenly, the camera angle changed as she switched the call. "Well, we both know how she gets. She's been upset you haven't called her again. I was thinking of seeing if she'd come visit for a bit. I know she doesn't have any training classes to teach right now."

I bit my lower lip. Either way she was going to be a pain to deal with.

"And Dad and I can keep her off you when she gets to be too much," Mother pointed out.

That was possibly an acceptable option, but... "I really need to get back to the main office. I've already got a backlog."

"We can discuss this later. Here, I think you remember this one. I want vocals also." The screen switched from Mother's face to a sheet of music as my phone opened the program she liked to use.

Narrowing my eyes to see it clearly on the small screen, I said, "I remember this, but why?" I turned my phone to landscape so the lines would be easier to read before scrolling through it quickly. It had been a long time, but I was fairly certain I could remember it without the sheet in front of me. She had made me practice it enough times on piano specifically.

"Just trust me on this one," she said cryptically.

Typical of her. Though she never gave me a reason to distrust her intuition. I bit my lower lip again and glanced to the side as a second presence appeared, trying not to turn and alert the people lurking nearby, but wanting to confirm who it was. Unfortunately, they were both out of my sight so I only knew one was Silver.

"Ketayl?"

I shook my head. "It's nothing."

"Then put on a show for me." I swore I could hear the grin on her face with those words. It was only fair that someone entertained the Elven songstress, but why did it have to be me?

I rolled my eyes and scrolled the music back to the top. She could not possibly mean including using magic. "All of it?" I knew I was whining and I had not particularly cared.

"Yes. I'll start the play through."

I groaned and hurried to get my fingers in place as a line began scrolling across the bars. Between the relatively unfamiliar instrument and trying to keep up with reading at the same time blocked out everything else. My voice rang out with more emotion than I had intended, but the song struck hard at what I had kept hidden.

The pain at being used. The embarrassment of being tossed aside. Like the fool I was, I decided to help Silver when he asked. I trusted him. Now...

As more instruments were needed, I split my concentration further to creating vague illusions to fill those gaps. Before I hit the high point, I had already stopped paying attention to the scrolling sheet, losing myself in the music.

There was nothing but silence once I finished for several long seconds.

"Ketayl," Mother said softly, her face appeared on my phone again.

"Sorry, I got carried away," I said, my voice quiet. I kept my head down, but could see her in my peripheral vision.

"You needed it. It's been a while since you've put that much power into your music - your eyes shifted again. We may need to reconsider what causes that to happen when you get back. I wish I could be there with you." She reached toward the screen with her fingers. Normally she would gently brush my hair back when I got like this.

I frowned for a moment at the mention that despite the use of my arcane abilities, I had still managed to cause the blue and green to show. I quickly forced a smile and reached for my phone. "I should probably get going. There's still work to do."

She gave me a sad smile. "Doing something for yourself is more important. You know you can call me whenever - I don't care what time it is."

I nodded.

"Alright, sweetie, I'll talk to you later."

I picked up my phone and ensured the called ended before putting it face down. Then I closed the piano key cover before resting my head in my hands. Why did I feel so drained now?

I STOOD in the outside training area facing Silver. He was in his full TIO armor with sword and shield drawn. I was uncertain why I had agreed to Marzena's idea of fighting it out. Last night it sounded like a much better idea than when I got up this morning.

Probably because I would not listen to him. I wanted nothing to do with the person who had been not only my partner but also my best friend for the past two and a half years. The closest friend I had ever had.

I just needed to stay calm and in control of the fight. Get this over with and then I could go back to ignoring him outside of the times we needed to work together.

Riva and Roh both rested in the shade of the trees. While I had said no audience, Savanas demanded that they at least be nearby to be able to go get help if needed.

"What's the matter? Don't want to get even?" Silver taunted. "You can't keep running away."

"*I can try,*" I muttered to myself. Though it was far too late for that right now. I took a deep breath and pulled my shrunken staff out of its holster, extending it. I had started to become numb to most things and this morning only left me feeling more drained and empty.

Silver threw his shield. I held my hand up, using my shield spell. I grunted against the hit, but otherwise did not move. There was no reason for this fight. He had made himself perfectly clear about how he felt when he threw me off the balcony.

Mechanically I blocked his attacks with my staff. After dodging a couple more strikes, about the time he would usually move to hit me with his shield, I used a quick flight spell to jump back several yards, landing softly on my feet.

He stood at the ready, but made no move to close the distance like he normally would. Instead, he simply watched. I had no idea what went through his head.

I turned away. It seemed our fight was over.

A familiar golden barrier formed up in front of me before I could take a step to leave. Apparently, the fight was not over. I sighed, my shoulders dropping. I looked back at Silver who stood holding his sword up behind his shield.

"I'd rather you be trying to kill me than this."

I shrugged and faced him fully. I knew better than to be caught unprepared if he wanted a fight. "*This* is what you're going to get right now. I trusted you and you used me just like everyone else. I'm tired of it, but I don't know how to change my situation."

Silver's face went from taunting to confused to something I could not make out before he walked over to me. He knelt down and placed his sword on the ground, the hilt to my right. He remained there with his head down. "My sword is yours. Use me as you will."

"What?" My question was barely above a whisper. Why the sudden change in attitude?

"I can't undo what I've done. I'm not even going to try to correct how you perceived what happened. All I can do is offer you myself and work endlessly to rebuild what I so carelessly destroyed. I am yours to use as you will." He spoke slowly and steadily.

"This is ridiculous," I said, wrapping my arms around my waist. "I won't take advantage of you like that and you know it."

Silver knelt there silently. His shoulders shook. "Then take my sword and strike me down."

I took a half step back, drawing my hands up and away from his sword even though it was on the ground. "What? No! Knock it off. I probably can't even pick up your sword."

My partner stayed where he was. I looked around. No one else was here to help me out.

"Silver," I said softly, walking around his sword on the ground carefully before kneeling down next to him. That was when I noticed tear tracks down his face. "I may be angry about what happened, but I'm not going to kill you. You've got too much still to do and you can't fix anything if you're dead."

He looked up at me. "I can't fix anything on my own. That's how I got myself into this mess."

I sat back on the grass and looked at the trees bordering the area, briefly noting that the two dogs still lounged in the shade. "No one ever said you had to do it alone."

Silver shifted, sitting also, but would not look at me. "Ketayl... Kela, I want you to know that I did not make that decision lightly. By the Gods, I wanted to ask you if you would continue to court me after this mess was over. It was everything I had ever dreamed of and more. And like a fool, I threw it all away thinking it was the only way to get you out of here and also get myself in the good graces of the Elders so I could find out the truth. I couldn't see a way out. They were going to kill you if I didn't do something."

"And then probably you as well." Logically it made sense. Once the emotions were gone from my perspective, it was clear to see why he chose the path he had.

He shrugged. "I wouldn't have cared at that point, but that would have put so many more lives in danger."

After several seconds, I said, "You should have told me of your plan. Then maybe we wouldn't be here right now."

"Yeah, I should have. There's a lot of things I should have told you," he said softly, still not looking at me. "I just wasn't sure if I told you if you'd actually leave."

I bit my lower lip, thinking through how we had gotten to this point. He was here trying and I had been behaving poorly. The least I could do was hear him out. "You still have time to tell me."

Silver turned and stared at me. His mouth worked and then he looked away. "I thought you wanted nothing to do with me."

"I didn't," I said flatly. "And I was acting no better than a child throwing a temper tantrum. I kept telling myself I needed time to think, but to be honest, when it comes down to it..." I sighed, unsure how to continue. "I'm not sure what my own thoughts are. I was so jumbled with the effects of your necklace that I have no idea what was really mine."

Silver stood up suddenly. "Will you take a walk with me?"

I raised an eyebrow at him as he picked up his sword and put it back in its sheath. Then it vanished along with his shield.

"Not far. Just away from the grounds. Being here may be affecting both of us." The lower part of his armor disappeared and he unzipped his jacket. Then I realized he was not wearing the clerical garments he had been, but rather the dress shirt and khaki pants I was used to seeing him in.

I could not argue with that logic. I stood up and signaled for him to lead the way.

Silver held his hand out as if he wanted me to take it.

I hesitated, staring at his hand and then sighed, taking it. Little would come from building a proverbial wall between us - the last week had shown me that much.

He brought my hand to his lips and kissed the back of it. His soft smile could not hide the tension in his face. Then he started off toward the tree line, away from where Riva and Roh rested. Neither seemed interested in moving.

While we walked, his hand was tight around mine. I considered telling him I was not about to run off, but breaking the silence might shatter the little we managed to rebuild. Besides, I had run from him so may times recently that even I would not trust myself with those words.

It gave me time to think. I knew he would not lie. Walk a fine line, yes, but his words earlier had been blunt and straightforward. In the end, I still trusted him. Perhaps it was nothing more than not wanting to lose the closest friend I had.

Or was he something else?

People often alluded to if not outright said that they thought we were romantic partners. I had always brushed it off. I never considered pursuing the notion as I had always been too afraid of accidentally hurting someone because I was an Arcanist.

Not that it mattered. He had been interested in someone else.

Silver led me to a small clearing. "I wasn't sure if this place was still here. It's been so long," he whispered. "In the spring there would be a wide range of colors of flowers, but it gets too warm for them come summer and the enchantment on the grounds doesn't extend this far."

I gave him a soft smile and stepped farther into the clearing, letting go of his hand. Given what he had said, this must have been a special place for him when he lived here. I turned when I heard a rustling of clothes.

Silver had slid his armored jacket off and was removing his metal bracers.

"Did you come here often?" His actions put me on edge, but we were not so far that I could not teleport myself back.

"Yeah. I found it by chance when I was... I'm not even sure I had reached my first decade. Initially I would come here when I was tired of being the outcast. I ended up spending more and more time here for different reasons," he said, putting his bracers with his jacket.

"Does anyone else know?" It was far warmer here than on the

grounds of the Central Seat, but it was summer. I turned my face toward the sun for a moment, closing my eyes before returning my attention to my partner.

Silver hesitated for a moment. "No one that's alive. My master found me out here once. It had always stayed between us. I never realized he seriously considered me one of his children." He walked toward me slowly, his hands up defensively. "I'm unarmed. Mostly anyway. I figured I'd give you the wrong impression if I took my belt off."

I shook my head. "You didn't need to do that."

"Yes, I did. I realized that while you're one of the rare people I ever let my guard down around, I've never let it all the way down. Not like this." He brushed my hair back with his fingers. "I wouldn't have brought you here or told you that."

I held his hand that was brushing my hair back and turned my cheek into it, closing my eyes. There was going to be a lot of work and doubting ahead, but after all we had been through it would be wrong to just give up.

"Kela, don't force yourself to do this." He went to pull his arm away, but stopped as I tightened my hold.

"I'm not," I said quietly. "I don't know what to do. I don't know what is right, only what feels right. I know what people expect, but you asked me about my future goals and I still don't have any. You're the only one who has ever asked."

He tugged on his braid with his free hand. "You are confusing as Hells. Earlier you wanted nothing to do with me and now this. I never know what you're thinking."

"Lately I don't know either. I just..." I trailed off, unsure of what I wanted to say. "I can't just throw this all away."

"Wait, stop. I could have killed you with my stupid plan." It seemed he could not decide what he wanted either.

"Silver..." I pulled his hand away from my face, but held onto it. "I've nearly killed myself a number of times. You've always been there to pick up the pieces. That you haven't thrown me off a balcony before now just for that is impressive."

He snorted and then laughed hard, pulling me into a tight hug. I wrapped my arms around him and held on. I had been so ready to turn my back on what we had built.

Fingers reached under the collar at the back of my neck. I looked up at Silver.

His face reddened. "I just wanted to make sure that I did in fact take my necklace back. I'm sorry I put you through so much making you wear it."

I rested my head on his chest. Despite the problems, his necklace had showed me that I was capable of more. More than the labels and titles that had been placed on me. I had always been too afraid of myself to try.

"Kela," Silver said softly after several minutes.

I pulled away from him, keeping my head down to hide my embarrassment. It was far out of the usual for me. Why had he let me stay like that for so long? "Sorry," I muttered.

"Don't apologize. We both needed it." He tried to tuck my hair behind my ear. "Should we start over? Try this again?"

I bit my lower lip for a moment, thinking through the idea. "No." I looked up at him. He stared at me with wide eyes. "We've done that once already. At this rate, we'll be stuck in this loop forever. I think it's time to move on. There's too much that time cannot erase." There was no conveniently forgetting the past as much as I had tried.

Silver tugged hard on his braid.

I cringed at the sight and stepped closer, putting my hand over his to get him to stop. "I'll have no idea what I'm doing. I hope you understand that." I could not bring myself to look up at him out of embarrassment. After all we had been through, why was this so hard?

His hand clenched tighter around his braid. "I don't understand what you're saying."

My face heated up as I thought through how to word it. Finding no appropriate way to say it, I took my hand off of his and tugged lightly on his braid, looking up at him.

Clouded blue eye searched my face while he lightly ran his thumb over my bottom lip. Silver opened his mouth to say something, closed it, then leaned down and kissed my cheek.

"Are you sure you want this?" I asked, as he rested his forehead against mine. I was not even sure what I was asking. As Elves, being physically close while remaining friends was common, but this might end up being something else.

"I really should be asking you that. I've never wanted anything more," he whispered, his eyes closed. His thumb stroked my cheek gently.

I shifted, moving to kiss him and paused for a moment wondering if this was a good idea. I shoved the thought back and committed to my previous thought, taking the initiative for once, having no idea if what I was doing was right. I knew the dangers of running on instinct, but there was no previous experience for me to fall back on.

Silver hesitated. I had started to pull away when he threaded his fingers into my hair and returned the gesture.

We spent our afternoon in that clearing, mostly him talking. At one point I had dozed off, resting against him. As it approached dinner time, he woke me up so we could head back before someone came looking for us.

"Kela?" Silver asked quietly as we reached where he had left his jacket and bracers. "Can we keep this between us for now?"

I tilted my head at him as he put his gear back on. "Um, sure, but why?" With as openly affectionate as he had been previously, this was an odd request.

He stood over me, running his fingers gently through my long bangs, his attention there. "It's not that I'm ashamed or anything. In fact, I would love nothing more than to show the world, but I don't think the others will understand right now. They only see recent events."

I bit my lower lip, mulling over his words. It made sense. Even I had gotten caught up on his recent actions and had not weighed the past. Kitteren had already renewed her dislike of him after explaining what happened. That was before I knew his reasoning. As for anyone else, I had no idea how they would react.

Silver tilted my head up and kissed me lightly.

"What was that for?" I asked, raising an eyebrow at him.

"I can't help it when you chew on your lip like that," he said, grinning broadly. "It's been utter torture these past couple of years."

I tilted my head, not following. "But you were interested in someone else."

Silver stopped and laughed. Once he calmed enough, he said, "Kela, it's been you all this time. I was too much of a coward to tell you. Or you were pissed and that was obviously the wrong time."

I pinched the bridge of my nose and shook my head. "You're impossible."

He gave me a broad, mischievous grin. "I strive to be." Then he tugged lightly on his braid. "It didn't help that I wasn't sure how to approach you about it. I had always been the one approached so..."

Silence fell heavily between us for a few lengthy moments. Had I been that off-putting that he could not bring up the topic with me? I usually kept people at arm's length out of habit, but I had always thought he never realized that I did that.

"How long?" I finally asked. How long had I not noticed? People had called me oblivious at times. Now I was going to be spending time going through my memories to figure out the clues I missed.

"Not as long as you think and longer than you'd like," Silver said cryptically.

I scrunched up my nose at his response. "A straight answer would be nice."

Silver leaned over and kissed my nose before he stood up and took a step away. "I guess I owe you that much. Um..." He moved away, tugging lightly on his braid. "The guys in Ocean's Edge had been teasing me about it from when I first met you, but I figured I was just fascinated with someone who saw me and not my title. I guess I stopped fighting the idea that I was interested in you while we were in Mystic Port. Can we change the subject now?"

That was when I noticed his cheeks had reddened. I smiled softly at him. At least now I had a timeframe, but it was still quite a bit of time to analyze. "What do we do now?"

"That's a good question." Silver took my hand and tugged me toward the edge of the clearing. "Guess we'll just have to figure it out as we go."

I frowned at the thought. I preferred to have a plan in place. Even a partial one to have a starting point.

The entire way back I churned through ideas, trying to come up with something.

Silver silently held my hand while I worked in my head, leading us back to the grounds for the Central Seat. He stopped just before we broke the tree line behind the training grounds. "Hey," he said softly, "you're overthinking this."

I raised an eyebrow at him. What had he expected?

"Yes, I know that's what you do, but this isn't something you can plan." He brushed my hair back before kissing my forehead.

"Does this mean what I think it means?" a familiar female voice asked.

I jumped and backed away from Silver, turning to see Marzena walking toward us in the forest with a broad smile on her face. My mind raced through various things to say, but nothing made it out of my mouth.

Silver pulled me into a tight hug, resting his chin on my head. "Mine."

Marzena put her hands on her hips. "Yeah, I was fairly certain I didn't have a chance in any of the Hells. I'm just glad to have my family back together."

"Marzi, we discussed this. No more lines," Silver said, sounding exhausted. His hold loosened, but not by much.

It was enough to get my hands between me and my partner. I pushed, needing air from the tight hug.

"Yes, I know, and I agree, but I still get to choose those I consider family. And I'd prefer it if you didn't smother her to death."

Silver let go and I stepped away, only to have him wrap his arm around my waist.

I scrunched up my nose at him. "*I thought you wanted to keep it between us,*" I muttered in my dialect of common.

He kissed the top of my head. "*We got caught.*" Then he looked to Marzena. "Can you keep this quiet? I think too few would understand right now."

"Yeah, but it's not going to take long for people to figure it out. You're not the most subtle, brother," she said in a teasing tone and signaled for us to follow her.

I took a deep breath, knowing I would have to answer questions. For now though, I could push all of that and concerns about the future aside.

EPILOGUE

I FROWNED, staring at my screens. It was too quiet in the office without Silver around. He had stayed behind at the Central Seat to act as a go between for them and the TIO. It had already been a month. We had no idea when he would return.

The fight had thrown the Order into disarray and they needed as much help as possible to recover. Not that there were many left and they needed to go through their people at other churches. The group in Ocean's Edge had already been recalled and the church closed at least temporarily until they could determine who, if any, were oath keepers.

Silver was also tasked with collecting evidence while he was there. If it had been only recent events he would have been done by now, but he was going back as far as he could to find how long the corruption had been going on. At least all records from the other churches eventually returned to the Central Seat and more recent documents were digital.

Before I left, I had peeked at some of the records from the vaults and the Elder's library at the Central Seat, but had not had time to read much between needing to catch up on work and the sheer amount of reports and meetings that followed my return. I always seemed to go back to Blaise Sutton's journals anyway. The words he wrote about raising Silver were entertaining.

It was probably unfair of me to have gained this level of insight into my partner. Partner did not seem right, but I was unsure what label was appropriate anymore.

All of the records from the Central Seat were now in our database. It had taken me most of the month and much arcane energy to get it done. They were working on building a translator into the program so anyone could read the documents written in divine text. As for Marzena's request to have a copy for themselves, I had been left out of that discussion.

I wondered how that was going...

As if in response to my thoughts, a call from the Central Seat popped up in front of me. I sent it up to the wall screen before getting up to answer it. "Marzena," I said, not having expected her. She would sometimes hop on during my calls with Silver, but I had never gotten just her.

"Oh good, it worked," she said, letting out a sharp breath. "Hi! Haven't started one of these before so..."

I laughed lightly, hiding my amusement behind my hand. "What's the occasion?"

The Human woman tugged at her collar. Her uniform shirt had changed to that of an Elder's. "I wanted to thank you for doing all of that work. It's certainly made it easier to cross-reference public records to those that had been kept in the vaults and by the Elders. There's a lot of our history that will need to be corrected."

"That bad?"

"Ugh, you don't know the half of it. I take it you haven't gone digging through yourself."

I shook my head. "I haven't had the time to." It was a small lie - I likely could have gone through some of it, but I really needed to focus on my own work. "Should I ask about the change in uniform?"

Marzena tugged at her collar again. "You know, I had my other shirts all nice and broken in and they want me to wear this thing now." She sighed. "I'm not entirely certain how I ended up as the head of the Order, but it's not going to be permanent, I can tell you that. I have no patience for the endless prattling of a politician." She tugged at her collar again. "Though I'm going to make it a point to do something about our dress code and the uniforms themselves before I step down."

"That doesn't seem fair to put everything on you."

She laughed. "It's not just me. Silver's stuck with one of these also when he's here. There are three others as well. We figured an odd number made the most sense, but for some reason I get to be the speaker for the group. This is just temporary until we can figure ourselves out."

"For your sake I hope a solution comes quickly," I said, smiling at her candidness. It was nice to hear how things were going. Silver never wanted to talk about the ongoings there.

"Oh, are you sure it's not so my brother can get back to you sooner," she teased.

Heat rose to my face quickly. "Marzena!" A piece of information she had dropped kept nagging for my attention. "Speaking of, you said Silver wasn't there?"

She nodded. "He took a ferry to the mainland this morning." A mischievous grin graced her face. "Since I have you captive for the moment, how long until I should expect an invitation to your... oh Hells, I have no idea what the Elven version of marriage is and I lived in Ocean's Edge most of my life."

If my face could possibly turn redder, it probably had at that point. "We're nowhere near that." I knew whatever it was, the ceremony was a private affair for only the two, but the details on what happened at the different levels of claiming a mate were outside of my knowledge.

"You're so much fun to embarrass." Marzena smirked. "And don't worry - I got the full story out of my brother. Including a couple of reasons for me to kick his ass around the training room."

I rolled my eyes. I could only imagine what Silver had said.

"Well, it's late and I should probably get some sleep. I've got more meetings in the morning and I'll have my hands full until my brother gets back."

"Goodnight, Marzena."

She winked at me. "Make sure you rest up yourself. We'll have to do this again sometime." Then she ended the call.

I sighed and cleared the wall screen, going back to my desk. I spent the next few hours thinking through the strange conversation. Silver obviously was not returning that day on the ferry. What would keep him away?

The sound of the door unlocking broke me out of my thoughts. Lockonis strode in, smiling as usual. "Hey, kid."

I nodded to her. At least she had not called me by my rank.

"How do you feel about getting out of the office for a bit?" She stood in front of my desk, bouncing lightly on the balls of her feet.

I raised an eyebrow at her, waiting for more information.

"Could you answer with words or should I start calling you 'Magus' again?" She crossed her arms and stared down at me.

"Please don't." I sighed, resigned to playing her game. "Where am I going?" I started shutting the system down since it was the end of the day, figuring I needed to go pack after this and request a fleet vehicle. Likely I would depart in the morning. Not that I had been focused enough to get any work done anyway.

Lockonis uncrossed her arms. "You're heading to the Gods' Coast in Human Territory. This is a direct request - they asked for you specifically. Your contact will pick you up at the airport. You leave as soon as you have a bag packed."

"What? Who? How long?" I asked. She had come in here so nonchalantly, I had not expected the immediacy of the assignment.

"I've got you scheduled out for a week. There's a Shrike being prepared for you as we speak so off you go." She shooed me out of the room.

"Wait," I said as she chased me out the door, trying to slow down. "Who is my contact?"

"No time to waste. I can send you details en route. Get going." She was smiling broadly.

Why did she have to get like this? I swore most of the time she withheld information for her own amusement.

It did not take me long to pack and get in the air. Looking at the map, I would be fairly close to where the Central Seat was. I wondered if I could get some time after this to go see Silver. We spoke almost every day, but I missed him.

That would mean admitting to the change in our relationship. The people who knew of what happened at the Central Seat were limited, but I still preferred privacy in this matter.

I messaged my partner that I was going to be away from the office before I left, but in the half day it took for me to get out to the Gods' Coast, he had not responded. I stared at my phone as I got off the plane, searching for the information of who I was to meet and the details of the assignment. *So much for Lockonis sending me information en route.*

As I passed the gate, someone grabbed my shoulder, causing me to spin around. There was an arm around my waist by the time I realized it was Silver who had grabbed me.

"Don't do that!" I smacked his chest. I must have sensed it was him otherwise I would have reacted to fight back.

He grinned down at me before stealing a quick kiss. "I couldn't resist, Magus."

"Don't call me that," I grumbled. He had also teased me about it since I had gotten the news. Pretty much everyone had. "What are you doing here?" Had he been requested also? I looked around for the person I was supposed to meet. Who was I supposed to meet? It would be hard to explain if they caught us like this.

Silver used his fingers under my chin to get me to look back at him. "I'm here to pick you up. We'll stay the night in the city. It's going to be a long drive to our destination and I know how you are when you've been traveling."

I blinked and then stared at him. "You requested me?"

"Come on, I'll explain on the way." Silver took my bag and my hand.

I rolled my eyes. "Please tell me you haven't flown me almost halfway around the world for no reason."

"The order came through Lockonis, right? It had to get approval first." Silver seemed almost as giddy as Lockonis had been when she sent me out the door.

I scrunched up my nose. He was being difficult.

Silver laughed. "You can't stand it, can you?"

I hesitated before I answered, "No."

"Well then hurry up. This isn't something I care to discuss in public." He pulled me along faster. All through the ride he avoided directly saying what this assignment was about.

All I really got out of him on the way to the hotel was that we needed travel to a remote area south of where we were and that there would be hiking and camping involved.

We had just walked into the hotel room when I finally gave in and cut him off. "Why am I here?"

Silver sighed, closing the door. He put my bag down next to him. "While this is tied to the Central Seat, it's more of a personal nature." He tugged hard on his braid. "I was going to do this alone, but..." He came over to me and took my hand, drawing the anchor with his finger on the back.

I looked down at our hands and then back up at him. Why would he need me to be his anchor? "What's going on?"

He shifted, tugging on his collar. "I, um... I think I found where I was born. Satellite images show something there, but it's hard to make out with how overgrown the area is."

I brushed the loose strands of hair back from his face. No wonder he was too nervous to do this alone. He likely had no idea what he would find. "Well, you managed to get me here."

He turned his face into my hand, kissing my palm. "That I did. Did you miss me?" He gave me a mischievous grin.

I grabbed his braid and pulled him down to be eye level with me. "While I can appreciate not having pens in my ceiling, yes, I did." Then I pressed my lips against his, needing that connection he teased me with all too briefly at the airport.

Silver grinned against my lips. "Hm. Someone's feisty."

I pulled back after a minute, needing air. "So, how did you manage to get me out here?"

He moved away to set my bags with his. "Mostly it was the Central Seat paying for the expenses. Part of it is that Lockonis knows about us. Probably more people than we want to know already do, but at least they're respecting our privacy on the matter."

I could feel my face heating up at the thought of anyone knowing. Kitteren would be ruthless when she found out.

Silver came back over and kissed my forehead. "It was going to happen eventually. Okay, let's get you fed and then rest. I'd like to leave just after dawn tomorrow."

I nodded - I was famished and in no mood to argue with him for the sake of arguing. "Why did you want me instead of Marzena?" He had known her for far longer.

Silver took a deep breath. "Because while it will interest the Central Seat, my findings are being reported to the TIO. The people directly responsible for slaughtering my village may be dead, but it will provide evidence of long-term coverups by the Order among other things."

I folded my arms, chewing on my lower lip while I thought his words over.

"Personally though, I wouldn't have wanted anyone else at my side."

SILVER HAD MENTIONED that we were going to have to hike a bit, but he failed to mention how much. My legs were sore and I was falling behind. The terrain was relatively flat, but there were no paths.

"Kela?" He stopped and turned.

"Sorry, I can't keep up anymore." I paused to catch my breath.

Silver glanced at the device he was carrying. "We've been pushing hard since we started. We're probably well overdue for a break."

I found the nearest clear spot and sat down. I tried to rub the soreness out of my legs.

"How did you do that hike down and back from where the necromancers were and you're struggling with this?" Silver laughed, kneeling down in front of me. He took over working out the tightness in my legs.

The tension in my legs released quickly, but they were still going to be sore for a while. "I wasn't moving this fast and I might've used my power on the way back to help. I'm not sure. I was rushing pretty hard."

"There's times you don't realize you're using your power?" he asked, his fingers slowing as he looked at me.

I turned away from him. "Yeah. That's why I was having a hard time sparring with you while we were at the Central Seat and I was hiding what I am. It's too easy to use it."

"Hey," Silver said, kissing me quickly. "I'm sorry, I didn't know."

I shook my head. "How much farther?"

He paused and picked up the device he had been carrying to help locate our destination. "We're not far, I think. Maybe a couple of miles."

"You should've said that and we could have kept going." I shifted to get up, but was stopped by my partner.

Silver sat down next to me. "No, you need the break and..." he trailed off.

I tilted my head. Was there more that he had not told me?

He took a deep breath before responding. "I'm not sure I'm ready for this."

I rested my head on his shoulder. "Whatever we find won't change who you are."

A wrapped package appeared in front of me. "Eat," Silver ordered.

I raised my eyebrow at the abrupt change of conversation, but dropped it, taking the bar from him.

A minute or so later, Silver asked, "Why don't you like your rank?"

I rolled my eyes. I thought we had been over this, but I reiterated, "I think they overestimate my abilities. I haven't earned it."

He bumped his shoulder lightly against mine. "I'm sure you've more than earned it."

"You're overestimating my abilities," I said, shaking my head.

Silver grinned broadly at me. "I guess I'll just have to keep calling you Magus every so often until you get used to it."

"Please don't," I begged.

He continued to tease me about it through our break. After we finished our snack, we set back off on our hike, though the pace was slower this time. I wondered how I would be if we were on a path to finding the village I had been born in. I doubted much remained of it, but there would likely be something. I might get lost in the past.

Silver had been so young when he had been taken that he did not remember anything of it. Would it jog some sort of memory or impression?

My partner took off running as soon as shapes that looked like structures appeared in the distance.

"Wait!" I tried to run after him and tripped. I stumbled for several steps until I got my feet back underneath me. I used a flight spell to catch up with him. Being so much shorter, I had no chance otherwise.

He stopped at the edge of the village. Buildings had been burnt long ago and nature had been taking over the rest for the past six decades.

I took Silver's hand when he started slowly walking into the remains of the village. I hoped maybe he would not take off if I held onto him. He paused and looked down at our hands, giving me a blatantly forced smile.

The village appeared to have been built around a wide-open circle in the center. I had no idea if we would find anything of use here. Or perhaps finding it at all was the purpose: in order to give credit to Blaise Sutton's journals. Neither of us knew if this was even the place, but I trusted Silver's research.

In the center of the open circle, it looked like a structure had stood there once, but what it was had long since been erased. Perhaps someone else would have better luck figuring it out.

Suddenly Silver tugged on my hand, dragging me away from the center of the village toward the outskirts and stopped when we happened upon a large pile of metal armor. Every shield bore the sun symbol of the Order on it. They rested as if someone might have been wearing it when the body decomposed. I quickly mathed out in my head the time frame for the bodies to be completely gone given the environment. Roughly sixty years would have left nothing behind.

"Master's is the truth," Silver whispered, taking a step toward the armor and weapons.

I stood in front of him and put my hands on his chest before he could go to the pile. "We can't touch it yet. There are procedures to follow and tests that need to be done, but yes, I agree with your assessment."

His eyes were locked past me to the pile. I wondered if my words were even getting through. "And yet he still followed them. Why would he do that? Did he—"

I slapped Silver. Not hard, but enough to hopefully get his attention. "Would you snap out of it? I read those journals too. He believed in the path and he wanted you to as well. If he had had the chance to bring the corruption to light and get the Order back on the right path, he would have. I think he would be happy to know that you did what he could not."

Silver touched the side of his face where I had struck. "At least one of us is being logical about this."

"You were in requesting for me to come with you," I said flatly, folding my arms.

His attention went to the pile of armor and weapons behind me. "What did this village do to deserve such punishment?"

"Likely nothing," I said quietly. "It was a village of Moon Elves, right? They worshipped the wrong God for the Order and conquer the wrong race for during the war. Especially in this region." The story of my village had been similar, though I had no idea if who each side worshipped was part of it.

Silver dug something out of his pocket. He held a necklace up, wrapping his arm around my waist. It was a decorative silver-colored crescent moon with a white gem hanging in it. As the light hit the gem, iridescent colors danced across its surface.

My eyes followed the sparkling thing he held. "It's beautiful. Where did you get that?"

He brought his arm down, flipping the pendant so it would lay in his palm. "The letter my master left for me. He said he thought it had belonged to my mother. He had been unable to find anything with my name, but that I should have something when the time was right."

I had no idea what to say and a couple of minutes went by in silence. I squirmed and asked, "What are you going to do now?"

Silver sighed. "I'm just here to scout out and see if there's anything worth pursuing. There will be another team sent to handle anything else more in depth. Come on, there's one more place I want to go before we set up camp."

I made a face at the mention of our current situation. I hated the idea of camping, but hiking back today was out of the question.

He led me through the village to a house on the outskirts of town opposite of where we had found the armor. He had gone to a few houses before stopping at one. He had not spent long searching as they had deteriorated enough that we did not need to step foot inside.

"Have you ever wondered what your life would be like if you had been able to grow up in your village?" Silver asked, staring into the one he stopped at.

"I doubt I'd still be there if that's what you're asking." It was not something I had truly considered, but given the disdain my biological mother and I had gotten, I had a feeling we might have left if things had been different. Or at least I would have regardless if she had lived. Though it would have been hard to leave Kitteren and a couple of others.

Thinking of Kitteren, my sister likely would have followed me.

"Hm, I wonder if I would have been content here or wanted to travel." Silver seemed lost to his thoughts again.

"Well, I'm certain you wouldn't have had to put up with my reck-lessness," I commented flatly.

Silver grinned down at me, wrapping his arm around my waist, stepping closer. "Well, you are the only person I've found who is more reckless than I am." He kissed the top of my head. "And I wouldn't trade it for anything."

I felt my face heat up and rolled my eyes. He was so open about his affections it was embarrassing. "What is this place?"

He paused, turning to stare at the dilapidated building. "I think this was my home. I'm not sure, but it's the best that I can gather from master's journal."

I was unused to being tactile and realized late that Silver probably needed it to help remain grounded. I put my hand on his back, but remained uncertain if this was right. It might not be enough with his armor in the way.

"Let's go set up camp before it gets dark. I don't know about you, but I'm kind of hungry," he said in a rush and moved away.

Had I done something wrong?

Silver found a spot not far that was clear enough. He pulled out a couple of nutrition blocks and I scrunched up my face at the thought of having to eat one.

He laughed and patted the grass next to him. "I'll treat you to a good meal when we get back, but I don't want to make a campfire if I can help it. It'll stay pretty warm overnight. We won't need the tent. Not that I know how to set it up."

I rolled my eyes and sat down with him, taking one of the blocks. "I thought you told me once that you knew how to camp."

My partner laughed. "I never said I used a tent before. I would just find whatever was around for shelter. The weather will be clear tonight, so we won't need it."

I unwrapped the block and took a bite, cringing at the pasty texture and bland taste. It was highly unlikely I would be able to finish this.

Silver laughed. "It's not that bad."

"I remember someone once calling them 'nasty blocks.' I think I agree. I miss your cooking." I had not the opportunity to eat anything my partner had prepared since we had lived together in Ghost Forest which was over a year and a half ago.

He stopped eating and stared at me. "You never said you liked it before."

I shrugged, fighting down the heat rising to my face. "We both know I'm not good at voicing things."

"Well, you need to tell me what you liked so I can make it again."
He pointed at me with his own food.

I bit my lower lip, trying to think back. "I don't know. Let's just finish this and then gather images. I don't want to be eating these for too many meals." I held up my nibbled-on nutrition block.

He gave me a sympathetic grin. "At least give me credit that I was trying to keep our packs light."

I sighed and shook my head.

Silence fell between us as we ate. We barely spoke while gathering images - only to point out things that we should capture to each other.

Even once we decided to rest for the evening, I laid awake in my sleeping bag, staring up at the stars. With no lights around the view was incredible. The waxing crescent moon the only thing drowning out part of the sky.

I closed my eyes, pretending to sleep when I heard Silver's sleeping bag rustle. The lecture I would get if he caught me awake would not help me rest.

My partner got up and left. I kept pretending to be asleep, waiting for the sound of his return.

And I waited.

And waited.

I had no idea how long I waited, but he should have long since returned. I got out of my sleeping bag, deciding that I needed to make sure he had not gotten into trouble. I could deal with his lecture about being up.

First, I searched the immediate area, but he was nowhere near where we had set up camp outside the village. My path took me into the village. I followed the circle of the outermost houses and found him standing in front of the one he thought might have been his home, staring up at the moon.

Silver had an etherial glow about him. There was not enough moonlight to be able to create the effect off his loose hair. It had been a long time, but I remembered seeing the effect before on him. It was during my first field assignment when he was just a divine consultant. At the time I thought it had been an enchantment on his original armor, but now he only wore the lightweight white pants he slept in.

I stepped lightly, closing the distance slowly. When I was close enough, I reached out and touched his loose hair, wanting to know more about the glow.

He jumped and spun. "Kela, don't sneak up on me like that. What are you doing up?"

I noticed the moon necklace was in his hand. "I couldn't rest and I was worried when you didn't come back."

"I'm sorry, I just..." he trailed off, turning back to the house. "No matter how hard I try, I can't remember anything."

"You might have been too young," I said softly.

Silver shook his head. "I was hoping for an impression or something. Nothing seems even remotely familiar."

I reached up to brush his hair back. "Have you considered that you might be trying too hard?"

He caught my hand and brought it to his cheek, closing his eyes. "Maybe you're right. And someday I'll get used to this."

"Get used to what?" Should I not be doing this?

"You touching me."

I pulled my hand back. "I'm sorry. I don't really know what I should be doing. I thought—"

Silver's lips on mine stopped my rambling. "I'm grateful for it. We're both going to be fumbling trying to figure this out for a while yet."

I tilted my head at him.

He kissed me lightly before taking my hand and leading me further into the village. We stopped in the center.

I looked around, unsure of why he wanted to come here.

"Kela, can I ask you a favor? Well, a number of favors really."

I folded my arms. "You really want to ask me this in the middle of the night?"

Silver tugged on his hair. "I know this is... What I'm saying is... Ugh!"

"Just say it. I'm already here." I never understood why he tripped over himself like this sometimes.

"I've been trying to figure out how to tell you since I found out." Silver paced. "I'm returning with you when we leave here, but only for a short trip."

"They still need you at the Central Seat?" It would be hard, but workable.

Silver stopped, hanging his head. "Yeah. Since we don't know how long it'll be, they asked that I clean out my quarters. Can I leave my things with you?"

"Of course," I replied automatically, the rest of my mind trying to wrap around the fact that we would still be separated.

"Hey." Silver strode up to me and cupped my face. "We've made it a month so far. I'm not leaving the team - I'll just be even less help than I had been. If you go out on assignment, I'll be going with you, okay?"

I nodded, still unconvinced.

"And I'll have to come back every so often to the main office. We'll make this work." Silver rested his forehead against mine. "I'm not giving this up. And you can be damn sure I'm coming back as soon as I can."

I took a deep breath, closing my eyes. "Do the job right."

"I will. There is one more thing."

I rolled my eyes.

Silver stood up and held up the moon necklace in the moonlight. "I really don't know who this belonged to. Master said my mother, but it could have been any woman really that he had taken it from and simply assumed. Regardless, would you keep it?"

"Me? Why?" His request made no sense.

"Actually, I want you to hold onto both this one and mine. You don't have to wear either, but I'd feel better if they were in your safe keeping. Consider it a promise to return if you wish."

Silver handed me the moon necklace and I put it on. I had no pockets at the moment. When I looked back up at him, he was smiling. "It looks good on you. I hope that one doesn't give you the problems mine did."

"Let's hope not," I said, rolling my eyes.

As we walked back to our camp, the sky had begun to lighten to predawn. We had both been up all night. Hiking back was going to be miserable.

Silver picked up his sleeping bag, unzipping it and laying it open before grabbing mine and doing the same.

"What are you doing?"

"We need to rest before heading back. I thought it might be easier if we share."

"I can make it." I was going to hate every second, but I could do it.

He got into the makeshift bed. "We've shared before. It'll be fine." He waved for me to climb in next to him.

I sighed and conceded that it was a better idea to rest before that trek, but we still had the drive back to the city. Though that did not match the timeframe I had been given. "Was there anything else here you needed to do?"

"Hm? No. Why?"

"Lockonis said I'd be out here for about a week."

Silver grinned, getting himself up on his elbow. He lightly traced my ear with his finger. "So, we have some time then. Do you think you could teleport us back?"

I raised an eyebrow at him before measuring the distance with my power and calculating how much I would need to teleport both of us. "Not from here. We'd be a couple of miles or so too short and I would be completely out of energy."

"We'll hike until we're close enough and then you can rest on the drive back."

"What's the hurry?"

Silver leaned over me. "I'm not going to waste the time we've been given."

I shoved him off. "Ugh! Just rest already." I never knew what to do when he got like that.

ACKNOWLEDGMENTS

Joshua Jackson and Brandi Burns who both kept me moving. There were some (joking) threats to my personal well being.

And all of my friends and family who have been cheering me along.

ABOUT THE AUTHOR

J.C. Jackson is originally from New England and currently lives in southwestern Idaho with her husband and daughter.

On top of writing, she enjoys gaming whether that is picking up a controller or throwing down some dice in a tabletop RPG (as well as other board games). She has also been a fan of science fiction and fantasy since she was little.

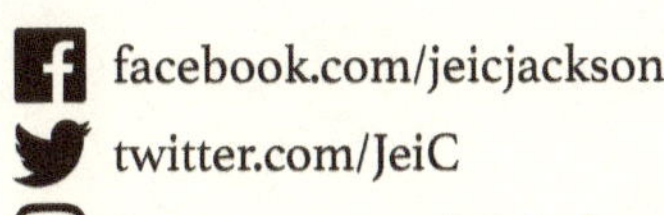

ALSO BY J. C. JACKSON

Terra Chronicles

Twisted Magics

Shattered Illusions

Twice Cursed

Conjured Defense

Mortgaged Mortality

Divine and Conquer